FUN TIMES
IN A DYSTOPIC
HELLSCAPE

ISBN: 978-0-9982120-9-8 (print)

ISBN: 978-0-9982120-8-1 (e-book)

Fonts: Plane Crash (licensed from WMKart.com), Garamond, Miscellaneous standard Apple fonts.

Visit the author's website at www.martina-fetzer.com.

Cover by okdoodle.net. Edited by Tom Williams.

Billy Joel slander is intentional, and if he finds out about this, he can challenge the author to a duel.

FUN TIMES
IN A DYSTOPIC
HELLSCAPE

* *

MARTINA FETZER

CONTENT NOTE

This series is meant to be funny. Many of the characters have traumatic backgrounds and gruesome events sometimes happen, but none of these are described very graphically. That said, content warnings for each book are available at the author's website: martina-fetzer.com.

TABLE OF CONTENTS

For the hell of it

RECAP

Agency for Detecting Horrible Occult Crimes (ADHOC) is a Brooklyn-based paranormal detective agency, run by Arturo Brooks (a cyborg) and Edward Smith (not a cyborg). The detectives are married, and have two time-displaced teenage daughters: a former Puritan from 1691 named Patience Cloyce and a former moon dweller from 2202 named Lemon Jones. They had a third daughter—a baby named Maria—who disappeared thanks to a genie. Technically, she never existed. It was a whole thing. Genies, y'know?

With over a decade of experience in the industry, Brooks and Smith have fought countless terrifying monsters (vampires, wraiths, ghouls, goblins, ghosts, etc.), as well as non-monster threats (including time travel, religious fundamentalism, interdimensional rifts, bad PR, and the horrors of venture capital). Their exploits became public knowledge when Smith staked a vampire on live TV. Now, the world's population is aware of supernatural hazards. This means creatures are much more careful with their illicit actions. It also means there are new detective agencies competing with ADHOC for cases. Capitalism, y'know?

Unrelated to their fathers' decreased workload, Patience and Lemon are now adults, and the two spend most of their time gallivanting through space and time in a time machine they borrowed from a philandering physicist. That's not as dangerous as it sounds. Both girls are immortal, unless they're in the presence of their cyborg father, whose technology interferes with their superpower. If that seems nonsensical and bothers you, you've chosen the wrong book. It's one of the less stupid developments in this series.

Anyway, Brooks and Smith are bored empty nesters. Let's go from there...

PROLOGUE

There are countless realities, spread across countless timelines. In our world, for example, Ronald Reagan is burning in Hell. In another world, it's still the 1980s and the Gipper is actively ignoring the AIDS crisis. But there are alternatives that don't align with our history at all. In some universe, it's the 1980s under President Mondale. In another, it could be the 1980s and everyone died when the Cold War went hot. It could be the 1980s and no human life ever existed on Earth to record it as such.

Forgetting the 1980s, as many would like to, there are realities where physical constants—gravity, the speed of light, electron mass, and so forth—differ from our own. It's not outside the realm of possibility that in one universe the only sentient beings are walking, talking corn cobs with names like Ty Cob, who eat cob salads and play *Cob of Duty*. There may even be realities where starting a book with a prologue isn't considered passé. But there's no point in thinking about it too hard because no one ever crosses from one reality to another, right?

Wrong.

Hieronymus Hardtack, founder of the popular chain restaurant Biscuit Bucket, lived a perfectly normal life. After serving in World War II, he created the first of the traditional country stores that would someday pervade America's highway exits from sea to shining sea. He lived in a normal suburban house, with a normal suburban wife. They had the average number of children for that period in history: 2.33.* They went to church on Sundays, ate jiggling aspics and tuna noodle casseroles, and sat in loveless silence in front of their

---

* The Hardtacks didn't like to discuss their "third child."

black and white TV for the evening news. The definition of normal.

That's why the whole world entered a state of shock when Hieronymus disappeared in 1972. Decades' worth of True Hollywood Stories, Unsolved Mysteries, and Ghost Hunters had speculated about the disappearance, but none had ever come to a solid conclusion. Billionaire CEO Maxwell Naples had taken to the mystery like James Cameron took to the Titanic, but even his seemingly endless resources couldn't crack the case.

The gist of the story was: Hieronymus went out for last-minute Christmas gifts, parked his car at the local Sears, and never returned for it.

Some say he abandoned his family and started a new life somewhere else. That didn't seem to check out. When authorities located Hieronymus's car, there were presents in the trunk; among them were an expensive handbag, an Easy Bake Oven, and a Bee Gee's Board (a non-blasphemous alternative to the Ouija board that allowed one to communicate with the disco music group). These were items that checked off his wife and kids' Christmas lists—presents he'd intended to bring home, but never did.

If it wasn't abandonment, the situation could only be grimmer. Some suggest that Hieronymus was murdered by one of the many burgeoning serial killers of the 1970s. In that story, his body was dumped in a nearby forest. But that didn't check out either. There were no signs of struggle and the most thorough manhunt in history hadn't found so much as a single footprint. It was as though he'd vanished into thin air.

Decades passed and no information ever emerged. By the 2000s, everyone assumed Hieronymus was dead, either from an inciting event or from the passage of time. No one, it seemed, would ever know the truth...

1 / APRIL FOOLS

If Edward Smith had read the entirety of the employee handbook at his previous employer before burning the building to the ground, he would have known what happened to Hieronymus Hardtack. But that would have been uncharacteristic of him, and he hadn't. Smith reclined on the couch of the Brooklyn brownstone he shared with his husband and work partner Arturo Brooks, a Norfolk terrier named Widget, and two time-displaced daughters who crashed there on occasion. At this moment, on April 1, 2018, Smith was the only one home.

That could be a dangerous proposition. Readers of the first three books in this series will recall previous times when Smith was left to his own devices. Once, he'd gone on a decades-long bender in upstate New York. A few times, he'd attempted increasingly bizarre methods of suicide, knowing they couldn't possibly work on his immortal self. One had. That was a doozy. There was another occasion when he'd wandered off in the heat of an argument and gotten capped by a genie, forcing his entire family into a war of genie-on-genie violence. On one particularly uneventful afternoon in the 1990s, Smith had even decided to dye his dirty blonde hair a putrescent shade of green and wear it in a sidehawk.* All in all, there were things you could trust Smith with, like captaining a team for Tolkien trivia night or staking a vampire. Being left alone wasn't one of those things.

But history was history. Life had gotten better. Smith took a deep breath and reminded himself of that as he sat watching a D-grade science fiction movie about a giant, killer sea bream. The fish wasn't particularly upsetting, but the notion

---

* Like a mohawk, but from ear to ear. It looks as stupid as it sounds.

that he might soon be a father again was.

It was one thing to—as Smith and Brooks had—take in a pair of teenagers who could look after themselves and who'd already been traumatized by their own tumultuous pasts. It was another thing to—as Smith and Brooks were planning—adopt a young child and intentionally subject it to their parenting. They'd done a trial run, thanks to that genie, but it didn't make him feel any more up to the task. Smith began nervously tapping the end table next to him as he thought up more than a few specific ways he could ruin someone's life. Drugs. Abandonment. Dying (yet again). Serving undercooked shellfish. Forgetting about a food allergy.

How did a giant fish movie bring about this introspective spiral of anxiety? A few moments earlier, a marine biologist—played by former pop sensation Tiffany—had shoved a child aside in a moment of slow-motion self-sacrifice.

"Idiot," Smith had said, then grimaced at his response. The moment was supposed to have been poignant, but he'd only been annoyed. That, he decided, was the latest sign he was a terrible human being.

Smith's thoughts of how he might traumatize a child varied in severity. Screaming. Hitting. Losing the kid in public. Forgetting to lock the bathroom door. Forgetting to lock the bedroom door. Not giving them enough money for a field trip. Unintentional displays of apathy. A series of crappy Christmas gifts...

His finger tapping grew faster and faster.

Jingling keys interrupted the spiral as Brooks entered, with Widget in tow. He unhooked the leash, and the dog scurried across the room to the man who hadn't betrayed him.

"*Butchers*. What have they done to you?" Smith rubbed Widget's shaved head, then turned to Brooks. "He looks like a rat."

"It's just this once," Brooks said. After tomorrow, Widget's fur could fly free once more.

Smith whispered to the dog as he scratched his ears. "Don't ever forgive him."

Brooks rolled his eyes, then noticed something across the room. A picture frame on the wall rested slightly askew. He hurried over to fix it.

"I don't think they're gonna be that picky," Smith said.

"They might be."

"They're *overflowing* with orphans. They'd probably let us take a dozen if we wanted 'em." He added, "I don't want a dozen."

For context, 'they' referred to Adopt Shop, a child adoption agency founded by Millennials with the goal of 'disrupting the adoption industry.' Brooks and Smith didn't understand what that meant or how holding the same interviews and in-home studies as every other agency was disruptive. What they did understand was that tomorrow's visit was the last step in the vetting process.

Crucially, nothing untoward had happened in the sixteen weeks since they'd used Adopt Shop's handy mobile app to sign up. Brooks and Smith were on the cusp of parenthood thanks to a tip sent to bs@adhoc.org that claimed there was 'something screwy' going on at the agency following its recent acquisition by the megacorporation Shoppli. The men agreed that they would investigate and either uncover something horrible, or adopt a child.* Either way, they needed to pass the next step, so Brooks straightened another picture on the wall.

Smith patted the seat next to himself. "I have to ask you something."

He sounded serious, so a wary Brooks took a seat and composed himself, assuming that Smith would attempt to renege on their nonsensical agreement.

---

* It may seem casual, but this is actually more thought than most people put into having kids.

"What is it?" Brooks asked.

"If there was a giant killer fish—"

Brooks relaxed. "Oh, thank God."

"What?"

"Nothing. I'm relieved it's a stupid question."

"No, it's not. If there was a giant killer fish—"

Brooks interrupted, with a grammar correction. "If there *were*. What kind of fish?"

"Does it matter?" Smith huffed. "A sea bream. Anyway, if a giant murder fish was about to murder some kid, would you jump in front of it and let the fish eat you to save the kid?"

"Just some random kid?" Brooks answered with confidence. "No."

"Now say it was our kid..."

"Ah." Brooks glanced at the screen, where Nicholas Cage was harpooning the creature in question, then back to his husband. "I don't know. I like to think there's a third option other than someone getting eaten by a giant fish."

Smith shook his head. "Uh uh. No weaseling. It's a Kobayashi Maru—"

"A what?"

"One or the other has to die," said Smith.

Brooks shrugged. "I don't know."

"They played the sad instrumental and everything." Smith lowered his head. "I don't get it. At all. I didn't feel anything but annoyed. You're a marine biologist. When it comes to slaying giant fish monsters, the world needs you a lot more than it needs little Brayden."

Brooks put a tan hand over Smith's very pale one. "Eddie, it's a bad movie."

"No shit. It's got Tiffany in it. But I should get it, right? I should be able to see myself doing that if we might be bringing some kid into this house." Smith pulled his hand away so he could mope alone.

"I don't think you should beat yourself up over a hypothetical sea monster. No one knows what they'd do in any situation until they do it. I mean... until last year, I didn't think I'd ever kill a human being."*

Smith sank deeper into the couch. "Yeah. Maybe don't mention that tomorrow. It's just... I'm not nice to begin with. What if it's a hop, skip, and a jump from here to Abuse Town, and the next thing you know I'm spitting Copenhagen into a Mountain Dew bottle and yelling at some kid to bring me another Coors."

"That's weirdly specific." Brooks stared deep into his husband's eyes and added a phrase he'd repeated often. "You are not your parents."

Smith broke the eye contact. "They weren't always assholes. I don't know what changed between me being born and them blowing themselves up in a meth lab."

"Probably the meth."

"Oh, well..." Smith's voice became heavy with sarcasm. "Good thing I've never had any problems with drugs."

"Maybe don't mention *that* tomorrow."

Smith let out a desperate laugh. "We're a mess."

"Everyone is. At least we know it. Besides, the fact that you're worried about this means you do care. You are not your parents."

Smith remained unconvinced. His face went cold.

Brooks tried to get something out of him. "Can you be a jerk? Sure. But you're not cruel. You've never gone out of your way to make someone hurt. You've saved so many people over the years..."

Smith waved his hand in a dismissive gesture. While time and therapy had lessened it, self-loathing still occupied about twenty percent of his waking thoughts. To wit, he outlined the ways in which he was a walking, talking TV-MA rating.

---

* That happened. In fairness, the dude sort of had it coming.

"Addiction? Yep. Pissiness? Yep. Internalized homophobia? Check. Excessive risk-taking? All there, babe. I have night-mares about killing Widget, just like they killed Jesse."

"For God's sake, Eddie. You'd never kill a dog. You'd kill yourself first."

Smith, having accidentally killed himself once, reacted with a knowing glare.

"I don't know what I'd do. I've never planned anything in my life. I could turn out like them *or worse.* Whatever was broken in them is in me, only I've got an extra decade of living with shitty foster parents on top of their shitty genes, and then a few more of staring at crime scenes and hacking apart demons on top of that."

Brooks smirked. "Would it help if I reminded you that you're super old and you've already turned out?"

Smith scoffed. "Barely older than you." He was forty-one to Brooks's thirty-five.

Smith's phone began to vibrate on the coffee table. He grabbed it and checked the caller ID.

"Speaking of demons..."

"Who is it?" asked Brooks.

Smith ignored him and answered the phone. "Hello?" There was an extended pause, during which his facial expression didn't change. "Okay. Thanks for letting me know. You know—"

Brooks could hear the harsh dial tone that ended the call.

"Who was it?"

"Lyla," Smith said, naming his stepsister. "Her parents are dead."

Brooks reframed the statement. "So... *your* parents are dead?"

"Sure. I guess." Smith shrugged.

When he was ten, Smith had been adopted by the O'Grady family, who ended up being the last and best in a long line of foster care. That wasn't saying much, and he hadn't spoken to them since he skipped town at age sixteen.

"I'm sorry," Brooks said. "That must bring up some complicated feelings..."

It did, and Smith's instinct was to lighten the mood. "April fools."

"What?" Brooks blinked a few times.

Smith's eyes shifted. "I don't know why I said that. They really are dead."

At that point in history, the fastest man-made object was NASA's Parker Solar Probe, which zoomed around the sun at speeds of 430,000 miles per hour. The second fastest was Brooks's palm launching toward his forehead.

2 / SCHEDULING CONFLICT

Technology progresses quickly, sometimes frighteningly so. Brooks had only been a cyborg for four years, and already some of his enhancements had become obsolete. A dedicated friend—Erin Burroughs—routinely patched his software, but without access to the scientists who cyborgified him in the first place, hardware updates were a lost cause. His USB port, for example, was Micro-B rather than USB-C. His cellular service would forever be stuck on 4G, and he suffered a single dead pixel in his right eye. He did, however, still possess a number of advantages over regular humans. Chief among them: hands-free internet access.

Smith hadn't gleaned much information from the quick phone call with his stepsister and he didn't care to.

"Let it go," he said.

Brooks refused. Via Wi-Fi, he could find almost anything he wanted to know. His normally expressive brown eyes took on an empty look as he stared beyond reality.

Smith hated that look. "You know, you could just use your phone."

"Why?" Brooks didn't break his focus.

Smith found himself conflicted, as usual. That his husband no longer anguished over being a cyborg was a good thing. That he was all-in on using his cybernetic abilities for even the smallest task... probably wasn't. It seemed a bit like addiction, but he was in no place to judge.

"Got it," Brooks said.

The notice ran in the *Clarksville News & Tribune*, whose website was ninety-two percent obituaries, five percent advertisements, and three percent news. Brooks paced back and forth across the living room as he read from it.

"Charles O'Grady (84) and Lucille O'Grady (82), both of

Clarksville, passed away on March 31, 2018... looks like they got into a car accident..." Brooks skipped ahead. "Beloved members of the community... kids and grandkids..."

"Did they list me?" Smith already knew what the answer would be.

"No." Brooks stopped pacing. "There's a service Friday."

"And?" Smith, still content on the couch with Widget, didn't care.

"We should be able to make it."

Smith couldn't do a dramatic spit take because he wasn't drinking. Instead, he narrowed his eyes to the narrowest squint he could muster. "Are you *high*?"

"I'm not high. You should go." Brooks corrected himself. "*We* should go."

"Why?"

"Because if you don't, it'll just give you another thing to beat yourself up over—"

"I'll always find something."

"—And—"

Smith crossed his arms. "Don't care."

"—And—"

"Don't. Care."

Brooks, determined to get his point across, sped up his speech. "And it's the respectful thing to do."

Smith snorted, then stood to look into his husband's eyes. "They're dead. Who cares? It's not like they're gonna know one way or the other."

"They showed up when *you* died."

From upstairs came a THUNK. Widget leapt from the couch and began barking at the staircase as two young women descended it. In front was Lemon Jones. Having traded her cuffed jeans and military jacket for an orange, bell-bottomed jumpsuit and rainbow-striped platform shoes, she looked like she'd just emerged from a Blaxploitation film rather than a time machine.

Hidden behind Lemon was Patience Cloyce. The tiny, freckled Puritan wore her usual floor-length brown dress, but now her curly red hair sat under a loose, mustard-colored crochet hat.

"Who's dead now?" Lemon asked.

Everyone in the house had died at one point or another, except Widget, so they'd arranged a solution. When a member of the family uttered the word "dead" more than three times in the span of five minutes, an alarm in Lemon and Patience's smart watches told them to come back and investigate.

Widget parked at Lemon's feet, awaiting some quality scritches. She rolled the dog onto his back and obliged.

"Where have you been?" Smith asked.

Brooks eyed their clothes. "*When* have you been?"

"1974, sirs," Patience chirped.

"I went to CBGB," Lemon bragged. "I saw the Ramones."

"I was nearly trampled in a riot concerning gas rationing," Patience said.

That was par for the course, and no one reacted with surprise.

Lemon looked from an alive Brooks to an alive Smith and back. "Who died, though?"

"No one important," Smith said.

"*Just his parents*," Brooks contradicted in a sarcastic tone.

"Oh no," Lemon said. "Wait, which ones?"

Smith faked a laugh. "Har har. Eddie had twenty-six families. Let's all laugh."

"I was actually asking, ya glorbdink," said Lemon.

"The O'Gradys."

"Aw, they were kinda nice. How'd they die?"

"From being in their eighties," answered Smith.

Brooks elbowed him.

Smith amended his previous statement. "Car accident, but I stand by what I said. Old people shouldn't drive."

Patience frowned. "You seem unconcerned by your parents' demise."

"I *am* unconcerned." He counted, using his fingers for emphasis. "One: they were older than dirt. Two: they sent me to a kooky religious indoctrination camp. Three: we haven't spoken in twenty years. Except for that time a genie changed reality and they became great parents and grandparents... goddamnit."

That satisfied Brooks. "See? You do care."

"That's not caring. That's being... gaslit by a genie."

"Gaslighted," Brooks corrected.

"No *fucking* way. I didn't 'lighted' a cigarette. I lit one."

"I mean, you could have 'lighted' one. Or lit one. They're interchangeable."

"Then why couldn't I have been gaslit?"

Brooks laughed. "I'm messing with you."

"*In my time of grieving*," Smith said, with dramatic flair.

Lemon tapped at the watch on her wrist and cleared her throat.

Brooks stared at her. "Do you have somewhere to be?"

Lemon answered with time-displaced slang. "Yeah, we gotta skitty. We'll catch you crazy cats in Indiana."

"We're not going to Indiana," Smith said.

Lemon shrugged. "Yeah, you are. Last time we saw you was there."

Smith groaned.

Brooks shook his head. "If you keep spoiling things, I'm going to take that time machine to the dump and have it compacted."

Lemon responded with a smug smirk. "You can't. We use it again in—"

"No spoilers!"

"*Fine.*"

"We'll see you there," Brooks said.

"Groovy." Lemon threw her fathers a peace sign as she

hurried toward the stairs.

"Peace out," Patience added, raising the wrong two fingers.

"Wait." Smith raised a hand to object, but Lemon and Patience were already halfway upstairs. "I'm not—"

"Guess you are," said Brooks.

The stomping of platform shoes let them know Lemon had done an about face. She re-descended the stairs. Patience, holding her dress high to avoid tripping, followed.

"I almost forgot!" Lemon said.

She ran over to Brooks and leapt into a hug that would have sent any non-cyborg falling backwards.

Patience, meanwhile, tiptoed over and patted Smith's arm.

Brooks broke free. "Why are—"

"We won't see you for a while, so... hug."

The girls swapped fathers. Lemon squeezed Smith extra tight, and Patience gave Brooks a gentle pat on the arm. It was affectionate for a Puritan.

In seconds, Lemon and Patience were scurrying towards the staircase. Brooks and Smith eyed each other with apprehension.

"Love ya! Later!" Lemon shouted down to them, and the two disappeared up the stairs.

"That seems sus," Smith said.

"*Sus?*"

"I can't keep current with slang?" Smith asked.

Brooks sat next to him. "You don't even keep current with our bills."

Smith took a deep breath. "You *really* wanna go to Indiana?"

"Of course I don't. No one does. I just think we should."

"Okay."

"Okay?" Brooks shot him a skeptical look. "Kind of thought you'd push back a bit more on that. I was thinking up a whole rationale..."

"No, it's fine," Smith acquiesced.

He wouldn't admit it, but part of him was curious to see whether Indiana was as horrible as he remembered. Another, larger part was too tired to argue. There was a good chance that, if he let Brooks continue convincing him, he'd have to listen to the entirety of some journal article about the psychology of grief. Having an internet-connected spouse could be annoying like that. It was better just to go with the flow.

3 / DISRUPTING THE INDUSTRY

At six o'clock the next morning, Brooks's internal alarm clock woke him up with a friendly neural chime. He rolled over and gently shook Smith, who hadn't slept in the first place. They went through all the standard morning rituals. Standard for them. Not the standard morning rituals of the Cult of Brachyura, which involved crustacean sacrifice and a lot of butter.

At eight o'clock on the dot, the doorbell rang. Brooks and Smith were clothed and ready, seated on the couch. To the casual observer, they might have appeared overdressed in their suits and ties, but they almost always dressed like that. For one, suits made them seem like authoritative professionals rather than frenzied improvisers. Then there was the preferential treatment. Catch someone in sweatpants trespassing? That's an arrest. Catch someone in a suit doing the exact same thing? Clearly a misunderstanding, officer.*

Widget—the victim of a melatonin treat—rested in his memory foam bed near the door. Brooks and Smith walked by him on their way to answer, but the dog was too busy dreaming about chasing squirrels to acknowledge their presence.

Brooks opened the door to reveal a peppy, bespectacled zoomer of ambiguous gender, who didn't introduce themselves and declined to shake either man's hand, on account of a clipboard and pen occupying theirs. The blue-bobbed zoomer remained in the doorway, looked up at the

---

* Results may vary based on skintone.*
* Because cops are racist^, and that's a bad thing.
^ Some cops.%
% A full collection of apologies can be found at the author's blog.

investigators who towered above them, and asked a single question.

"What's the worst name someone could give their child?"

Brooks, nosy detective that he was, glanced at the clipboard to see what other questions were forthcoming. There were none. The page included a header (Adopt Shop: a Shoppli Company), the lone query, and a large, empty space for... notes? Drawings? Charts? It was unclear.

The zoomer shot Brooks the stink eye and pulled the clipboard close to their chest.

Smith answered first, and thoughtlessly. "Khaleesi."*

"Whatever their name is, Junior," Brooks answered. Unlike his husband, he'd put thought into it and decided that burdening a child with their own name was the worst thing a parent could do. This did not apply to legacy names that skipped a generation, like his own, which had belonged to an *abuelo* he'd never met.

"Interesting." The zoomer jotted down some notes, then pushed through the pair with a surprising amount of strength.

Brooks was himself the bearer of a surprising amount of strength, but he let the obvious intern pass.

Without saying a word, the zoomer inspected the kitchen, stairwell, and coat closet before returning to the front door to measure its width with a tape measure. Then, almost as abruptly as they'd entered, the zoomer exited the Brownstone.

"Um, there's another floor," Brooks said.

"I know."

That was all the acknowledgement the zoomer gave before leaving in silence. The adoption industry had been thoroughly disrupted, and the detectives had been thoroughly

---

* This was stunningly prescient of him, considering the *Game of Thrones* finale wouldn't air for another year.

confused. Smith shut the front door, and exchanged looks with his husband. They began talking at each other instead of holding an actual conversation.

"That was weird," Smith said.

"I think we answered okay..."

"Why measure the front door?"

"... *Oh God*, what if that kid was a Junior?"

"Why so much focus on the toaster?"

"... I was wrong. Someone's name *the Third* is worse than Junior..."

Widget, awakened by an unfortunate dream squirrel incident, let out a short bark. It snapped the men out of their self-absorption and reminded them they had things to do, and flights to book for the long week ahead.

4 / TS, EH?

Because they had no problem starting their journey on the worst possible foot, the detectives took a cab to LaGuardia Airport. The funeral wasn't for three days, but Brooks and Smith knew how this would turn out if they waited until the last minute. To avoid yet another time-related disaster, they'd packed their bags, left Widget with reluctant dogsitter Erin Burroughs, and headed straight over. Their plan was to fly to Cincinnati and spend a few days eating chili and doing whatever people in Cincinnati do, before heading into the hellish nightmare that was Indiana.

Nothing ever went as planned.

The terminal greeted them with industrial tile that looked like concrete, and fluorescent lights that flickered intermittently. Mere feet from the entrance, beneath a partly illuminated 'Wel me to New ork' sign, were two rolling trashcans and a handful of plastic trays lined with garbage bags. Each was intended to catch water falling from holes in the ceiling, but several had already overflowed. A bold yellow 'Caution/Cuidado' sign let them know that no one intended to mop the floor any time soon.

ADHOC—the detectives' agency, for those who struggle with acronyms—distinguished itself from competition by presenting as a luxury brand. Brooks and Smith had convinced New Yorkers with more money than sense that their exorbitant fees were worth it to ensure the ghosts and ghouls that plagued them never returned. In fact, they had a money back guarantee that had only been utilized once. They were doing quite well and could have easily flown out of JFK or Newark, but as Adopt Shop looked like it might pull through, there were future childcare expenses to consider. Cheap was cheap.

An airport's appearance wasn't important anyway. What mattered was the total airport experience. Omega Airlines checked them in without incident, and the Departing Flights board showed that—miraculously—their flight was on schedule. Funeral aside, things were looking just fine.

But they still had to go through airport security.

Low, stifling ceilings gave the area an ominous air. The cement-like floor transitioned to rough, worn-out carpeting that hadn't been updated since Smith wore his hair in a green sidehawk. Nearly every traveler-to-be tripped over the lack of a threshold as they moved from one surface to the other and approached the security line. And what a line it was!

Due to past incidents, neither man could ever qualify for TSA PreCheck. They were lucky they weren't on a No-Fly list. Two hours until departure ticked down to ninety minutes, and then to an hour, all spent trapped in an agonizing line between Midwestern tourists who couldn't stop babbling about *Wicked,* and a Canadian businessman who wouldn't get off his cell phone. Big Maple, it seemed, just couldn't wait.

By the time they made it to the scanners, Smith was thirsty and Brooks was anxious.

Smith and his bag passed through fine, as did Brooks's luggage, but Brooks himself was pulled aside. A surly agent in a bright blue shirt and even brighter blue gloves waved a wand in front of the cyborg's pants.

"Sir, I need you to *empty your pockets*," she said.

"I don't have anything in my pockets."

"Sir, I don't need your attitude. Empty your pockets."

Brooks spoke slowly, enunciating each word as if communicating with a small, stupid child. "I. Don't. Have. Anything. In. My. Pockets." He turned them inside out to prove the point.

A different agent poked his head up from behind the scanners. "Sir, do you have any medical implants?"

"Well, I'm a *cyborg*, so... yes."

"Sir, I don't need your attitude."

Brooks turned to Smith, perplexed. "Am I giving them attitude?"

"No more than usual." Smith shrugged and moved toward a nearby fountain. "I'm gonna refill my bottle."

The first agent repeated herself. "Sir. Empty your pockets."

Brooks reached down and gave his empty pockets another tug. "They are literally inside out right now."

A third, taser-wielding agent hadn't been paying attention to the conversation, but noticed Brooks's motion. He hovered one hand over his weapon while he pointed with the other.

"He's got something in his pocket!"

"What?" Brooks stammered.

The agents swarmed.

Brooks was furious, but—unlike REO Speedwagon—he could fight the feeling. He remembered what he'd read in books like *So You Committed Murder* and *Self-Flagellation for Dummies*. Rather than murder them, he let himself be overtaken. The next thing he knew, he was tasting matted grey carpeting at the bottom of a pile of under-bathed, overzealous agents.

From the scanner queue, the businessman complained in a thick Ontarian accent. "Gosh, is this gonna take all day? Some of us have got flights to catch."

"Oh, I'm sorry," Brooks spoke from underneath the pile. "Is this inconvenient *for you*?"

An agent shouted in his ear. "Sir, stop resisting!"

Brooks's ears started ringing, thanks to supersensitive hearing. He grunted as the agents dragged him to his feet. "I didn't *move*. Eddie?"

Smith stopped sipping his water. "Do you want me to escalate this or de-escalate it?"

Brooks shook off the agents encircling him.

"Honestly don't care," he said.

Smith grabbed his and Brooks's bags, made eye contact with the agents, and motioned toward the airport exit. "We're just gonna drive instead. Can we leave?"

"C'mon now. You're holding everything up," the Canadian complained.

The TSA agents glanced back and forth at each other, mumbling. "Is that fine?" "I think that's okay." "We can let them leave, right?" "We don't have to detain them?" "I don't remember anything about cyborgs in the training." "There was training?" "I think so?"

Finally, the one with the taser nodded.

"You're free to leave."

"C'mon now," the Canadian whined.

Brooks and Smith turned to leave the airport. As they made their way toward the exit, Smith unscrewed the top of his water bottle and splashed water all over the Canadian's shirt.

One of the agents glanced at the soaked Canuck and screeched. "He's carrying more than an ounce of liquid on his person!"

There was a soft PZZZZZT as the armed agent jabbed the Canadian's side with his stun gun.

Smith broke into a mischievous grin. "Hey. Heyyyy."

"*What?*" Brooks snapped.

"I think I just disrupted the maple syrup industry."

Brooks ignored that. Near the automatic doors, he noticed a little stand with a laminated sign. It asked: 'How was your visit?' Beneath it were three buttons that would have been illuminated, had their bulbs not burned out: a green smiley face, a yellow indifferent face, and a red sad face. Brooks slammed a fist down on the sad face, cracking the button on his way out the door.

5 / ADDITIONAL FEES MAY APPLY

Cyborgs make excellent multitaskers. While Brooks was giving the airport a firm sad face rating, he simultaneously searched the internet for rental cars. Every company but one had sold out, and that company wouldn't take same-day online reservations. Neither Brooks nor Smith had ever heard of Waco Car Rental, but they sauntered over to be greeted by a yellow sign which read 'CARS FROM $19/DAY*^⌘℉' in dull blue letters. No explanation was given for the asterisk or for the other symbols.*

Smith pointed at the sign. "If Omega refunds our flight, we're gonna save a ton."

"Big if," said Brooks.

More likely events than an airline granting a refund include: being struck by lightning, winning the Pick 5 lottery jackpot, and the world coming together to solve climate change before it's too late.†

Brooks and Smith stepped toward the desk and plopped their bags onto the ground.

A young customer service agent looked up from her computer to greet them.

"Hi, there. Do you have a reservation?"

"No. Our flight got cancelled, so we need a car," Brooks replied.

"Okay. Let's see what we can do for you..." She mashed the keys on her keyboard. "We don't have any standard or

---

* The answers were buried on the Waco Car Rental website, which was down for maintenance daily between 8AM and 8PM EST.
† That's a joke. Humanity isn't doomed. Probably.

midsize available, but we do have a premium sedan."

"Do you have any compacts? It's just the two of us."

"Unfortunately, our compacts are all booked. I can get you a minivan or a truck..."

Both men grimaced.

"The premium is fine," Brooks said.

"How much is it?" Smith asked.

"The base rate for the premium level is seventy dollars a day," the agent replied. "How long are you going to need the car?"

Brooks wasn't sure. "Two days out, a day for the funeral, two days back?"

"Five days," Smith confirmed.

"Okay. Three fifty for five days. You'll be returning the vehicle here?"

The men nodded.

"And who'll be driving?"

"I will," they said together, then shot disgruntled looks at one another.

"Okay, there's a ten-dollar fee per day to add a second driver..."

"Why?" Smith asked.

The agent offered a cheerful shrug. "Insurance reasons."

Brooks sighed. "That's fine."

"Now, you mentioned something about two days out. How far do you plan on taking the vehicle? Bear in mind the car does have GPS and if you exceed your stated mileage there will be a hundred-dollar fee."

Brooks sighed again. "Clarksville, Indiana."

"Okay..." The agent typed something into the computer. "Seven hundred thirty miles each way. That's fourteen sixty. Ten cents a mile brings the mileage total to one hundred forty-three. You can come in up to fifty miles over that without incurring any charges."

"How generous," Brooks said.

"And will you be needing insurance?"

"No," Brooks and Smith said at once.

"Okay, so I'll need to see your current insurance."

They didn't have any.

Brooks acquiesced. "We'll take the insurance."

"Okay. It's fifteen a day, so seventy-five for the insurance."

Smith's head began to ache from the math.

"Yeah, that's *fine*," Brooks said.

"Great. And just so you know, there is a fee if you bring it back with less than a full tank of gas."

"Of course there is," said Brooks.

"Is there a full tank in it now?" Smith asked.

"No," said the agent. "It says here it's at two thirds. Can I see your driver's licenses?"

They slid them across the counter, and the agent typed and typed. When the clicks and clacks were finished, she looked back up at them.

"Will you be needing transportation over to the garage?"

"How far is it?" Smith asked.

"Six miles."

"Yes," Brooks and Smith said.

"Okay. With the ten-dollar shuttle fee, your grand total including tax is—"

Fifteen minutes and $726.16 later, Brooks and Smith were standing at space 61 in the Waco garage, staring at the rear end of a grey Toyota Avalon. Its lopsided bumper bore numerous dents, presumably from previous renters' attempts to parallel park.

"*This* is the premium model?" Brooks huffed in disbelief.

Smith opened the driver's side door and recoiled, coughing.

"What?" Brooks narrowed his eyes.

Smith coughed into his hand, like the horrible disease vector he was. "I think the last driver left takeout in there."

"You want to go back to the airport?"

"Nah."

Smith pulled his shirt up over his nose and dove into the car, probing for the offending container. Brooks began his search at the trunk, but found nothing in there but an empty spare tire well and some EZ Kidnap brand zip ties. Smith found the food—eventually—under the passenger seat, wrapped in a brown paper bag, with dark, wet spots where spoiled sweet and sour sauce had seeped through.

"Got it," he gagged.

He opened the bag, revealing a styrofoam container, and the smell hit Brooks, even from two yards away. "Ugh."

Smith held his nose and peeled back the container's lid, then dumped its molding contents onto the hood of the identical Toyota Avalon in space 60.

"Why would you—?"

"Because fuck Waco. That's why." Smith stood tall, pleased with himself for ensuring the next customer's experience would be as unpleasant as his own.

This was how Waco perpetuated an endless cycle of misery. The takeout container had been left in the detectives' car because the previous renter, after being charged an exorbitant 'food in the car' fee, had tucked their leftover sweet and sour pork under the front seat in an act of spite. "Food in the car!" they'd exclaimed. "I'll show them food in the car!"

Brooks tossed their bags into the trunk, and slammed it shut. As he did so, he eyed Smith adjusting the position of the driver's seat.

"What are you doing?"

Smith froze. "Getting into the car?"

"In the driver's seat?"

"I have a *driver's license* and we paid the two-driver fee, so... yeah."

"You drive like a maniac, and you don't have cyborg reflexes," Brooks noted.

Smith scoffed. "I drove to the first case we ever worked together."

"And you got into a fender bender."

"Yeah. A fender got bent," Smith said. "Who gives a shit?"

"I'm just saying my driving record is perfect."

"And mine has *one fender bender*?"

"Also the time you ran over a mailbox," said Brooks.

"To be fair, I was very high."

"... That's not the defense you think it is."

"*Fine.*" Smith rolled his eyes and tossed the keys over to Brooks. He circled around the front of the car to get into the passenger seat.

"Tell you what," he said. "If you can make it twenty miles without raging out, I won't ask to drive again the whole trip."

"I don't rage out," said Brooks.

Smith stifled a laugh.

"I *don't*," Brooks said, his voice raising a couple of octaves. He nodded and pointed a defiant finger. "You've got a deal."

He put the car in drive and exited the parking garage without cursing at any of the tourists who cut him off. He didn't honk at the car that remained stationary at a green light or flail his arms at the many pedestrians who wandered into his path. He didn't grumble about NYC DOT closing a lane during peak hours. He didn't even raise his voice when a Shoppli delivery van double-parked, forcing him to sit in the middle of a one-way street and stare at its stupid winking logo while the driver made a delivery to a sixth-floor walkup. All in all, his effort was admirable; he'd managed to get them out of the city without so much as mutter of disapproval.

But the next state over could corrupt even the kindest soul. Two miles into New Jersey, on Interstate 78, Brooks's left hand shot out the window, its middle finger raised at a black BMW passing him on the shoulder.

"*¡Chinga tu pinche madre, cabrón!* It's called a turn signal! I put it on so you'd know I was getting over to let you pass, you fu—"

Brooks glanced at the passenger seat, where Smith was staring with raised brow.

"*What?* Did you see—Ugh. Fine. You win."

Smith didn't gloat, but no one had ever looked as smug and satisfied as he did in that moment, except maybe Gwyneth Paltrow at the launch of her line of pumpkin spice-scented sanitary products.

6 / PA WELCOME CENTER I-78W

With the sun setting in their field of vision, the detectives pulled up to the Pennsylvania Welcome Center, both to avoid being blinded and to swap seats. It was a red stone building with a redder tin roof that jutted out at sharp angles. Out front, a friendly blue sign decorated with a yellow keystone boasted, 'Pennsylvania: It's Okay.'

There were ample trash cans, all empty, as well as ample discarded bottles and cans, all scattered on the ground. Brooks eyed an abandoned diaper on the sidewalk with disgust, and shriveled his nose as they entered the building.

In the lobby, a large travel map showed them just how far they hadn't traveled. Brooks pointed at a faded yellow 'you are here' marker.

"That's it?" he asked.

Smith chuckled. "You haven't left New York in a while."

"Neither have you."

"Yeah, but Midwest trash never forgets."

The entrance to the Welcome Center smelled faintly of bleach and echoed with the sound of flushing toilets, causing a Pavlovian response in one of the men.

"I'm going to use the restroom," Brooks said.

Smith stepped toward the food court. "Snacks."

"You don't have to go? After all that water?"

Smith shrugged. "Nah."

"I'm not stopping again in half an hour," Brooks warned.

Smith waved him away into the bathroom as he entered the food court. The name was a misnomer. Every stall was closed, except for Starbucks, which had a line twenty people deep—weary travelers in sweatpants and flip-flops, all of whom looked as if they might suddenly fall asleep where they stood. Smith shook his head at the queue and turned around, bringing him face-to-face with something marvelous.

"And what are *you*?" he wondered out loud.

A row of vending machines stood before him. One offered an alternative to Starbucks' extortionate prices: cheap but terrible quality coffee and hot cocoa served at one thousand degrees Fahrenheit. Another held rows upon rows of chips, cookies, and other road snacks. A third, labeled ROMANTIC ENHANCEMENTS, sold ranch dressing flavored condoms for fifty cents (quarters only).

There were two more machines that piqued Smith's interest with their explosive all-caps font: GUNS and AMMO. He wandered over to the GUNS machine and poked its fingerprint-smeared touchscreen. It presented a question:

HAVE YOU EVER BEEN CONVICTED OF A FELONY?

Beneath the question were two square icons: a green NO and a red YES. Smith stared at them for a moment before his mind resolved the incongruency between the words and colors. There were only misdemeanors and international incidents on his record, so he tapped NO.

Another question appeared:

ARE YOU CURRENTLY A FUGITIVE FROM JUSTICE?

Another NO generated another prompt.

HAVE YOU EVER BEEN DIAGNOSED WITH ANY OF THE FOLLOWING: ANTISOCIAL PERSONALITY DISORDER, BIPOLAR DISORDER, DEMENTIA, DEPRESSION, PTSD, or SCHIZOPHRENIA?

Smith tapped YES.

HAVE YOU EVER BEEN DECLARED LEGALLY DEAD?

It didn't ask whether he was still legally dead, so that was another YES.

HAVE YOU EVER ABUSED ANY OF THE FOLLOWING SUBSTANCES: ALCOHOL, BENZODIAZEPINES, COCAINE, HEROIN, or ANY OTHER CONTROLLED SUBSTANCE?

There was no ALL OF THE ABOVE button, so Smith tapped YES. The price of his gun increased by a hundred dollars, but there were no other barriers. He swiped his credit card. The vending machine's spiral released his gun—a Chekhov 0.38—which landed with a THUNK in the collection tray, just as Brooks returned from the restroom.

"Look!" Smith grinned, waving his new gun.

No one in the vicinity batted an eye, though one member of the Starbucks line appeared to adjust their bulletproof vest.

Brooks responded with the facial expression equivalent of an ellipsis. "Why?"

"Why not? When in Rome..."

"We're not going to Rome." Brooks paused. "Wait. Are you saying most of the people at this funeral are going to have guns?"

"Yeah. Probably." This didn't faze Smith at all.

"The funeral full of people who hate you? That funeral?"

"Yeah." Smith shrugged.

Brooks threw up his hands in defeat. "Don't forget the ammo. I'll be in the car."

He wandered away while his partner jabbed at another screen.

When Smith emerged from the Welcome Center, his pistol tucked into his pants and ammo and potato chips in hand, Brooks was nowhere near the Toyota. Instead, Smith found his husband in the company of the truck driverest truck driver ever to drive a truck. If there'd been a trucker in the

Village People, it would have been this guy, with his blond handlebar mustache, bald eagle belt buckle, and faded flannel button-down shirt. Judging from their body language, the trucker appeared to be hitting on the cyborg, who was loathing every second of it.

Smith approached with a bemused look. "If you're having car trouble, I wouldn't ask him."

"—there he is." Brooks slid toward Smith, desperate to exit the conversation.

The trucker eyed Smith from top to bottom and back. "There's room for two."

"Room for two for—?" Smith wondered.

Brooks waved his hand, begging his partner to cut it out, but it was too late. The trucker was thrilled to provide an answer.

"Follow me," he said with a wink.

The mustachioed man stepped around the side of the Welcome Center, and waved for them to follow him across the overgrown lawn. Smith obliged, moving in a serpentine pattern to avoid deserted piles of dog poop.

Brooks followed, reluctantly, still searching for another out. "We really should be heading—"

"We've got a few days. I wanna see," Smith said.

"No, you don't," hissed Brooks through his teeth.

Behind the building, in the dim light of sunset, was a group of twenty or so truckers engaged in all sorts of classic sexual formations—the Double Dip, the Doggy BJ, the Tag Team, the Cowboy Couplet, the Three Seater, the Aperol Spritz, and the Middle-Class Tax Burden, to name a few. The detectives weren't close enough to see or smell the most lurid details, but the grunting and sloshing sounds pervading the air were enough for them to get the gist.

Smith frowned. "Oh, it's just a trucker orgy."

"Just a—" Brooks lost the rest of his sentence.

"No thanks," said Smith to the trucker, who simply

shrugged and began unbuckling the eagle as he headed in to join the fray.

Smith averted his eyes from the man's junk, roped his free hand around Brooks, and scooted him back toward the car.

As they approached their respective doors, Brooks paused.

"*Just a trucker orgy?* Have you—"

"Been spit-roasted behind a rest area? Oh yeah." Smith climbed into the driver's seat. "Don't act surprised."

Brooks entered the passenger's side. "I'm not surprised. I mean... not at that part. I just thought the whole truck stop rest area thing was a myth."

"Well, then you were myth-staken."

Brooks groaned so loudly that neither man noticed the sound of a large drywall nail piercing the Avalon's left rear tire as they backed out of the parking space.

7 / CAR TROUBLES

Modern vehicles can last a surprising distance with a tire puncture. The detectives didn't realize anything was wrong with the Avalon until two and a half hours beyond the rest stop, when a loud POP prompted Brooks to pull their luxury model to a stop on the side of the Pennsylvania Turnpike, a short walk from the middle of nowhere.

They'd just passed through Amish Country—a booming metropolis compared to the unincorporated community of Willow Hill. It would have been a great place to isolate during a pandemic or to hide a dead body, but since the men weren't trying to do either of those things, it was far from ideal.

The night was pitch black, and there was nothing but a field of cattle as far as Brooks's enhanced vision could see. A cursory, lagging internet search located one local mechanic, whose shop was closed. A call to Waco revealed that one of the many fees they'd paid included roadside assistance, but that the nearest eligible body shop was more than thirty miles out.

"Don't worry," the Waco representative had said. "With the Waco Guarantee, we'll get it towed there in no time! If it isn't fixed within twelve hours, we'll send a replacement rental."

'No time' turned out to be over two hours, and Brooks and Smith passed the time cozied up in the backseat, reading and mocking the celebrity memoir *Don't Look at Me!*, by Godwin Zane. The luxury model was roomy, and Smith laid on his back with his knees bent and his head in Brooks's lap. He'd gotten some satisfaction learning how Shoppli CEO Maxwell Naples had displaced Godwin Zane from the title of World's Richest Man, but the book was about to take an uncomfortable turn.

Brooks read aloud. "...finally, at age thirty-two, I lost my virginity..."

"Let's skip this part."

Brooks did not. "... just as my birthday was unfairly made somber by 9/11, so too was the joyous occasion of my cherrypopping. To begin with, the only person willing to accept my magmatized seed was not a large-breasted woman, but..."

Searing headlights spared Smith this recounting of his personal low point.* As the tow truck pulled up behind them, its beams shone through the Avalon's rear window and beyond the windshield.

Smith did a little fist pump. "Thank you, Waco."

"We're going to read the rest later," Brooks said, stuffing a bookmark between the pages.

Brooks shut the book and tossed it into the footwell. He emerged from the vehicle, ready to get anywhere but Willow Hill.

Smith followed, but not before reaching down, tearing out the bookmarked page, and stuffing it into his coat pocket.

The tow truck's driver—a very large, muscular woman with a blonde mullet—inspected the scene for about thirty seconds, before reaching her verdict.

"Burst tire."

"Um. We know," Brooks said. "Did you bring a spare, or...?"

"Waco didn't give me any info, so best I can do is take her back to the shop. We do carry just about any size tire you can imagine, though. Can have her ready first thing in the morning."

If you've ever seen a vehicle lifted onto a tow truck, you know how tedious it is to describe a vehicle being lifted onto a tow truck. If you've never seen a vehicle lifted onto a tow truck, know that it happened and it was tedious.

---

* If you want to read about it, pick up *Time Purge* and *The Bedazzlers*.

When the job was done, the truck driver—whose name was Louise—opened her door and stepped up into the cab. The two men followed after her, presuming they'd be given a ride to the shop. Smith reached for the door handle but was rebuffed.

"What do you think you're doing?" Louise asked.

Smith gave her a questioning stare. "Getting to the shop?"

"Sorry, boys. Waco's guarantee provides a ride for the *car* to get to the nearest shop. It doesn't cover transportation for you two."

Brooks reached for his wallet. "Well, can we just pay you for a ride?"

"Nope. Insurance reasons."

"We're not rapists," Smith blurted out.

Brooks slowly resettled his wallet and stabbed Smith with his eyes. "What are you—"

Smith continued. "I mean, there's two of us. If it's a safety thing, I'm just saying."

The driver laughed. "Even if you were, I think I could take you two in a fight."

"Hey! Maybe me, but he's a cyborg," said Smith defensively. "He could totally—"

He realized what he was saying, and backtracked.

"—but he wouldn't. Because we're not rapists... Also, he's gay."

Brooks pinched the bridge of his nose. "Can we at least grab our bags from the trunk before you go?"

Louise nodded. "Sure thing."

Moments later, Louise and the Avalon were gone. Brooks and Smith stood on the side of the highway, with their bags at their feet. At this point, it was close to midnight.

"*We're not rapists*?" Brooks scoffed.

"It was worth a shot." Smith eyed a set of headlights in the distance. "Hitchhike?"

"Are you insane?"

"What's the worst that could happen? Someone kills us?"

"*Yes.*"

Smith shrugged. "Wouldn't stick."

"Let's just walk."

"To...?"

Brooks searched the internet, barely holding back his rage at its achingly slow speed.

"The nearest hotel is... twelve miles away. They have a vacancy. I think. The page won't load all the way."

Smith gestured at the field beyond. "I'd rather sleep on a cowpie than walk that far."

Brooks rolled his eyes. "Hi. I'm a cyborg with cyborg strength and cyborg speed, remember?" He bent his knees and gestured behind him. "Come on."

Smith groaned. "No."

"Yeah." Brooks grinned.

"Let's just hitchhike and get murdered."

"I'll carry the bags. You just piggyback and hold on tight." Brooks insisted at glowering eyes. "Come on."

Smith sighed. "Giddy up."

He hopped on and threw his hands over Brooks's shoulders, finding the whole situation humiliating. "You're lucky you can't see my face right now."

"Let me guess. Pursed lips, little wrinkle between the eyes?"

"I don't know. I can't see it either," Smith admitted.

With that idiotic remark, they were on their way. Brooks didn't make the fun CLIP CLOP noises that a horse's hooves would have, but occasionally, his knees creaked like they needed lubricant. Not because he was a cyborg, but because he was in his late thirties.

8 / ALL SOUTH FROM HERE

Pennsylvania had never been a part of the Confederate States of America, but that didn't stop the Glory Inn from proudly flying a Confederate flag out front. It waved back and forth at the top of a rusted flagpole, with a smaller American flag a foot beneath it. Though it was pitch black out, the owners were thoughtful enough to make sure the display was the only well-lit area of the property.

Smith patted Brooks's chest. "Whoa, Brooksy. Whoooa."

Brooks came to a stop. He dropped their bags, then dumped Smith off his back.

Both men stared up at the pole.

"Ugh... *Vete a la mierda, pendejos*," Brooks complained in Spanish.

Smith dusted himself off and adjusted his clothing, which had ridden up during transit. "We're not even below the Mason-Dixon. This is the only hotel around?"

"Yeah. For another *fifty miles*."

In sync, they looked up at the flagpole, across the dark lawn to the dimly lit hotel entrance, and back toward each other. Smith spoke first.

"Well, I'm white, so..."

Brooks's voice reached peak sarcasm. "You're a great ally."

"You wanna carry me another fifty miles, Seabiscuit? I'm being *practical*. We don't even have a car to sleep in. Let's just say we're brother-in-laws and swindle these rednecks out of a bed."

"Brothers-in-law," Brooks corrected.

"You know, I felt bad about you having to carry me until just now."

Brooks shook his head. "I'm going to have to make a huge donation charity to feel okay about this."

"Do what you need to, babe. I'm goin' in."

Smith led the way down an overgrown cobblestone path to a set of double doors fronting an enormous manor. It was an old colonial with six pillars and an ornate iron door-knocker in the shape of a fancy plus sign. It wasn't any symbol they recognized—and the cell service was too spotty to check—but both men got the impression it was probably racist. Next to the door stood a stone statue of Rhett Butler, his nose chipped off like some sort of segregationist sphinx.

"Look." Smith pointed. "Maybe they're just big *Gone with the Wind* fans."

"Still a problem."

Smith shrugged. "Never watched it."

"Really?"

"Four hours of rich assholes whining about their problems, and Clark Gable doesn't even hang dong? Hard pass."

"But you saw *Seabiscuit*?"

"Elizabeth Banks," Smith explained.

He opened the door to an empty lobby that smelled like wet newspaper. Along the wall to their left were framed, yellowed photos of Confederate military officers, each caked in a layer of dust. To their right was a worn letter board:

GL0RY INN:
THE SOUTH SH4LL RI$E AGAIN
BUT OUR RO0M RATES WONT

Brooks and Smith shared a glance as they continued straight on to the unmanned front desk. A corroded brass bell sat next to a sticky note that read, 'Ring for Service.'

Smith did. Repeatedly.

BING. BING BING.

BING BING BING BING BING.

Brooks pulled his husband's hand away from the bell and shot him a murderous look.

Smith reached back toward the bell and grinned.

BING BING.

An old female voice wheezed in the distance. "Just a minute."

After what felt like an hour but Brooks's internal clock registered as three minutes, an octogenarian emerged, hobbling with the assistance of a walker. She wore no fewer than three layers of sweaters over a pair of powder pink, elastic waist pants. Her eyes looked enormous behind a set of ultra-thick glasses secured around her neck by a tasteful cord.

Smith whispered to Brooks. "Now I get the Civil War theme..."

"*Eddie.*" Brooks was hesitant to mock the elderly, even if they were a white supremacist.

Smith, on the other hand, had no reservations.

"... it's *nostalgia.*"

When she reached her spot at the front desk, the old woman—whose nametag identified her as Ruth—looked up at them. "Sorry about that. I dozed off watching *Wheel.* Are you looking for a room?"

"Yeah. One night," Smith said.

"Will that be—"

"A double? Yeah," Smith said.

"Oh. I reckoned you two would want a King."

Brooks and Smith exchanged a wary look.

Ruth's giant pupils shifted toward the Confederate generals and then back to her potential customers. "I inherited this place from my parents, who inherited it from theirs. All this Southern hullabaloo is just a gimmick. I don't give two toots about those traitors, but it goes over well with a certain demographic. And remodeling is far too expensive."

"A King then," Smith confirmed.

"Alrighty. It's forty a night."

Brooks and Smith eyed each other. Brooks mouthed "*forty?*" before asking out loud, "You mean two forty or three forty, right?"

"I mean *forty*."

Brooks responded under his breath. "You could probably afford the remodel if you raised your rates..."

Ruth scrunched her face. "Where are you boys from?"

"Brooklyn."

She nodded in understanding. "How long did you want to stay again?"

"Just the one night. We're passing through," Smith said.

A hop, skip, and a credit card swipe later, Brooks raised an old-fashioned skeleton key to the door of a suite labeled 'The Carpetbagger's Chambers.'

"This feels like a personal attack," he said.

"I might agree with you if I knew what a carpetbagger was," said Smith.

"It's an insult from the Civil War," Brooks explained as they made their way into the room. "Southerners used to... holy crap."

"They used to...? Oh."

They both stopped in their tracks in awe of the room's decor. It was normal, for the most part. There was a four-poster bed with burgundy curtains ready to be drawn around it, an antique desk and dresser, gaudy out-of-date carpeting in red and gold... then there were the room's other occupants.

Between the bed and a window that overlooked the parking lot stood four life-sized wax figures: Abraham Lincoln, seated in a chair, and three Union soldiers standing at his side. Honest Abe was in the direct path of the evening sun, and his stovepipe hat had melted and re-solidified over and over again, giving it a bumpy, dribbling appearance like a stalagmite.

"They're staring into my soul," Brooks said.

"Souls aren't real. Ask me how I know."

"How do you know?"

"Because if I had one, it would have just left my body."

Smith removed his jacket, walked over to the figures, and draped it over Lincoln's head. Then he pulled his shirt off over his head and used that to cover the dead-eyed face of one of the wax soldiers.

"Good plan." Brooks followed suit, using his own jacket and shirt to cover the last two figures.

"That's better," Smith said.

Brooks shuddered. "I can still picture their faces. Ugh."

Smith eyed his husband lecherously. "I'm picturing something else."

"No. Not until I find a shower." Brooks felt (and smelled) like he'd just run the Preakness Stakes. He opened the only door in the room, expecting to find an en suite bathroom. It was a closet. He tossed his bag inside, then turned toward the room's entrance, dismayed and checking heat signatures to locate the bathroom.

Smith reached for his shoulder. "Who cares? Come on. You. Me. *Spur* of the moment..."

Brooks ignored what must have been Smith's dozenth horse reference. "Shower."

"Fine, fine."

Brooks stepped into the hallway and Smith followed. Floorboards creaked as they moved toward an open door that was glowing with fluorescent light.

It was the bathroom, all right, and Brooks ran face-first into the person exiting it.

"Sorry," Brooks said.

"Hey!" said the man in recognition.

Smith snickered to himself. "*Hay.*"

Brooks, in a stroke of terrible luck, had just collided with the trucker who'd previously offered to Eiffel Tower him.

"I didn't catch your name before," the trucker said.

Brooks spoke through a fake smile. "That's because I didn't give it to you."

The trucker gave him a friendly slap on the shoulder. "I'm

in the Bull Run Room, if you wanna stop by." He turned to Smith and winked. "Still room for two."

"We're good," Brooks said, in a tone that said "I'm dreaming of homicide."

Smith adored that tone. Minutes later, once they'd scrubbed the turnpike filth from their bodies and room was thick with steam, he found his eyes wandering back to his husband's soapy body.

"You, uh... *hot to trot?*"

"Neigh," Brooks said dryly.

"Hey..."

Despite his brash nature, Smith could be charming when necessary. He deemed horny-in-a-community-shower one of those moments.

"... sorry about the horse jokes."

"What? I don't care about those. I just have a lot on my mind with Adopt Shop and—"

"Let me take it off your mind." Smith smiled softly and kissed his shoulder.

Brooks always fell for that smile, and he chuckled at himself. "How do you do that?"

"Lotta tongue," Smith said, sliding to his knees.

Brooks startled. "Wait."

He brought his husband back up to eye-level and pulled him close.

"That trucker is peeping," Brooks whispered and nudged Smith's head toward a gap in the shower door.

Smith could make out just enough to tell that Brooks was right... but he didn't care.

"Let him peep," he said.

Fun, explicit times were had.* An undisclosed length of time later, Brooks and Smith exited the shower stall, wrapped

---

* Sorry if you thought this was the kind of book that would describe them to you.

in undersized hotel towels. Outside, they encountered a problem. Not one of the bathroom's old problems, like its dripping sink, cracked mirror, and rusted floor drain. This one was brand new.

"Where are our clothes...?" Brooks asked.

Smith glanced around. "Well... I'm guessing that pervert made off with them and is currently sniffing your *chones* while he tugs one out to 'Goodbye Horses.'" He paused. "That was a *Silence of the Lambs* joke, not a horse joke."

Brooks sighed. "It's fine. We have more pants."

"Who are you trying to convince here? 'Cause I couldn't care less."

"At least he left the key..."

The pair left the bathroom, still half naked, and tiptoed down the hallway to the Carpetbagger's Chambers. They found the door already cracked open.

Smith stepped into the room first. His face twisted in disgust. "There is no god."

"You don't have to be a dick about... oh."

Brooks realized his husband wasn't giving an atheist screed, but reacting to the wax figures—visible once more. The detectives' jackets and shirts had gone the way of their pants and underwear.

Smith pulled open the closet door. "They didn't get our bags."

"Or our phones." Brooks eyed the nightstand, where his Zanephone still rested on its charging pad. Next to it was a piece of paper, torn from a book.

"Did you remove your sex scene from *Don't Look at Me*?"

"Yeah. Guess even the perv who nicked our clothes didn't wanna read that."

Brooks flopped onto the bed. "Ugh. This is a disaster."

Smith took a seat on the edge of the bed. "This is what road trips *are*."

"Have you ever even taken a road trip?"

"No... but I watched the *National Lampoon* movies. Have you?"

"Have I watched the—"

"Have you ever taken a road trip, smartass?"

Brooks paused for a moment, lost in thought. "Yeah..."

Smith stared at him. "So... you got a story to tell, or are you gonna sit there looking like you just got a blowie?"

"I *did* just..." Brooks laughed it off and sat up. "Okay. When Tasha and I were ten or eleven, our dad saved up enough money to take us to Disney World. The three of us and our grandparents all loaded into this minivan and drove the whole way there. It took *forever*, and my dad never wanted to stop. He just kept on checking the clock and saying we were making good time. I had to pee in a soda bottle at one point."

"Sounds great..."

"I *hated* it... the whole trip. We stayed at a campground, and it was hot and miserable and there was no shower pressure. The parks were nothing but lines. But... looking back, I wouldn't change a thing. It was perfect."

Smith scoffed. "Pissing in a bottle was perfect?"

"Yeah. You know how memories are just... like that sometimes? Rose-colored?"

"No." Smith shook his head.

"I don't just mean from childhood. They can be from whenever. There's nothing you look back and appreciate in hindsight?"

"No."

"*Nothing?*"

Smith was silent for a moment, pensive.

"You're thinking of something," Brooks said.

Smith nodded, then looked away. "I'm kinda glad I accidentally killed myself."

"Oh my God. Are you serious?" Brooks's eyes widened. His shoulders tensed. He was ready to call some sort of hotline.*

"Calm down," Smith said. "*Not like that.* I'm glad I'm not dead. But it forced me to own up to my bullshit, and it made us a lot closer."

"Okay. That's... less bad. Still don't love it, though."

Noting the disconnected look on his husband's face, Smith apologized. "Sorry."

"Well... I asked." Brooks fell backwards onto his pillow. "Let's just go to bed."

Smith rolled over to the other side of the bed and began scooting under the covers.

"At least tonight can't get any worse," Brooks muttered under his breath.

Smith froze in place, then tapped his partner across the arm. "Are you kidding me?"

"What? It can't."

Brooks's phone responded at that exact moment with loud vibrations. Smith shook his head and turned to face the ceiling.

"It's Adopt Shop," Brooks announced.

"At two in the morning? They really do disrupt the industry..."

Brooks grimaced and tapped at the phone. "Hello?"

"Hi, this is Kharisma with Adopt Shop."

"Hi. You're on speaker."

"Wonderful. Sorry to call so late, but we just finished up your paperwork."

"Oh, okay. So how—"

"You and your husband are approved!" she announced

---

* Which is, y'know... what you should do if you're suicidal. Don't kill yourself.^

^ Also, don't take advice from comedy books.%

% Except this advice.#

Fuck.

cheerfully.

The looks of fear briefly left Brooks and Smith's faces, but they probably shouldn't have. Much like the Church of Scientology, Adopt Shop kept the breadth of its insanity under wraps. Only when a couple had been approved for adoption did they truly learn the ways in which the company 'disrupted the industry.'

Kharisma explained the next steps. "We need to see you in our office next Tuesday. It'll be fifty thousand dollars, cash only."

"Cash only?" Smith mouthed.

Brooks raised a finger to his lips.

"There will also be a standard contract and Non-Disclosure Agreement."

"A Non-Disclosure..."

"Totally standard. It just states that you won't share any information about our process, that if you leave any online reviews that you must first send them to us for vetting, that you can never take your child to Des Moines... et cetera, et cetera. I've emailed a copy to both of you."

Brooks pretended all that was normal. "Great. Thanks."

"Congratulations again, and thank you for choosing Adopt Shop!"

Brooks and Smith exchanged an awkward glance in awkward silence as the dial tone rang out.

Smith was first to break it. "I don't wanna be a Debbie Downer, but... this seems sus."

Brooks shook his head. "Please stop saying that. It is, though."

"Yep." Smith tapped at his phone to find Adopt Shop's email.

Brooks shifted his eyes. "But... does it have to be?"

"You saying we should ignore something shady going on for our own benefit?" asked Smith.

"Ugh. No. Obviously not. But maybe—"

"Babe, you can't even handle the old country inn. How are you gonna feel when you find out Adopt Shop is into child slavery or something?"

"Yeah... we have to investigate. I know." Brooks sighed.

Smith stared at the documents. "Oh. Definitely. Have you seen—"

"The part about fake social security numbers?" Brooks nodded. He'd been reviewing the email in his mind.

"I was gonna say the part about getting the kid micro-chipped like a pet..."

Other highlights included mandatory barcode tattoos and registration in the Epstein Registry of Vulnerable Youth.

"It's bad," Brooks said. "They have to know that, right?"

"They sure as shit should."

"Then why would they allow two *detectives* to get this far in the process? They know what we do for a living."

"Doesn't make sense," Smith said. "Could be a trap?"

"There's a lot of easier ways to trap us." Several monsters and a grey billionaire had managed to kidnap them over the years, without the need for an elaborate ruse.

Adopt Shop had finally taken the turn they'd been expecting. Now it was a matter of unraveling the thread of corruption until it was a big messy pile of corruption on the floor.

"What are we going to do?" Brooks asked. "Obviously we're not adopting some slave kid, but... do we show up with the fifty thousand dollars and just see where it goes?"

"You know I'm a big fan of looting the retirement fund, but how about we just pretend we have the money, show up, and do some breaking and entering?"

"Works for me." Brooks's words didn't match his despondent demeanor.

Smith scooted closer to him. "You knew there was a good chance this place was shady."

"Yeah. I guess now you don't have to worry about the sea bream," Brooks said bitterly.

Smith put a hand on his arm. "Hey..."

"Eddie, I swear—"

"Not the horse kind." Smith took his husband's hand and intertwined their fingers. "Just 'cause these guys are shady... it doesn't mean never."

"You're just saying that to be nice."

"Well, *yeah*," Smith admitted. "I think it's a disaster waiting to happen, but—"

"If—"

"Let me finish."

Brooks nodded.

"I'm fucking terrified. But you're not, and I trust you. If you think I can do it, then I can do it. So... we'll do it."

Tears began forming in Brooks's eyes.

"What? What's wrong?" Smith wondered.

"Happy crying..." Brooks wrapped his arms around Smith and squeezed, unaware of the mischievous grin that had worked its way onto his husband's face.

"Easy, there. We still have to solve this case. *Don't put the cart before the horse.*"

No number of horse jokes could have robbed Brooks of his joy in that moment.

9 / BISCUIT BUCKET

Brooks and Smith's road trip soon improved. When they awoke six hours later, their freshly laundered jackets, pants, and shirts were hung neatly outside their room: a free service, included in the forty-dollar room rate. Some unseen staff member had taken care of the cleaning while the two were being perved on in the shower. On a suspicious note, their underwear was not with the laundered goods, but a seventy-five percent recovery rate was much better than the police recovery rate for stolen items, which has hovered around twenty-six percent for several decades.*

The detectives tidied themselves once more, and made their way to Appomattox, the on-site restaurant in the basement. Its dining room radiated an aura of sadness. Think Waffle House at three o'clock in the morning. The cement walls had been painted pink thirty years earlier, and had never been touched up. The tables were cafeteria-like, covered with aged white vinyl tablecloths, with antique, hickory Windsor chairs providing the seating. In one corner, a bar that seated four was nestled beneath green glass pendant lights. The bar stools were identical to the dining furniture, only taller. They didn't swivel because that would have been one blessing in this forsaken place.

A wistful Smith stared at an illuminated Jack Daniels sign behind the bar.

Brooks caught him looking.

"It's ten o'clock in the morning," he said.

---

* Source: FBI Uniform Crime Reporting Program. Now you can tell your friends you're reading something educational instead of ruminating on the nature of satire and failing to explain what the hell this book is actually about while they stare through you with dread in their eyes.

"The heart wants what the heart wants."

A sign shaped like a downward-pointing arrow dangled from the ceiling over the worst seats in the house—a diner booth for two tucked between the men's restroom and a swinging two-way kitchen door. It read:

> Sit at the John Wilkes booth and we'll take
> a Lincoln ($5) off your bill.

They shrugged in unison, and took the crappy seats. Appomattox's single-page menus looked like they'd been photocopied from a photocopy of a photocopy.

Smith squinted to read the fading text. "Dred Scott's Dred Tots...?"

Brooks's face twisted in disgust as he perused the drinks menu. "Our drink special is the... Fieldhand's Tears...a southern-style mix of seltzer and tobacco-infused bourbon garnished with cotton candy..."

"Okay, even I know that's fucked," Smith said.

Brooks fell into his dead stare.

"What are you doing?" Smith asked.

"Making that huge donation..." The dungeon of a restaurant had Wi-Fi, at least.

Ultimately, they decided on coffee—the cheapest menu item, and the only one without an appalling name. As they downed their third refills, Louise called to let them know the Avalon was ready.

Smith tossed two dollars onto the table and stared at his husband, struggling to hold back a smile.

"What?" Brooks asked.

"That's all I have in my wallet."

"And?" Brooks asked.

Smith grinned. "*Pony up.*"

"You're lucky you're pretty."*

Brooks tossed three more dollars on the table, and the two were on their way.

This time, they took advantage of the hotel's complimentary shuttle service. Brooks had been prepared to give the Glory Inn a one-star review on Trippr, but taking into account the sheer hospitality of the place, he forced himself to rate it one and a half, with the added comment: "Would be a nice hotel if it weren't for all the racism." Smith, meanwhile, rated it three stars with no explanation. According to some study Brooks once read to him, that was the worst thing a reviewer could do, as it left the business with neither affirmation nor constructive criticism. An unexplained three-star review might be stewed over for days, maybe weeks...†

"Ohio lasts *forever*," Brooks despaired later that afternoon.

It wasn't the widest state they'd end up crossing during their journey, but it was the most boring. There's a reason many of Ohio's best-known celebrities are famous for finding creative ways of leaving Ohio. The Wright Brothers took to the sky. Neil Armstrong went to the moon. Charles Manson went to prison.

"You've got this," reassured Smith, while swiping through faces on a new adoption app called Adoptr. "How about this one? A-A-A-A-Ayden. Six months old."

Brooks glanced over at a picture of a smiling child that looked the same as all the others, then returned his eyes to the road. "Did you develop a stutter or are there really five A's?"

"There are f-f-f-f-ive A's," Smith stuttered. "Oh, it says

---

* Smith was neither.

† Maybe years. Are you listening, Gary? You son of a bitch.

he's addicted to crack. *Left.*"

"Someone has to give the crack baby a chance."

"Yeah, but *we* don't." Smith kept swiping. "Rayleigh, age two... not good with pets. *Left.* Tallahassee, seventeen months, no known problems... *Right.* Caleighmari, age three... yiiiikes that's a big scar. *Left.*"

Brooks ran his hand along the mark on his neck, just under his left ear, and frowned.

Smith backtracked. "This was really, really big. Whole body big." He moved on. "Anna Marie Maria Anne, two years old, straight couples only. Well fuck you too, Anna."

"I doubt the kid put that there," Brooks said.

"The kids on this app *suck* compared to Adopt Shop."

"Well, they don't have Shoppli's backing..."

Smith looked up from the disappointing faces for a moment to blurt a single word: "Food."

Brooks eyed a blue FOOD NEXT EXIT sign in the distance. He zoomed in on it, in hopes that this exit would be different from the last four. It wasn't. Nothing but Biscuit Bucket. He sighed, louder than usual.

"Have you ever *had* Biscuit Bucket?" Smith asked.

Brooks answered in a smug tone. "No."

"Okay, Maxwell Naples." Smith raised a pretentious pinkie finger. "It's not that bad. And since it's all we've seen in sixty miles..."

"You want to go to Biscuit Bucket."

"Yes."

Brooks tapped the turn signal. "Fine."

"You're not gonna regret it."

Brooks doubted that as he took the exit and pulled into the Biscuit Bucket parking lot. Packed with vehicles that outsized theirs, the lot seemed to stretch for miles. Brooks circled the building twice before stuffing the Avalon into a space between two minivans that had parked right on the lines.

"Babe..." Smith cracked his door, and gestured at the sliver of space available for him to exit.

"Okay. Which of these vans do we hate more?" Brooks asked.

"The one on the left had a stick figure family on the back."

"Works for me."

Brooks backed the Avalon out of the space, then sidled back in so the car was almost touching the left minivan. Soon, a family with four child lacrosse players would be furious.

Smith threw open his door and hopped out.

Brooks followed, struggling to maneuver his six-foot-one frame across the front seats and out into the parking lot.

FLAP FLAP was the sound that greeted them outside the car. FLAP FLAP FLAP.

Patriotic vinyl bunting hung around the perimeter of the yellow building, and the Ohio winds that had once helped the Wright Brothers take flight now lent the Biscuit Bucket an enchanting soundtrack.

FLAP FLAP.

Smith soaked it all in. "You feel that?"

"Anxiety?" Brooks wondered.

"Americana."

Brooks eyed some locals swaying back and forth in rocking chairs on the building's expansive porch. "I feel like I'm going to get hate crimed here."

"Nah," said Smith, dismissing that with a handwave. "They're doing better."

A few years earlier, Biscuit Bucket had faced a PR nightmare when it was revealed that its founder, Hieronymus Hardtack, had been a member of the wildly evangelical Church of Smite. The Church had some problematic fire and brimstone beliefs, which they'd shown explicitly through the restaurant chain's treatment of its employees. As a result, the internet had embarked on a virulent social justice crusade against Biscuit Bucket, using hashtags like #BisQuit and

#ButterTogether. It had impacted sales, forcing the chain to make some changes.

Brooks and Smith entered the lobby of a friendlier, more politically correct Biscuit Bucket, past a large wooden plaque with a chain of linked hands etched into it. The sign read:

WE'RE DOING BETTER

Here at Biscuit Bucket, we respect the money of all customers, regardless of age, race, sex, gender, national origin, orientation, disability, religion, voting preference, weight, height, eye color, or any other characteristic, immutable or not.

Smith gestured at the sign. "See?"

"Charming," Brooks replied.

To their left stood a host station, manned by a frazzled teenager in a red and white striped apron. To their right was the restaurant's gift shop, where a few locals with nothing better to do were browsing products they didn't need.

Smith hurried into the gift shop.

Brooks called after him. "What are you—"

The gift shop looked as if someone had loaded a game of Boggle with cheap, sweatshop-made trinkets. There was no coherent order to anything.

"Look at this!" Smith gestured at a four-foot-long To-blerone. "And this!" A foam cowboy hat. "Holy shit!" He grabbed a bottle of dill pickle flavored soda and held it up like a trophy.

Brooks shrank in embarrassment as he stepped reluctantly into the gift shop. "I thought you were hungry."

"I am hungry... *for a bargain.*" Smith's eyes lit up as he rushed toward a display of poorly executed primitives. "Wooden signs that say things!"

"We are *not* buying primitives."

"I wouldn't dream of it. But *look at them.*"

Brooks looked, in horror.

I keep trying to loose weight but it keeps finding me

This house is:

Happy

And

Uplifting

Never Empty

Together

Empathetic

Delightful

If mama ain't happy, everyone's food is gettin' poisoned.

When life gives you zombies, make zombie friends!

Wine: It's Cheaper than Therapy

Vampires: Live, Laugh, Love, Live Again

The signs were awful, but Brooks couldn't help but smile. It wasn't often Smith showed his giddy side, and if a ludicrous gift shop did the trick, it was a gift shop worth perusing. Brooks sifted through a rotating stand of typo-ridden bumper stickers and snickered.

If you can read this, your too close

Pigeon Mom

The best things in life are free (if you have a gun)

My other car is the Bedazzlemobile

"We should road trip more often," Brooks said.

"Agreed." Smith put on a pair of pink, star-shaped sunglasses. "What do you think?"

Brooks shook his head. "Were you even hungry?"

Smith shrugged, then darted toward a stand of summer-themed snow globes.

An hour later, a server directed the detectives past walls covered in tin and patrons covered in gravy to a booth large enough for four. Smith slid his bag of tacky souvenirs into one side, then scooted in next to it with ease, while Brooks wedged himself into the small space opposite. The tabletop dug into his stomach.

"Ugh. Can we move this thing toward you a little?"

He pushed and Smith pulled, but the table wouldn't budge.

"You wanna switch sides?" Smith hoped not, since he'd end up even more squished than Brooks.

"No." Brooks gave the table a good cyborg shove. It didn't move.

"Performance issues?"

"Shut up." Brooks shoved harder. "What the hell is holding this thing together?"

Smith patted the seat next to him. "Come be gay with me. Biscuit Bucket doesn't discriminate anymore." He looked up, addressing a portrait of Hieronymus Hardtack above their booth. "Cope."

Brooks dislodged himself and moved across the booth, nestling in next to his husband. He glanced up at a TV on the dining room wall. On screen, a typical blonde twenty-something was reporting on a plane that had been hijacked out of LaGuardia. Brooks acknowledged the TSA's failure with a discerning snort.

Smith took a laminated menu from the display stand and unfolded it in front of them. Then he unfolded it again. Then he unfolded it yet again. Once fully opened, the menu spread all the way across the booth, like battle plans for the fight against healthy living.

"Look, they have your favorite." Brooks gestured to the words. "Spaghetti pie."

Smith groaned.

Brooks traced his finger down to a small box in a corner labeled 'Healthy Options.' There had originally been six items there, but four had been marked out with Sharpie, leaving only the Simp Salad and Nitwit Nachos.

"They really don't want people to order these, do they?" Brooks asked.

Smith shrugged. He ended up ordering the Geezer Sunrise from the all-day breakfast menu. Brooks ordered the Nitwit Nachos, with carrot chips.

Smith eyed his phone screen while they waited.

"That's weird..." he said. "I tried to reopen the NDA we got and it's gone."

Brooks tapped at his own phone. "Gone for me too. Hang on..."

His eyes shifted to a dead stare as he cyborged his way into Adopt Shop's servers.

The number of cyborgs in the world at this point was unknown, but it was fortunate that none had executed any sinister plans. With a little more time and a little less morality, Brooks could have hacked into anything. He could have started wars, crippled economies, crashed satellites. Instead, the most malicious thing he'd done was use his powers to circumvent Shoppli's convoluted return process by hacking into their servers and issuing himself a refund for a stoneware gravy boat that had arrived broken.

Brooks put those skills to work again as he rifled through Adopt Shop's records.

"There's no mention of us on their servers. There's nothing about *any* adoptions on there. Just administrative stuff like instructions for requesting time off and an announcement for the annual chili cookoff."

"That seems sus..."—Smith held the pause just long enough to annoy—"...picious."

"There was definitely stuff there before." Brooks maintained his glassy stare as he scoured the internet. "There's something called a self-destructive email that becomes unreadable after a certain amount of time, or after an action... like, say... opening and signing an NDA..."

"Just what you want to see in an adoption agency."

Brooks furrowed his brow. "I can't find anything. They must have moved their records somewhere..."

"Check Shoppli?"

The parent company was a reasonable place to look.

"Already did. There's nothing about Adopt Shop there either. Damn it!" Brooks tightened his grip on his drink, shattering the plastic cup and sending a flood of water and ice cubes across the table. He grabbed a stack of napkins and blotted the mess.

Smith put a hand on Brooks's leg. "You know you don't have to be useful, right?"

"What? Of course I do."

"No. You don't. I love you because you're you."

"Yeah, I know. But being a cyborg has to be good for *something*, right? Otherwise, what's the point?"

Smith startled at the sentiment, but moved past it. "So... you think they're keeping *paper records*?"

"God help us if that's the case. I think they're probably keeping everything digitally, just offline. In which case...

when we get there on Monday, I'll see if I can access their local network and poke around."

Finally, the food arrived. A humbled Brooks had to admit it was delicious.

Before leaving, Smith insisted on a second trip through the gift shop, just in case they missed anything. The detectives had spent so long in Biscuit Bucket that, once they emerged, Smith had earned himself a rewards card. Also, it was evening...

"Oh shit," said Smith, feigning disappointment. "Guess we're gonna have to call it a night."

"Why? I have night vision."

Smith let out a dramatic yawn. "It's too bad it's so late."

"It's seven thirty."

They reached the Avalon, which sported a fresh dent on the driver's side door. Smith leaned against the trunk "You're gonna make me say it, aren't you?"

"Oh yeah," Brooks said.

Smith had been trying this new thing where he'd actually describe his emotional needs, and he hated it. He exhaled. "I don't wanna be in Indiana tonight."

"You don't want to be there ever."

"No... I don't. But can we... call it a night? There's a Nights Inn across the street. I wanna push this back as long as I can."

"Of course."

"Yeah?"

"Yeah. See how easy it is when you tell me what you want?" Brooks asked.

Smith grew ornery. "But what if what I want is to not tell you what I want."

Brooks just shook his head.

10 / HOOSIER DAMNED

As the Avalon traversed the Ohio-Indiana-Kentucky tri-state area, the hellfire billboards became more and more frequent. They usually appeared in sets. First, a black sign would ask a loaded question in bold white letters. A few hundred feet down the road, another would answer the question with righteous fury. A few hundred feet further, a third sign would offer an alternative. It was formulaic, but must have been profitable for someone, as the signs infested the landscape like Bradford pear trees.

Feeling **LOST**?
HELL is REAL
JESUS has the **MAP** out

Smith pointed at the sign. "That bastard stole our map."
Brooks snickered.

Imagine NO RELIGION?
So did **STALIN**.
Better **DEAD** than **RED**.

"Do you think most people around here even know who Stalin was?" Brooks asked.
"By 'around here' you mean 'in America'? Not a chance."
"Do *you* know who Stalin was?"
Smith grew quiet.

Are You **SAVED**?
Don't ask me, I'm a billboard
Only **GOD** knows

"Oh my god, they're becoming self-aware!'"

The signs and mockery continued like that for a while.

At the end of a long bridge spanning the Ohio River, they passed a much more ominous sign: a small blue square with a picture of a red state. It read:

Welcome to Indiana: The   State

Ample space between 'The' and 'State' gave the impression that a word had faded or been scratched from the sign, but it was actually a placeholder. No one in Indiana had ever figured out what they could fill it with other than 'Jesus,' and that was 'unconstitutional' according to several hell-bound law nerds.

"Pull over," Smith said.

Brooks's voice combined concern with annoyance.

"Again?"

"*Pull over.*"

Brooks dutifully did so.

His husband leapt from the car and pulled a pack of cigarettes from his pocket. Smoking was the only vice Smith had left, and he'd set himself a deliberate limit of one pack per month. He regretted that small bit of self-care as he gave the pack a little shake and counted. There were two left, and it was only April 5th.

For a brief moment, he considered saving them, but the thought went through the rental car, back out the window, and was hit by a passing semi. Smith didn't plan. He lit one of the cigarettes and tucked the other away for later.

Brooks waited for a caravan of Shoppli trucks to pass before opening the driver's side door and joining his husband.

"Welcome to Indiana." Smith gave a despondent chuckle. In the distance, he could see the single water tower that marked his hometown's skyline.

"Do you want to go home?"

Smith took a deep drag and shook his head. "May as well enjoy the shitshow."

Brooks glanced around. "At least it's clean."

"Yeah, thanks to the..."—Smith squinted to make out an ADOPT A HIGHWAY: LITTER PATROL sign in the distance—"...KKK."

Brooks responded in rapid blinks. "I always thought you were exaggerating, but the signs and the bumper stickers and the... *ugh*. I'm sorry you grew up here."

"Hey," said Smith, feigning offense, "you don't get to shit talk it yet. Not until you've had the authentic Indiana experience."

"Sorry... the authentic Indiana experience?"

"You'll see."

When Smith was finished with his coping mechanism, he tossed the butt to the ground and pressed it into the gravel with his shoe.

Normally, Brooks would have objected to littering, but in this instance, leaving trash on the side of the road would force the racist litter-pickers dangerously close to oncoming traffic. He let it slide.

They resumed the drive, passing such varied scenery as a Dollar Tree, a Dollar General, and a Family Dollar on their way to the Clarksville Nanotel—a chain hotel that looked like every other chain hotel. It stood on a dusty, flat street between two shuttered gas stations and across from an empty field. There was one other car in the hotel's parking lot, and its hood had been painted with busty erotica and a fading Guns N' Roses logo.

On the inside, the hotel appeared to be clean unless you stared at any one element too long. That's when the cracks in the plaster, the pubes in the shower, and the tears in the carpet would become apparent.*

Brooks quoted Wikipedia as they sat on the edge of their hotel bed, bored out of their minds. "Did you know... Clarksville has the largest exposed fossil beds from the Devonian period?"

"Yeah, that's like the only thing it has." Smith didn't look at his husband; he was busy flipping through TV channels.

"Not true. It also has the seventh largest clock in the world."

"It was the second largest when I lived here..." Smith looped through all eight stations and groaned. On screen, a local news anchor reported on a Shoppli warehouse strike.

"—CEO Maxwell Naples was quoted saying 'I don't give a shit.' Workers, meanwhile, say conditions are dehumanizing, with Shoppli offering only one five-minute restroom break and one twenty-minute social media break per shift. Last week, one employee was crushed by a loading robo—"

Smith turned it off.

Brooks continued. "Clarksville is also home to the second-largest Trout Pro sporting goods shop in the United States at the Green River Mall."

"That one's new to me. Don't get me wrong... *I don't care*, but at least it's new."

Brooks frowned. "I'm beginning to see why you started drinking."

"Cheers to that." Smith raised a bottle of water to the air before stopping to reminisce. "Believe it or not, this was the best town I lived in."

During his stint in Indiana's foster system, young Smith had the pleasure of living in such places as Shelbyville, Remington, Monrovia, Seymour, and Bloomfield.†

---

*You decide whether that's 'tears' rhyming with 'bears' or 'tears' rhyming with 'beers.' Both were present.

† If you've heard of any of those, you know too much about Indiana.

Brooks shook his head in disbelief. "So... which awful chain restaurant do you want for dinner?"

"Let's just order pizza to the room and go to bed."

"Yeah?"

"Yeah. Then I'll pretend I'm asleep so you don't try to talk to me about my feelings, until you eventually drift off, at which point I'll wallow in existential dread for a few hours until my eyes physically can't take anymore and I pass out against my own will."

Brooks stared at him. "You know I can tell whether you're asleep, right? From your heart rate?"

"Great. I'm married to a Fitbit."

Brooks ignored that, and adopted a serious tone. "Are you going to be okay?"

"Probably."

"Are you sure? Because when you start making dark jokes—"

"Who's joking? That's exactly what I'm gonna do to-night—"

"Eddie..."

"—and that's fine. It's okay. I'm self-aware or whatever."

"Okay." Brooks wasn't sure the concept of self-awareness was meant to lead to total resignation, but he decided to change the subject. "I'm going to put something out there and you're probably going to say no, but—"

"Spit it out."

Brooks feigned offense. "*Never.*"

Smith smiled. "Really, though."

"Should we visit some of... I don't want to call them your family, but..."

"No," said Smith.

"We drove all this way—"

"Yeah. We did. And if we're lucky, no one will recognize me tomorrow and we can get back to driving and be out of this shithole by noon."

"Do you want to at least give me a tour of the town?"

"Oh, sure," Smith said sardonically, as he hitched his voice up to a higher pitch, "—over here on your left is the school I dropped out of... and over there's a house I lived in for two months where I had the shit kicked out of me. That spot over there? That's where a kiddy diddler lives. Wanna know how I know?" He faked a laugh.

"Okay, I get your point."

Smith's voice returned to normal. "Good."

"It's just... I doubt we're ever coming back here, so if there's *anything* I can learn about you while we're in town... I'd like to. That's all. I know your life here sucked, so if the answer is no, it's no."

Smith's demeanor softened. "Actually, you know what... there is... one place that didn't suck."

Brooks responded in an instant. "Take me there."

Not long after, the detectives were standing on the bank of the Ohio River. It was evening, and the brown water glimmered with purple—reflections of the lights from yet another bridge spanning from Indiana to Kentucky. There were so many bridges—enough for hundreds of people to jump from at once.

Smith seated himself on a patch of dead grass and tapped the ground next to him, waiting for Brooks to join.

The park, like many things in Indiana, was full of unrealized potential. If someone cleared out the driftwood and installed a few benches and trash cans here and there, it could have been nice.

"That's it." Smith gestured across the river at a skyline much more impressive than Clarksville's.

"That's what?"

"Louisville, Kentucky. Population half a million, give or

take."

Brooks fact-checked. "Over six hundred thousand."

"Whatever. When I was a kid, it was the biggest place I'd ever seen. The O'Gradys hated going there. Said it was too crowded. But once in a while they'd take me, Teddy, and Lyla across the river to go to the zoo or a monster truck rally or whatever, and I thought that city was *huge*. When I got a little older, I used to come down here and think about crossing that bridge and just... disappearing. Getting lost in the crowds. First time I ran away from home, that's where I went."

"Really? You never told me that."

Smith laughed. "Yeah, 'cause they found me two days later. It's not that big."

"Then what?"

"Then... nothing. They just kept trying to talk to me about it, and... I never could explain myself. I can't even explain myself now. I just... had to get out. I knew if I didn't, I was gonna fucking die here." Smith snorted. "Well... I died anyway."

Brooks stayed silent, but noticed his husband rubbing his hands together for warmth. He put an arm around him.

"They really did try, and... I kind of hate them for it..." Smith removed Brooks's arm from his shoulder.

"*Why?*"

"Because. It'd be a lot easier to explain who I am if no one ever cared. Instead, it's on me. The reverse Midas. Everything I touch turns to shit."

"You've been saving people's lives for *two decades*."

"Not *them*. There's like this thing where... the closer I am to people, the worse I make things."

"That's—"

"You're gonna say it's not true, but... if you hadn't met me, you'd never have joined the Reticent. You wouldn't be a cyborg, and you wouldn't have to spend every day of your life dealing with my bullshit..."

Brooks closed his eyes. "Eddie—"

"I wis—" Smith stopped himself from saying the 'w' word. "I love you, but I... sorta hope... that one day you'll leave me."

"No, you don't," Brooks said. "We're in Indiana and you're spiraling." On a dime, the cyborg's face switched to its hollow expression as he googled his way through his husband's crisis.

Smith shook his head. He glanced over his shoulder at a town full of bad memories. After a minute or two of brooding, he turned back around, reached into his pocket for his last cigarette, and lit the tip.

"Yeah. You're right."

"I'm always right," Brooks said.

Smith had no reply.

11 / FAMILY TIES

It was a good thing Brooks and Smith were almost always dressed for a funeral, since that's exactly where they were headed. Following a nice night's sleep for Brooks and a nice night's existential dread for Smith, they tossed their bags into the Avalon's trunk.

Smith wedged a pizza box in on top of the luggage.

"Why are we bringing leftover pizza?" Brooks asked.

"It's a Midwestern funeral. Everyone brings food." Smith squinted. "Did you wanna make a hotdish at the Nanotel?"

"No. I mean... they're not going to think it's weird that it's half eaten?"

"Two thirds," Smith corrected, "and if anyone opens it, they'll assume someone else got to it first. It's the perfect crime."

"And who *doesn't* want to pull one over on the bereaved?"

Smith shrugged.

Brooks checked his watch. "You'd think the girls would have shown up by now."

Smith didn't share his concern. "Lemon said they saw us in Indiana. She didn't say when. For all we know, it was 2045."

"I hate that time machine."

"Oh, *you* hate it?"

Brooks groaned. "I am *not* in the mood to argue with you over which of us has been more traumatized by time travel. *Again.*"

"Me neither," Smith said.

"Good."

"It's me, though."

Brooks held his tongue. They were heading to a funeral, and he knew Smith was holding on by a thread, but he could have made a good case for himself. The same wacky caper that had put his husband on a decades-long bender had given Brooks the worst gift this side of a gym membership—knowledge of his date of death. When the time came, he didn't die (obviously), but there was still something to be said for spending a decade of one's life counting down the days to its expiration. It had left Brooks a neurotic perfectionist. Accordingly, he adjusted his tie in the side-view mirror.

"You look fine," Smith said.

"Fine?"

Smith upgraded his assessment. "Good?"

"Better."

"What do you want, 'sexy'? We're going to a funeral."

The funeral went as non-sexy funerals go. Some pastor quoted Bible verses that no one but he would remember in a few hours' time. Some people who were clearly uncomfortable speaking in front of a crowd spoke in front of a crowd, telling heartfelt stories that went on too long and jokes that weren't remotely funny.* Some people who were bad at singing sang. Tears were shed by folks that neither Brooks nor Smith knew.

Thanks to the structured schedule, they'd managed to avoid any confrontation. They'd arrived just as services began, sat quietly in the back, and shot out the door as soon as it was all over. Everyone in the procession wondered about the jalopy with New York license plates, but no one saw fit to bother its occupants while there were still more events to come.

The procession drove down one flat Indiana road after another, until it reached the Kraft Cemetery—no relation to the

* I'd tell you one, but I'm incapable of writing jokes that aren't funny.

processed cheese product. If one ignored the unkempt trailer park across the street, it was a lovely spot, well-maintained and dotted with hickory trees.

More words were said. More tears were shed.

Eventually, it was time to lower the O'Gradys' coffins to their final destination.

The pastor folded his arms and addressed the crowd. "Everyone ready your weapons."

Everyone complied, including the children, revealing their guns and pointing them up at the sky.

Brooks blinked a few times. "What?"

Some stranger—a greying redhead who thought an Indianapolis Colts jersey was appropriate funeral attire—turned to Brooks with an alarmed expression.

"You don't have a gun?"

"Um... I left it back home."

"Here, you can borrow one of mine," said the Colts fan, pulling a loaded weapon from his ankle holster and handing it to Brooks.

"Uh... thanks." Brooks had left college a few credits shy of a chemistry degree, and while physics may not have been his strong point, firing loaded weapons into the air struck him as wrong. He whispered to his husband, "Isn't this super dangerous?"

Smith shrugged, then cocked his Chekhov. "Probably."

"Ready... aim... fire!"

A cacophony of gunfire exploded, honoring the dead. For a quarter mile in all directions, bullets rained down from the sky, shattering a handful of windshields. One unlucky groundhog—a third cousin of the famous Punxsutawney Phil—was killed.

Thus concluded the funeral.

Smith, whose brand-new pistol had jammed upon firing, began dismantling it in search of the cause. Whilst he fiddled with the cheap vending machine firearm, Brooks returned his own, borrowed weapon to the stranger, who promptly introduced himself.

"I'm Teddy, by the way." He extended a chubby, calloused hand.

"Oh, for fuck's sake," Smith muttered to himself, realizing the vending machine had issued the wrong type of ammo.

Brooks ignored him and shook the man's hand. "Arturo Brooks. Nice to meet you."

"Arturo. That's an interesting name."

The Spanish and Italian version of Arthur wasn't all that interesting, but Teddy had clearly never met another.

"It's a family name," Brooks said.

"So... how'd you know my mom and dad?"

"Uhh..." Brooks had no idea what kind of family drama he might get himself into, so he turned to his husband for rescue. "Eddie?"

Teddy squinted. "Almond Joy...?"

Smith took a deep breath and turned to Brooks. "Don't ask."

"Holy heck!" Teddy roped Smith into a bearhug. "I thought you were dead!"

"I was," replied Smith.

Teddy laughed as if it were a joke and beckoned to an unknown party. A blonde woman and small girl—also dressed in Colts jerseys—came forward.

Teddy wrapped an arm around the woman. "This is my wife, Marcella. And that's Tessa."

The girl's eyes stayed glued to her tablet. He gestured at the men in front of him.

"That's Eddie. You know, Almond Joy. And this is his... friend? Arturo."

"Oh, that's an interesting name," Marcella said.

"It's a family name."

"Not a friend." Smith threw an arm around him. "We're married."

"*No mames,*" Brooks swore under his breath.

"Hey, that's totally cool," Teddy said, raising a palm.

Marcella nodded in agreement. "Absolutely."

"It is?" Smith sounded almost disappointed.

"We're like Biscuit Bucket," Teddy said.

"Doing Better...?" Brooks wondered aloud.

"He gets it!" Teddy reached toward him to offer a high five, which Brooks weakly reciprocated. "Any Biscuit Bucket fan is all right in my book. What's your favorite dish?"

"Uh... the Geezer Sunrise?"

"Ohhh, that's a good one. I'm on the Simp Salads myself. Doctor says I gotta watch my cholesterol." Teddy patted his stomach.

Brooks blinked a few times.

"I'm hungry," whined Tessa without looking up.

"You two going to the reception?" Teddy's eyes widened in anticipation.

Smith started to answer but was quickly interrupted.

"Wouldn't miss it," replied Brooks.

Smith glared at him.

"We gotta get over there a-sap and get this little one fed," Teddy said, "but I can't wait to catch up."

He hugged Brooks, who squeezed back, then Smith, who tensed.

"Almond Joy..." Teddy chuckled to himself as he and his family headed back to join the other mourners.

When they were out of earshot, Smith turned to his husband, exasperated.

"*Wouldn't miss it?* There's nothing I'd rather miss."

"They seem nice enough. Besides, you just outed me in the middle of Indiana, surrounded by people with guns..."

"... who you could crush with your bare hands." Smith sighed and raised an eyebrow. "So what? You're punishing me?"

"Little bit. Mostly I was being polite." Brooks changed

subjects. "Why do they keep calling you Almon—"

"I said don't ask."

A redheaded woman in a skirt suit approached from the crowd, cutting their conversation short. Her pale face bore a look of total disdain. "Why are *you* here?"

"Lyla," Smith said, not even attempting to hide his sneer.

"Your stepsister?" Brooks wondered.

Lyla eyed the unfamiliar man from head to toe. "Who are you?"

"Arturo Brooks," he replied, extending a hand. "Eddie's husband."

She ignored it. "'kay. Good luck with that."

"Good to see you too," said Smith, deadpan.

"I called you as a courtesy. You didn't visit mom and dad when they were alive so I assumed that—like always—you'd ignore us."

"Believe me... I wanted to."

"You see them?" Lyla gestured across the lawn at a tall, strapping man and two tall, strapping twin tweens. "That's my family. I don't need you here finding a way to fuck up our lives like you do everything else."

"'kay," Smith mimicked, refusing to let her see how she'd just nailed him right in the insecurity.

Lyla stormed off toward her Peloton-honed family.

As they filed into a Jeep Grand Cherokee and sped away, Brooks shot Smith a sly smile. "You want me to change her email password?"

Smith barely registered the question over his loud, disparaging thoughts. He shook them from his head. That was everyone he considered a relative, as much as circus peanuts can be considered food. Once everyone else had left for the reception, he found himself drawn back to the gravesite.

"I don't know what to do with this. Do I say something? It's not like they'll hear it."

"Stranger things have happened..." said Brooks. These had

included several instances of the dead resurrecting.

"Good point," said Smith.

Brooks placed a hand on his shoulder. "You don't have to do anything."

"Gimme a sec, okay?"

Brooks nodded and started back toward the Avalon.

In movies, the moments after a funeral are quiet and peaceful—the perfect time for the main character to have a heart-to-heart with the recently deceased, preferably during some soft, somberly lit rain shower. In reality, the moments after a funeral are filled with the sounds of backhoes and cemetery workers in neon safety vests barking orders. Those were the sounds that filled the air as Smith stood at the O'Gradys' grave. There was no ambient rain, just the ever-present Indiana prairie dust.

Smith searched for something to say. "Uh…"

"Hey! Watch it!" shouted one workman, as another steered his equipment over a bed of fresh flowers.

"*WHAT?*" shouted the driver over the vehicle's rumble.

Smith stumbled along. "… I sort of hated you both… uh… but…"

The gravedigger flailed his arms wildly, gesturing for the driver to move over. The driver, unable to see his coworker from the cab, continued rolling over daisies.

"*MOVE OVER!*"

"Thanks for trying…" offered Smith, in an attempt at honesty.

BEEP BEEP BEEP BEEP.

News travels quickly when the people transporting it have little else going on in their lives. By the time Brooks and Smith arrived at the local VFW hall for the reception, everyone there knew who they were, where they came from, and what they did for a living.

Smith set the pizza box on a table next to a bowl of potato salad.

Brooks gestured in horror toward a row of gelatinous dishes at the buffet.

"Eddie, what the hell is that?" he whispered.

Farthest left was a bowl of sea green fluff, dotted with marshmallows. In the center sat a pile of unidentifiable, vomit-toned lumps topped with mandarin oranges and maraschino cherries. To the right was a bowl of green grapes and walnuts, floating in a dubious white substance.* All of it seemed inedible.

Smith pointed at them one-by-one. "Seafoam salad. Ambrosia salad. Waldorf salad."

"Those aren't salads..." Brooks poked at the Seafoam with a serving spoon.

A random man—somewhat older than the pair and one hundred percent more mustachioed—came rushing toward them, and grabbed Smith's hand for a shake.

"I knew you looked familiar!"

Smith tensed. "Do I know you...?"

The man ignored him and kept on shaking. "You were on *Entrepreneurity Hour* a few years back! The vampire guy!"

"Yeah... TVs only work the one way..."

The man had a true aversion to negativity, and he ignored that remark as well. "You two work in monster hunting, huh? What's that like?"

"It's a job," Smith replied.

Brooks turned to his husband. "Eddie, this one has *celery* in it."

"And you're gay," the stranger continued. "What's that like?"

This comment caught Brooks's ear, and he turned his

---

* It was mayo. It's always mayo.

attention from the 'salads.'

"Bi," Smith corrected.

"Well, what's *that* like?"

"It's like being straight, but I also fuck dudes."

Brooks snorted.

"I wish that could be me, honest to God," rambled the mustachioed man. "If I could fall in love with someone who was into football and fishing and not all that girly crap, I'd do it."

Brooks gave a bewildered look. "That's somehow progressive and sexist at the same time."

The man ignored him and waved to his friend. "Carl! Come here!"

Smith rubbed at his temple.

"Who's Carl?" Brooks asked.

"I don't know. I don't even know who the fuck *this guy* is."

Carl—mid-60s with a hard face and a grey buzzcut, looking fully at home in the VFW—hobbled over with a shit-eating grin plastered to his face. "These the ones Teddy was telling us about?"

"Sure are," the still-unnamed man replied.

Carl eyed Brooks up and down and tilted his head. "Weren't you one of them Bedazzlers?"

Brooks was used to the question. For a very brief stint, he had been a superhero, but it was shockingly easy (and best for everyone involved) to throw people off.

"No," he lied. "I get that a lot, though."

Carl's handlebar-wearing friend chastised him. "You idiot. That guy had the weird eyes."

"Well, what's it like being detectives?" Carl asked, ignoring the comment.

"It's a job," Brooks and Smith said together.

Thus began wave after wave of Hoosiers, all with questions for the men whose lives were nothing like their own. Well-intentioned but irritating questions about city life. "You really don't have a car? How do you get groceries?" "How much is your rent?" "How do you deal with the crowds?" "Aren't there rats everywhere?" "Did you ever meet Al Roker?"

Brooks and Smith alternated answering questions and stuffing their faces to avoid having to do so. Irrelevant people came and went, introducing themselves and asserting that they were accepting of the detectives' 'lifestyle' in a way that made it seem like they really weren't. Minutes dragged to hours, until Brooks and Smith had spoken to almost everyone in the room—besides Lyla, who continued to snub them. Once their popularity had worn thin, they reconvened at the salads.

"Have you met Harold?" groaned Brooks.

"Yeah. He keeps talking about stuff that happened while I was still in my dad's balls."

Brooks spotted the man in question approaching and quickly suggested more food. "Tater tot?"

"If I eat one more tot my heart's gonna give out."

"You ready to get out of here?"

Smith responded with desperate, rapid nodding.

"Need to say any goodbyes?"

"*No.*"

Smith held his empty pack of cigarettes high, so that anyone still paying attention would assume he was out for a smoke. He made his way out the door with Brooks close behind and nearly collided with group of children running around making WHIRR and PEW PEW noises at each other. Brooks chuckled, for a moment.

"Why do I always have to be the innocent child?" whined one of the kids. "I wanna be a drone!"

Playing drones and dronees was far more wholesome than many other popular children's activities in Indiana, such as hitting each other with corn stalks and throwing rocks from overpasses, but Brooks didn't know that. No longer amused, he turned away and headed toward the car.

Smith took the driver's seat and started the ignition.

"Letting me drive without a fight now?"

"I think you earned it around your third serving of jello salad," said Brooks.

"It's *ambrosia*." Smith put a hand on the shift knob, but paused. "You know... part of me always felt guilty for leaving this place because... they were decent people and I know I stressed them out being the piece of shit I am—"

"Stop saying that—"

"—but today has done nothing but remind me why I left. I mean, can you picture me at a church potluck talking about fantasy football?"

"Only ironically."

"If I never ran away to New York, and I never started doing the work we do... I'm pretty sure I'd be dead by now. For real dead, not us dead." He shook his head but his face read satisfied. "I don't think I feel guilty anymore. I can't stand their lives."

"I know you can't."

Smith offered a sideways look. "Is that why you made me come here?"

"If I could *make* you do anything, we'd have a much cleaner living room. But I did think it would be good for you to get some closure on a big chapter of your life. And to remind you that... as disconnected as you are from these people, you're *even more* disconnected from your birth parents."

"Yeah, okay..."

Smith reached down to put the car in drive. Before taking off, he glanced over at his husband, who was picking tater tot remnants from under a fingernail.

"I fucking love you."

"I know. I love you too."

Smith shook his head. "Now... let's get the hell out of here."

They sped off, leaving Smith's family behind them. At least, that was the plan.

12 / AIMLESS

Before departing Clarksville and ending their authentic Indiana experience for good, Brooks and Smith decided to check out America's second-largest Trout Pro sporting goods store. Smith wanted ammo, and the reviews claimed it had an unmissable shooting range—fun for all ages. They never found out, as the store was closed following yet another mass shooting. Rather than cross the yellow crime scene tape, the detectives returned to their car.

Parking for the Green River Mall was divided into three lots: East, North, and West. The East Lot had been converted to overflow parking for a nearby used car dealership. The North Lot hadn't been repaved since the 90s, and weeds grew three feet tall from breaks in the pavement. The West Lot was the only one that still resembled a parking lot, and was where Brooks and Smith were the only ones parked.

Before getting back into the car, Smith gave the mall a wistful look.

"This place used to be lit."

Brooks stifled the urge to criticize his husband's use of slang. "Yeah?"

"Oh, yeah. It had bumper cars. I gave my first handy-J in the movie theater over there."

He pointed to a boarded-up doorway. When the theater closed, it had been advertising *Star Wars Episode II: Attack of the Clones*. But all that remained of the title on the marquee was __A____S_____S.

"Lovely," Brooks said.

"Can't say I'm sad to see malls go the way of landlines, though."

"Really? I thought you'd be a fan. They're just a bigger version of the Biscuit Bucket gift shop."

"No, I like those because they're pit stops. A place to buy useless shit shouldn't be a destination."

"That's commie talk," said Brooks with a smirk. "Are you trying to turn me on?"

Smith rolled his eyes. "Cool your jets. I'm still never voting. I *am* gonna pop behind one of those pillars and take a leak, though." Smith had been hitting the bottled water hard. He tossed Brooks the car keys and made his way toward the North Lot.

While Smith dodged sprouting weeds on his way to a secluded spot, Brooks stepped around the car and seized the driver's seat. He turned the key to get some much-needed heat. Though he could access the internet using his mind, Brooks was not immune to the addictive nature of aimless scrolling. Once the was nice and toasty, he pulled out his phone and opened Adoptr.

Jaxxxxon, age three, open adoptions only.

"No thank you," Brooks muttered to himself, before swiping to the next child.

Safely behind a pillar, Smith unzipped his pants and got down to business. Alone again, his mind began to wander— mostly judging him for being a piece of shit and despising folks who'd been nothing but polite to him. He bet Teddy would have sacrificed himself to the sea bream...

Once his mind and bladder were emptied, it became quiet enough for him to hear a nearby whooshing sound— something faint and fanlike. He zipped up and went looking for its source.

He found it a few yards away. Inside an immense, three-foot wide pothole was a flat, circular void—swirling red and black, with a faint glow at the edges. Bits of dust and dirt floated in the air above it before being gently sucked in. Where they went was anyone's guess; once they reached the center they simply disappeared.

The whirring sound was soothing, almost entrancing.

Smith knelt to get a closer look because he was an idiot and, before he could register any kind of sensation, was sucked in, like lint into a vacuum cleaner.

Brooks, meanwhile, lost track of time as he scrolled.

13 / A-HOLE NEW WORLD

Smith didn't feel a thing inside the portal. One minute, he was standing in the dilapidated parking lot of the Green River Mall. The next, he was standing in the fully paved parking lot of the Green River Mall, its rows packed with Ford Escorts, Pontiac Fieros, and Buick Skyhawks as far as the eye could see. That wasn't very far. The sky was hazy, and anything beyond twenty or thirty feet was a brownish blur. Smith froze in place, both in confusion and because it was quite cold.

The entrance to the movie theater was no longer boarded up. Hundreds of incandescent bulbs shone through the pollution, and the marquee within them boasted the films showing throughout the day: *Halloween, The Wiz,* and *Jaws 2.*

The hottest films of 1978.

But the theater had never been able to afford new releases. It wasn't the 1970s. That was apparent. Beneath the display, large groups of hairsprayed adults dressed in high-waisted pants and colorful windbreakers chatted about the films they'd just seen or were about to see.

Smith had hated the 1980s the first time around.

"Not again..." he groaned.

He noticed something off about the litter on the ground and knelt to investigate a shiny, discarded pouch of Capri Sun: Cool Broccoli. As a child, he'd only been given generic drink pouches, if any, but he was certain they'd never come in broccoli flavor. Nor had Tab, as far he was aware, ever released a special edition clam chowder variety, despite what was printed on the crumpled soda can that lay a few yards away. This wasn't just time travel; it was a parallel universe.

"Shit."

He tried to think back to the Reticent's training manual

and what it had to say about parallel universes. If the information had ever been in his head, it had long since evacuated. All he knew now was a) how parallel universes worked in various works of fiction, and b) that he needed to get home.

Smith squeezed between cars, shimmying from row to row in search of another portal, but found nothing but more litter. Whatever journey he'd taken didn't come with roundtrip tickets; the hole he'd emerged from wasn't anywhere.

Way to fall into another dimension, dipshit, mocked his inner critic. *Just take a peek at the swirly portal. Christ, you're stupid.*

His more rational side chimed in. *That's not helping. Focus. Figure out what kind of world this is. Fuck...*

To familiarize himself with his new surroundings, he decided to investigate the mall. If it were a dangerous universe, he'd need to tread more carefully than if it were just a mirror image of his own with different snack food flavor profiles.

Smith approached the entrance and stepped into a thick cloud of cigarette smoke. He paused, closed his eyes, and inhaled a deep and satisfying breath. When he opened them and all the smokers were staring—in judgment, he assumed—he shrugged off the glances and continued through the doorway into the Food Court.

The place seemed normal enough. The air was loud with songs from the *Xanadu* soundtrack being pumped through the mall's speaker system, and potent with the smells of fast foods. There was the Wok of Shame, serving up samples of General Tso's... something. Smith eyed the samples as he passed and couldn't tell. Next to that, McDonald's still existed in this universe, serving up McNuggets made of by-product. A pretzel stand stood next to a Broccoli Julius, which stood next to a bun-free hot dog joint. Mostly normal. Different foods were to be expected. But were people staring at him?

Smith glanced down to check whether he'd left his fly open or had any mysterious stains on his suit. Nope. Granted, his suit didn't match the style of the era; it was neither broad-shouldered nor pastel, and he wore it over a button-down shirt instead of a crewneck. But it shouldn't have been enough to cause a scene.

In any context, Smith hated being noticed. In the context of another universe where no one in the mall seemed to buy anything, he hated it more.

What are they doing here? No one has any bags. They're walking around like zombies. Fuck. Maybe they're zombies.

No. I know what zombies look like... IN MY WORLD.

Shit... they could look different here. Stop sweating. Stop sweating. It's suspicious AF.

Aren't you a bit too old to say AF?

Shit... maybe it's a commie paradise and this is a capitalism museum. No, that's stupid...

The stares continued. It wasn't his imagination. Now people were stopping and whispering under their breath.

"Okay..." Smith muttered under his own.

He kept on walking, picking up his pace until the Food Court was completely out of sight, and encountered a long hallway of 1980s retail. Formal wear, tennis shoes, and sports caps all seemed normal for the time period. Some of the teams may have been different in this universe, but Smith wouldn't have known either way.

He counted five things that were off about this universe. One: The food. Two: No one carried shopping bags because no one had bought anything. Three: The terrible hair was worse than he expected for the era, and he could have sworn half the shoppers were wearing wigs. Four: The constant staring from every adult in the vicinity. Five: There were only adults in the vicinity.

He took a good look around. No screaming hellions demanding ice cream. No exhausted parents pushing double-wide strollers. No uncomfortable babies wailing at the overwhelming amount of noise. No Carter's or wherever people bought children's clothing in the 1980s. No KB Toys. No shitty little merry-go-round with only three horses. This universe didn't even have the Green River Mall's biggest draw—the bumper cars. But there were plenty of pregnant women.

That raised uncomfortable questions.

Smith checked himself again to make sure he wasn't somehow a child. That he was six feet tall and two hundred and twenty pounds suggested he was not. Then again, someone could have cast a glamour spell on him and made him look like anything. He didn't rule it out; at least it would be *an* explanation for the weird looks.

The staring became overwhelming. All around, more and more mall patrons were stopping in their tracks to point at Smith and gossip in hushed tones. Not wanting to recreate a scene from *Invasion of the Bodysnatchers*, Smith ducked into Tape World. As anyone born before 1990 would assume, it was full of cassette tapes.*

Naturally drawn to the S aisle, Smith pretended to browse through Social Distortion and Soft Cell cassettes. Browsing didn't make him seem any less suspicious. Unlike back home, stores in this world were fully staffed. Multiple employees in black and blue striped shirts began to reach for their walkie talkies. Before they had the chance to radio for help, half a dozen muscular men—wearing orange fluro pants, navy bomber jackets, and aviator sunglasses—entered the store. Each brandished a menacing-looking baton, and they were looking in Smith's direction.

They were dressed far too causally for police or military, as far as Smith could tell. They weren't Mall Security either, unless this universe was especially strict on shoplifting. But they did have an authoritative air about them—the kind of vibe that suggested they'd subdue and hold him captive rather

---

* Anyone born after 1990 can kindly close this book and not burden its author with thoughts of aging and mortality. Thank you.

than beat him to death.

Capture was worse than murder in Smith's eyes, and he checked his waist for his Chekhov. It was still there, but thanks to the mass shooting at Trout Pro, he'd never replaced the faulty ammo.

"Shit..."

As the armed force moved in, a sound emerged from within the S section.

"*Psst.*"

Smith scanned the rack but saw nothing. He turned to face the approaching gang and pulled out his gun, hoping to bluff his way out of capture.

"Don't come any closer!" he said, waving the weapon in their direction.

"*Psst.*"

Unintimidated, the attackers continued their approach.

"Shit."

"*Psst!*"

Smith glanced at the cassettes again, and noticed a green eye staring up at him through a gap in the display. As his eye and the mystery eye made contact, the base of the display split between the S's and T's as a hidden door cracked open. It contained a small opening, maybe two by two feet, but big enough for Smith to squeeze through.

Fuck it. Might as well.

He crawled in, hoping it might be a way home, or, at the very least, that he was Alice in this scenario, about to trip his balls off in Wonderland.

14 / URINE-SOAKED PILLAR OF THE COMMUNITY

Back home, Brooks was still fully immersed in his swiping session.

Awbreigh, age two, allergic to air. *Left.*

Lee-Oh, age Eighteen, literally an adult. *Left.*

Poppytart, age—

THUD.

A chunk of plaster peeled from the mall's exterior wall and fell to the ground. The sound pulled Brooks from his app-induced stupor, and he squinted to check the time. Nearly an hour had passed... that couldn't be right. Brooks synchronized his heads-up display with a handful of time servers, but the time remained unchanged.

"Oh, no..."

He threw open the car door and stormed through the weeds toward the urine-soaked pillar. Briars somehow made their way up into the leg of his pants, scraping at his ankles. He ignored them and pressed onward.

"Eddie?" he called out.

No response.

He rounded the corner of the building. Nothing.

"You're not funny!"

Brooks scanned the area and found more nothing. No heat signatures. No pulses. No one but him, standing alone in a dilapidated parking lot with bleeding ankles, shouting at no one. If he wasn't careful, he'd end up on a bus to California with a bunch of homeless people.

Brooks dialed Smith's phone in a light panic.

"BRRBRRBEEP. Your call could not be connected as dialed."

His panic began to increase, but he quickly composed himself. He was a cyborg, after all. He would embrace his cyborghood and cyborganize a solution.

Brooks had some experience investigating missing persons, and he walked himself through ADHOC's process.

Step one: hack into cameras. That was useless. The mall's security had skipped town a decade ago, and traffic cameras showed nothing. Smith hadn't gone anywhere. He'd disappeared.

Step two: check news reports. As usual, there were plenty of strange occurrences, but no men mysteriously appearing out of thin air.

Step three: review hospital admissions and arrests. He searched for people matching Smith's description, but none fit the bill.

Step four: contact the missing person's acquaintances. Brooks messaged everyone he could think of, at once. None had heard from his husband.

That's when Brooks experienced true, full panic. Step five was to alert the media, and in his experience, when investigations made it to that stage there was a 98.9% chance the missing person was dead.

He paced in the parking lot, fidgeting with his hands. His thoughts raced.

Oh my God, don't be dead...

You're not allowed to be dead, not again...

¡Mierda!

I swear to God if you're dead I'm going to kill you, Eddie...

Shit shit shit

Am I having a panic attack?

No, no... I don't think so... but maybe!

What am I going to do???

¿Por qué me pasa esta mierda?

Shit, I'm a widower!

Shit shit shit

You have to calm downnnn...
Ahhhhhhhhhhhhhhhhhhhhhhhhhh!
Seriously, calm down!
01000101 01000100 01000100 01001001 01000101
Shit shit shit
There has to be something...
¡Espere!
00100001

He stopped himself. There was a semi-rational way to work through this.

Brooks babbled desperately to the empty parking lot. "He's dead. Dead. Dead. Dead. Dead."

15 / LIKE A PRAYER

Sometime in the 2180s, Lemon and Patience were having the time of their lives in Pretoria, Mars. That is to say, Lemon was having the time of her life, which she stated so emphatically that Patience also agreed that it was the time of her life because she simply couldn't bear to argue.

Everyone reaches an age where clubbing becomes sad and exhausting rather than fun, but Lemon was far from it. The Space Bar—the hottest club on Mars—was heaving with dancers, with Lemon at the center of the massive crowd, swinging her braids wildly to the music as dozens of drones sprayed the room with colorful lighting.

At Alt Key—the adjacent restaurant—Patience read alone in a corner booth, waiting for her sister to become bored, declare the planet passé, and set their sights on a new destination. It was inevitable. Gallivanting around the universe kept the Lunan from thinking too hard about her goals and aspirations, and the fact that she had none.

Patience never sighed too hard, as it would be impolite. She checked her watch, let out a very short exhale, and continued reading *The History of Mars, Volume 7*. She was no longer as terrified of everything as she once was, but Patience still preferred studying the exploits of the daring to participating in feats of daring-do. One brief stint as a paranormal detective had been enough. Reading was far more enjoyable, and *Volume 7* contained some quality material. The mass guillotining of 2119 was as fascinating as it was horrifying. Patience trailed her finger across the text, engrossed and oblivious to the twenty-something man in a silver jumpsuit who had approached her table.

He brushed his chin-length brown hair away from his greyish face. "Wotcha readin'?"

The accent was unplaceable, to Patience or anyone else. It was some mix of South African, Canadian, and fifth-generation eccentric billionaire. Patience shifted in her seat, paranoid that she'd done something wrong.

"Hmm... I'm reading a book concerning the history of Mars."

"You don' 'ave to read about it," the man replied.

"Pardon?"

"I can giveya the royal tour."

It was clear he expected a reaction, but Patience had absolutely no idea who he was. "Have we met?"

The man scoffed. "You don' know me?"

"I'm afraid I don't, sir."

He extended a hand and introduced himself.

"X Æ B-13."

"Ex Ash Bee Thirteen?" she repeated.

He nodded. "Roit. You can call me any of 'ose for short."

"All right... Mr. Thirteen. I'm content to stay here and finish the book, if you don't mind."

"I do mind." Mr. Thirteen gave a lecherous smirk and sat down across from her. "Wot've you got to lose, eh?"

Patience considered the question. Not her life, since she was presently immortal. Her dignity, perhaps, though she hadn't much of that left following an embarrassing and short-lived marriage. It didn't matter. Naïve as she was, Patience knew enough to know when someone was, in her favorite father's words, 'a douchebag.'

She readied a classic escape plan, one that involved a visit to the restroom.

Before she could execute it, an exasperated Lemon strolled into Alt Key.

"This place is over," she declared to everyone in the room, before locating her sister in the corner.

"X Æ B-13?" she uttered in surprise as she approached.

"Ugh, Oi'm not signing any autographs, hoser."

Lemon gawked at her sister, impressed. "You know X Æ B-13?"

"We were just acquainted."

X Æ B-13 saw an opportunity, and he turned to Lemon. "This ya friend?"

"Sister. Kinda."

"Oi was just offerin' the royal tour but she says she don' wan' it."

"Patience... she, uh..." Lemon stammered. "She plays hard to get."

"I do?"

"Patience. That's a weird name," said X Æ B-13.

Patience's cheeks had turned almost as red as her hair. The unwanted attention made her long for the witch executions of Salem.

"We'd love to go on your tour," Lemon said, speaking for both of them.

"We would?" Patience wondered aloud.

Lemon pulled Patience from the booth, stepped out of the billionaire's earshot, and explained her excitement in as soft a tone as she could muster. "That's X Æ B-13!"

"That was my understanding as well."

"He basically owns this planet," said Lemon.

"I haven't yet reached that volume of *The History of Mars*."

Lemon's eyes widened. "We gotta go!"

"Are you certain? I thought you might want to go somewhere else..."

"Yeah, *after the tour*," said Lemon, almost shaking with excitement. "He lives in a space castle!"

Patience exhaled sharply. "If you insist."

By Puritan standards, hanging out with her sister all the time was so exhausting that it had to be virtuous. She wasn't a Puritan anymore—not exactly—but the principle remained.

Fortunately for her and unfortunately for Lemon, their

wrists simultaneously lit up and began vibrating with a message:

DEATH ALERT! COME BACK ASAP!
2018-04-06 15:45:21 GPS 38.3160401,-85.7637147

The two girls exchanged worried glances.

"Crudbuckets," cursed Lemon.

"We must return to Brooklyn!" Patience could barely hide her relief. She walked wordlessly over to the booth and retrieved her book.

"Hey, X Æ..." Lemon said, trying not to blow the moment. "We gotta go, but we'll be right back!"

"Why? Wot are you—"

The girls darted out of the room, leaving the Martian royal behind.

Some one hundred and sixty years earlier, the time machine materialized in a parking lot. Shiny, metallic, and tapered, with four bright red fins elevating it from the ground, it looked wildly out of place sitting on the cracked asphalt— like some rocket ship plucked out of a 1950s cartoon special had been spat out into the real world.

Brooks waved to his daughters as they exited the ship a few yards from where he was standing.

As they hurried through patches of overgrown weeds, Patience's frock snagged, ripping the linen. The garment's bottom already had contrasting stitches where she'd patched up dozens of holes, and she made a mental note to make another repair. She smiled slightly to herself; toil was virtuous, after all.

"Who died?" Lemon asked.

"No one, I hope," Brooks said, his voice wavering.

Patience glanced around the parking lot. "Where's Edward?"

"I... don't know." Brooks drew a narrow breath. "I need your help. I need you to go find future Eddie and—"

"You said no spoilers." Lemon frowned.

"I did. I'm a hypocrite."

"And a glorbdink," she added.

"Sure..."

Lemon held her head up, smug. "As long as you know it."

"*Please.*"

The Brooks-Smith-Jones-Cloyce family had always had a complicated relationship with time, but Brooks's reluctance to use the time machine was borne more out of past agonies than danger. There was no way in the universe to create a time paradox. If, for example, Lemon and Patience went to a future point in time to discover where Smith was, and then returned to tell Brooks that location, then that is what had always happened and what would always happen.*

Lemon and Patience scurried back into the machine, and vanished in a green glow.

In the brief moment he was alone, Brooks googled one hundred and thirteen stress management techniques, ignored all of them, and gnawed off two of his fingernails. They tasted like tater tots.

The machine reappeared in almost the same spot it had left, except this time one of its fins had landed in a pothole, causing it to lean slightly askew.

Lemon braced herself as she exited the crooked time machine.

"You're not gonna like this," she said.

"Where is he?" asked Brooks.

Lemon shrugged "I guess he went through a portal and it

---

* Don't think too hard about that, or its implications on free will. The people using the time machine sure didn't.

closed behind him. You're gonna find the next one in Akron, Ohio tomorrow, around 3:34 PM."

"Ohio..." Brooks groaned and considered his options. "Can you take me there?"

Time machines were, as a general rule, much faster than Toyota Avalons.

"Okay," replied Lemon, "but then we *really* have to go."

"Why?" asked Brooks.

"'Tis a spoiler," Patience said.

Brooks approached the machine with hesitation. Using it had never ended well for him. He told himself this was different, that it was just like taking an airplane. He closed his eyes and steadied his breathing. Then Brooks did something he told himself he'd never do again.

He climbed in.

16 / JUST THE TWO OF US

Somewhere beneath the S cassettes, in the underbelly of the mall, Smith crawled through a narrow passage in total darkness. A musty smell assaulted his nose as he crawled blindly along the concrete and through the occasional cobweb.

Just cobwebs, Smith assured himself. *If you can't see spiders, there are no spiders.*

"Follow me," said the voice that was psst at him earlier. It was redundant since the passageway only went in one direction, but the voice sounded young enough not to know about redundancy.

Eventually, light appeared in the distance—the narrowest sliver that opened out into a bright square as they approached. It grew closer and brighter until the passage emptied into the floor of a room about the size of a Claire's.

Smith picked himself up off the ground and dusted himself off. The room's walls were cement, just like the passageway; the smell, however, had improved, thanks to a handful of burning candles. Myriad scents combined to create something loosely fruity.

On the opposite side from the hole he'd just popped out of, Smith noticed a metal door, bolted several times over. Once his eyes had adjusted, he saw that the room was some sort of makeshift living quarters, with three sleeping bags on the floor, dozens of two-liter water bottles, and a large case of Mutant-B-Not anti-radiation pills. Next to one of the sleeping bags was a tape deck and a pile of comic books, presumably the property of the person standing in front of him.

"Thanks for opening that door," Smith said. "It only opens from the inside?"

"Yep!" said a diminutive voice.

His savior, visible by candlelight, was a small boy about

four and a half feet tall. Smith wasn't good at guessing children's ages, so he guessed this one was somewhere between six and ten. He believed the child was blond—based on his eyebrows—but it was hard to tell just what was under the bright red clown wig that shot off in coils from his head.

Smith gestured around the room. "You make all this?"

The child shook his head. "No, my parents made it."

"And... where are they?"

"They went out for food. They told me to stay here."

Smith shifted uneasily. "When was that?"

"A few days ago." The boy looked down at his stomach and frowned as it let out an angry gurgle.

Smith reached for his useless gun and aimed. "You don't eat people, do you?"

Children could be trained to kill just as easily as adults could, and he wasn't about to let his guard down in this leg warmer-infested shithole of a universe.

"No." The child raised his hands over his head. "Please don't shoot me."

"What year is it?" Smith demanded.

"1984."

"Little on the nose," Smith said with a smirk, but kept his weapon drawn. "What's your name?"

"Eddie."

"Me too."

Smith didn't think anything of that. He had the most generic name in the universe. He did, however, think something of the child's face, which eerily resembled his own. He thought even more of the fact that there was an uneaten candy bar—an Almond Joy, if he wasn't mistaken—lying on one of the sleeping bags.

A starving kid and an uneaten candy bar meant an allergy.

Same name, same eyes, same tree nut intolerance...

Same crappy parents...

"Where you from?" Smith asked, already suspecting the

answer.

"Clarksville," said the boy.

"When's your birthday?"

"December 4th."

Smith's stomach lurched. The littler Eddie looked healthy enough, but that meant nothing. Smith remembered all too well having to hide bruises from teachers and having to invent imaginary vacations to explain frequent absences.

He pictured having to rescue his child self from his own parents, and his stomach churned a second time.

"Your parents usually leave you alone for days at a time?" he asked, careful not to react in any way that might let the kid know they were alternate versions of each other.

"No, they usually come back in a few hours."

"Well." Smith lowered his gun. "You've got a mystery, I've got a mystery. A few minutes ago, I was in a different universe. I was with my husband, then I fell in a hole, and now I'm here. So, what's say we find your folks and figure out what the hell is going on?"

Eddie laughed. "You have a husband? Are you a girl?"

"No, but I could be. Don't be a judgmental little prick."

"But—"

"It's 2018 in my world. People get gay married all the time."

Eddie's face scrunched in confusion. "Gay?"

"I'm a man. I married a man."

"That's gross."

"*You're gross*," Smith said, mimicking him.

Eddie just giggled.

"Why were those guys after me?" Smith asked, changing subjects.

Eddie looked at him like he was stupid. "'Cause you don't have your wig on. Duh."

"Oh. Of course." Smith was already tired of this universe.

Eddie, meanwhile, was tired of being hungry.

"Can you take me to Biscuit Bucket?"

"Biscuit Bucket." Smith repeated the request in disbelief.

"Yeah. I'm hungry."

"There's a food court upstairs," Smith suggested.

"I can only go up there when the mall's closed," whined the child, "and I don't know how to use the deep fryers..."

"You want me to take you to Biscuit Bucket." Smith repeated again, just to be sure.

"Yeah!"

"No one ever taught you about stranger danger, did they?"

"What's that?"

"Nothing," Smith said, letting his own comment slide. "Where's the nearest Biscuit Bucket?"

Eddie giggled some more. "There's only one Biscuit Bucket."

Smith groaned. "Parallel universe. Yeah. Sure. Let's go to Biscuit Bucket. I can't wait to see what they serve here."

He did not add what he was thinking at that moment, which was: *Maybe we'll run into someone who's actually useful.* That was personal growth.

"Okay!" Eddie shuffled his feet into his shoes and velcroed them into place. Then, he scurried toward the metal door.

Smith grabbed a bottle of Mutant-B-Nots from the case, popped one, and tucked the rest into his pocket.

When he moved to follow the boy, Eddie paused and assessed his new companion.

"Wait, you really don't have a wig?"

Smith ran a hand through his still-full head of messy hair. "No?"

The child raised a finger. "One sec!"

He scampered a few feet across the room and began rifling through a battered cardboard box in the corner. After a moment, he pulled out a lank, shoulder-length black wig.

"Here, you can use this one."

Smith eyed the hairpiece with disdain. "Sure, and later on

we can start a My Chemical Romance tribute band."

"Huh?"

"Nothing." Smith scowled, snatching the offending item. "It was funny if you were over thirty and from my universe."

"You're weird..." said the kid.

"Yeah, and having a going-out wig isn't?" Smith begrudgingly pulled the obvious Halloween prop over his head.

Looking like the 'Before' picture from a hair volumizer ad, he pulled open the heavy metal door. But instead of strolling out, he paused as a momentary lapse in stupidity caused him to reach for his wallet.

Brooks would surely come looking for him, and he'd need a trail to follow. Smith rifled through, found what he needed, and dropped a clue for his husband to find.

Then, with his newest (or oldest, depending on your point of view) companion, he ventured out into a brave new world.

17 / COINCIDENCE, SCHMOINCIDENCE

Life is full of coincidences. Someone telling you about a band and you hearing them on the radio for the first time the next day. Two random people on a bus sharing the same birthday. This book mentioning a tardy Amazon Prime delivery and you experiencing one...

Ooh. Spooky.

Arturo Brooks, being both superstitious and a detective, didn't believe in coincidences.

He didn't believe in them generally, and he didn't believe in them specifically as he stood in front of yet another crumbling mall. This one—Rolling Acres Mall—had been condemned, and its parking lot appeared to act as a local dumping ground. In lieu of cars, there were worn-out tires, broken couches with springs bursting from the cushions, rusted appliances, and a whole bunch of used compact fluorescent lightbulbs, which no one knew how to dispose of.*

Designed in the 1970s by renowned architect David Allen Jade, the mall had all of his signature design features. It was a giant box, with one grand, boxy overhang at its entrance. Not a curve, pillar, or an arch in sight. Jade was a true artist with an eye for design, but he did not fully understand the importance of location. The mall had been built over a sinkhole, which had since sunk, leaving a nice place for snow to accumulate in the winter, melt in the spring, and become a bacteria-laden pool in summer months.

But that was inside, at the former location of the mall's seasonal North Pole. Brooks stood outside, staring at a

---

* Take them to your local home improvement superstore for recycling.

swirling, red hole in the universe that had materialized next to the fallen S of a SEARS. It was maybe two feet in diameter, its edges delineated by a faint glow.

"Have fun!" Lemon said, eager to get back to her Martian prince.

"You're not staying to—"

The time machine glowed its familiar shade of green and disappeared into nothing.

Brooks sighed, thinking about the days when Lemon and Patience were always around. He stepped toward the hole, ready to be sucked into some parallel dimension like his husband apparently had been. Instead, something—or someone—came flying at him from within.

A man collided with Brooks, causing him to fall backward onto one of the busted couches. Its cushion sank under the weight of two bodies, collapsing completely when a third person—a woman this time—came flying out and landed atop both men.

The woman rolled quickly off the pile of men and stood, her hand shading her eyes to take in the surroundings.

"Oh, crap," she said. Her hand moved from her forehead to the top of her head, and her thick crop of blonde hair.

"*Oh, crap!*" she repeated, with more panic.

Then she saw it, next to a toilet—a long, purple, chin-length polyester bob. The woman scooped it up and reapplied it to her head.

The man had a wig of his own—a large brown pompadour, which rested off-center on his head. He adjusted it, then lifted himself off the couch. He frowned, and glanced around like he was looking for something.

The woman knelt, picked up a metal cane that had fallen nearby, and handed it to him.

"Thanks, honey," said the man. "Wow, this place is even worse."

Brooks cleared his throat, but the pair ignored him.

"You think we should give it a chance?"

"I mean, the sky isn't red..."

Brooks heaved himself off the couch and assessed the new arrivals. Both were tall, in their late twenties, and blond beneath their respective wigs. The woman's green, somewhat bulging eyes were strikingly familiar. The man's blue eyes were not, but his sharp, upturned nose was.

He cleared his throat again, louder this time.

"Who are you?" he demanded.

"Who are *you*?" asked the man.

It had been a long day, and Brooks was over it. "I'm a cyborg who's about three seconds from kicking your toupee-wearing ass if you don't tell me what's going on with that portal."

The man hobbled forward and moved within inches of Brooks's face.

"Try it, old man."

Without hesitation, Brooks snatched the man's cane and bent it clean in half. The mystery man and woman exchanged fearful looks.

"Never mind," said the man, taking two steps back. "Name's Phil and that's my wife, Leslie. We came from another dimension, and we're looking for a new home."

"What's wrong with your current one?" asked Brooks.

Leslie scoffed. "What isn't?"

"This one doesn't look so sharp either," Phil said. "Look at the state of the mall!"

Brooks strangely felt the need to defend the universe that had always been a pain in his ass. "Oh, no, the mall just sucks because we don't really do malls anymore. And Akron just sucks because it's Akron. Most of our world is actually pretty okay."

Phil raised a hand to his chin. "Interesting..."

"You don't have roving gangs of kidnappers?" asked Leslie.

"Uh... not generally."

"So, where did the bombs go off?" she asked matter-of-factly.

"The what?" stammered Brooks.

"The nukes? Y'know... from the Soviets?"

"Um... they didn't," he said.

The couple looked a little relieved.

"How about the oceans? Are they rising?" Leslie asked.

"Well, yeah..."

Phil shook his head. "Like Meat Loaf says, two out of three ain't bad."

Brooks, neither wanting to discuss climate change nor power ballads, elected to change the subject. "This is gonna sound weird, but your last name doesn't happen to be Smith, does it?"

Both dimension hoppers stared at him.

"It does!" said Phil emphatically.

"And you have a son named Eddie?"

"We do!" Phil confirmed.

"Do we know... you?" Leslie asked.

Brooks shook his head. "No, but I'm pretty familiar with this universe's version of your son. For your sake, I hope you're better people than his parents were."

"We are," Phil said with confidence.

"How do you know Eddie?" Leslie asked.

Brooks paused. "Does it matter?"

Leslie raised her eyebrows. "I was just curious, but you not wanting to answer makes me even more curious."

"Um..." Brooks hesitated again. "...we're married?"

The fire in Phil and Leslie's eyes told him he should have hesitated longer.

"You... sick bastard," Leslie said.

Brooks sighed. "Okay, guess your universe isn't big on the gays."

Leslie seemed offended at the notion. "We don't have a

problem with *alternative lifestyles*. But our son is *eight years old!*"

"Oh!" Brooks frantically waved his hands about. "No!"

"No?" said Phil, taking a step forward this time.

"I mean, maybe *your* Eddie is. Mine's forty-one."

The two travelers relaxed.

"Oh, thank God," Phil said. "Regular ol' sodomy I can overlook."

Brooks glowered at him.

Leslie's sigh of relief became a sigh of confusion. "Did you say *forty-one?*"

"Yeah?"

The two exchanged a look that may or may not have been meaningful. Brooks couldn't tell, and he didn't care. What he cared about was solving the problem at hand.

"I think he might have gotten sucked into your universe."

"Crap," Leslie said.

"That's a problem," said Phil.

"I know," Brooks said.

"A *big* problem," Phil clarified.

"*I know!*"

"A huge fuckin' problem." Leslie flushed and covered her mouth.

"Swear jar!" Phil pulled a tiny spiral notepad and pencil from his pocket and added a tally mark.

None of this boded well.

18 / METH LAB FOR CUTIE

In Smith's normal universe, malls presented spots of disrepair in otherwise passable cities. In this other universe, which he was now mentally calling Hell World, the reverse was true. Malls were vibrant, clean places. Outside of them, Hell World was in rough, if not apocalyptic shape.

On the other side of the thick metal door was a sewer, which emptied—naturally—into the Ohio River... or what would have been the Ohio River, if any water remained. Instead, the river bed was dry and cracked, and littered with trash and skeletal fish remains. It was a disaster, like the Challenger shuttle, or ending a sentence with a conjunction.

Smith gazed across the river toward Louisville. If the city had ever existed, it had since been leveled. No trace remained. Even the bridges leading to it were gone.

Smith and his younger self walked along the shoulder of a crumbling road that ran parallel to the riverbank. They pushed onward toward farm country, where there was no vegetation to be seen. Not a single corn field. Not one soybean plant. Far from typical for Indiana.

"What happened here?" Smith asked in alarm.

"What do you mean?"

"Everything is dead." He gestured at nothing, and then more nothing. "Where are the plants? Where are the animals? Where do all the people who were at that mall *live*?"

That was too many questions for a small child, and Eddie only processed the first. "I dunno. The outside's always looked like this."

"You're very sheltered, aren't you?"

"Yeah, we just came from there."

Smith struggled with the remark for a second, then sighed. "How much farther is Biscuit Bucket?"

"Not much, I don't think." The child's face scrunched. "I know it's along the river, but I never walked there before. My parents drive a scooter. I ride in the sidecar with a blanket on top of me."

"Why?"

"I dunno. They said I'd understand when I'm older."

"Great. You really don't know anything, do you?"

"I know how to multiply and divide. Oh, and I just learned about magnets." The child grinned.

"Amazing," said Smith.

If Eddie caught the sarcasm, he didn't show it.

"You homeschooled?" Smith asked.

"What's that?"

"Who teaches you about math and magnets?"

"My parents. And books."

"That's... homeschooling."

"You know lots of words." Eddie pondered on something for a moment. "Do you know what a condom is?"

Smith wasn't sure he heard correctly. "A wha—yes, and I'm not explaining it to you."

Eddie scuffed his feet against the dirt and kicked a rock into the empty riverbed. "Darn."

There were no clouds visible in the reddish grey sky, but they were up there somewhere, sending down flurries of delicate snowflakes. There wasn't enough to stick, just enough to be cold and irritating.

No amount of picturesque snow would have made the area any more inviting. The few buildings that remained stood windowless and crumbling.

"Christ, it looks like Gary," said Smith.

"Who's Gary?"

Smith, of course, meant Gary, Indiana, the worst city in America. It was a town whose biggest attraction was its blight—where voyeurs from safe suburbs would come to snap pictures of abandoned factories and historic buildings before leaving to spend their money in another town. If they were unlucky, those dollars might end up going toward replacing a stolen vehicle. To revitalize the area, the city of Gary once put single-family homes on the market for one dollar. No one took them up on the offer.

Instead of explaining any of that, Smith just mumbled something to Eddie about how he'd understand when he was older.

Soon, Smith noticed that the child was slowing. He'd already fallen more than a few steps behind. They came to a stop in the midst of nothing.

"Mister... uh..." Eddie paused, needing more information. "What's your last name?"

"Uh... Brooks," lied Smith.

"Mr. Brooks... I'm tired."

"I thought you were hungry."

"I am."

Smith felt his patience waning. "Pick one, kid. Do you want to sleep or eat?"

"Can you carry me?" Eddie whined.

Smith rubbed his eyes. "Are you serious? How much do you weigh?"

"Twenty-seven kilos."

Smith didn't know how much that was, but he knelt down, thankful that Brooks wasn't there to see him become the horse. "Climb aboard."

Eddie cheered as he climbed onto Smith's shoulders.

The sound echoed in the... wait, that wasn't right. Smith glanced around, seeing nothing against which a sound could echo.

"Wooooo!"

It was louder this time.

"Wooooo!"

Smith swore it was getting closer. Despite the extra weight, he quickened his pace, hoping that any second the lights of the Biscuit Bucket would break through the haze.

The sound came again, this time from straight ahead. Smith would have judged it twenty meters or so, if Smith had been proficient with the metric system.

Instead of a Biscuit Bucket, three shadowy figures emerged from the dust and snow, intimidating in their obscurity.

Smith felt a chill run up the small of his back.

"Wooooo!"

Two appeared to be human men—stocky, wearing motorcycle helmets and leather, and carrying baseball bats. The third—the one wooing—was emaciated and wore a mullet. Although he might have been human, he scrambled across the ground on all fours like a monkey. He probably hadn't taken any Mutant-B-Nots.

The larger of the stocky men approached and stopped a foot ahead of his companions.

"Take off your wigs," he said.

"No," snapped Eddie. He was remarkably defiant for a tiny human sitting on a stranger's shoulders.

"There a reason I shouldn't?" Smith whispered to the kid.

Of course, Eddie didn't know anything, and he had no good answer. "We're not supposed to..."

Smith reached up and tore off the hairpiece, revealing his sweaty, matted head of blond hair.

The ruffians didn't react. Their eyes fixed over his shoulders.

"*Him*," said the one in front, clearly the leader of the group.

"Life lesson," Smith said to his younger self. "You are very small. You should listen to large people with baseball bats."

"But I'm not supposed to take it off!"

"I promise I won't tell your parents," Smith said.

Eddie hesitated for a moment, then reached for his clown wig. He mimicked the older man and dramatically tossed it to the ground.

"Hand him over," demanded the leader.

"Why?" Smith asked.

The man tightened his grip on the baseball bat. "Hand. Him. Over."

There was only one man in all the universes Smith would sometimes listen to, and it was not some helmeted Indiana wasteland thug.

"Nah, I don't think so."

"Do you want to die?" the leader asked.

Smith shrugged. "Sometimes."

He was in no shape to fight off three attackers, so he turned and ran, though he was in no shape to do that either. He was used to walking around with a chip on his shoulder, not a child. As he picked up his pace, he suddenly realized what it meant when the video game characters he'd played over the years were 'over-encumbered.'

"Fuck. You're heavy."

"Swear jar!"

They headed toward a twenty-foot-high pile of rubble that had once been an insurance agency. As he slowed, Eddie began to panic.

"You can't stop!"

"I can't outrun them either," Smith said. "But there might be a way to..."

He knelt down and shook the child off his back, then grabbed a large rock from the pile. He wound up and flung it square at his least favorite attacker: the mulleted monkey boy. It bonked him in the side of the face, and the creature fell to the ground, whimpering.

"Woo at that, you dick."

The leader stopped to assist his friend. The other helmeted thug—unfazed—approached the rubble.

Smith sent a second rock flying. There was no sense aiming for a headshot, so he directed this one at the man's genitals. It was a direct hit, but the attacker showed little reaction.

"Shit." Smith glanced around, pondering ways to stop a

junkless strongman, and found his window. The remains of a window, to be exact. A pane of glass and a cracked, triangular bit of concrete were all that was keeping the pile of rubble from collapsing on itself.

Smith knelt down and signaled for Eddie to hop back on.

"Here." Smith reached over his shoulder and handed the boy a rock. "I'm gonna let him get close and when I say 'Biscuit Bucket' I want you to throw it at him."

"I don't think that's gonna stop him, Mr. Brooks."

"Trust me." The irony of asking his younger self to trust him—when he didn't even trust himself—was not lost on Smith. But there'd be more time to think about irony if they survived.

"Hand him over," the junkless thug said.

Smith put up his hands. "Okay. Alright. You win."

"Hey!" Eddie objected.

"Sorry, kid. I know you were looking forward to *Biscuit Bucket*."

On his signal, Eddie tossed the tiny rock, which landed softly at the man's feet.

The man's helmeted head pointed toward the ground as he eyed the rock. Deep laughter emerged from within.

Seizing the moment, Smith grabbed the triangular rock and pulled as hard as he could. He dashed left as an avalanche of concrete and stone fell toward their attackers, filling the air with even more dust and buying valuable time.

Smith cursed his stupid, worthless gun as he continued running. It could have been worse. At least their attackers didn't have firearms. One point in favor of Hell World.

Adrenaline could only do so much. He had about a mile in him, at best. The wasteland warriors almost certainly had more.

"Hurry! Hurry!"

The voice over his shoulder didn't help. Smith's eyes shot around furiously, searching for another plan.

Abandoned buildings... Dust... More dust... Snow... Broken gun... Motocross dicks who came out of nowhere... More snow... Trailer park...

Bingo.

Smith darted past a charred sign for 'Riverbed Estates' and weaved between bits of garbage.

Most of the trailers were turned on their sides or rusted out. A few were not.

Lacy curtains... Birdfeeder... Kiddie pool...

He headed for a trailer with blackout curtains and a bright orange 'BEWARE OF DOG' sign on the door.

"Woo! Woo! Woo!" came a familiar cry, close behind.

Smith shrugged Eddie off of his shoulders, then kicked in the flimsy trailer door.

It was a standard model, one that Smith recognized. The front door put them in the living room, to the left of which was a narrow hallway lined in peeling floral wallpaper that led to some bedrooms and a bathroom. To their right was a tiny kitchen with avocado green cabinets and appliances.

The place still smelled like chemicals. In lieu of furniture, the living room had a long banquet table covered in bottles, beakers, and buckets. Around the room and overflowing into the kitchen were dozens of large plastic barrels, coiled up plastic tubes, crates of sugary soda and energy drinks, and discarded coffee filters. Classic meth lab chic.

Smith shut the trailer door behind them and pointed down the hallway.

"Go down the hall, smash out a window with whatever you can find, and get ready to jump out. I'll be there in a second."

Eddie's voice seemed unsure. "Okay..."

"Trust me."

As expected, the former owners had left behind a cornucopia of toxic chemicals. Smith grabbed a two-liter of Mountain Dew Broccoli Blast, twisted it open and dumped the flat, sugary liquid onto the shag carpeting. From a back room, a window shattered.

"Good kid."

For reasons that should be self-evident, this book is not going to describe any of the ingredients used to make meth. Just know that one lowlife production method involves dumping standard household chemicals into a two-liter bottle and giving it a good shake. Shake it the wrong way or pop the cap at the wrong time, and the bottle can explode.

Smith would never make it in the high-octane field of amateur chemistry. In the process of mixing up his makeshift batch, he managed to pour acid on his left hand.

"Fuck, that stings!"

There was no time to worry about it. With the last ingredient added, Smith got to shaking as the cheering started up again, just outside the front door.

He hurried down the hallway and into a room that was barren, aside from a deflated waterbed. Eddie stood next to the room's smashed-out window, holding the handle from a dismantled Radio Flyer wagon. He'd made a tiny, Eddie-sized hole.

THUNK.

Smith peeked out into the hallway as the three thugs came lumbering toward him. The smallest—in spite of the trail of blood trickling down his face—cheered again.

Smith glanced back to Eddie.

"Jump!"

He gave the bottle a final shake, twisted the cap halfway off, and sent it hurtling down the hallway at the attackers. He charged toward the window, sprinting harder than he had in a decade, and leapt toward it as half the trailer exploded behind him. He landed outside, crashing shoulder-first into the tangled remains of a swingset.

Still holding his wagon handle, Eddie stood nearby, wide-eyed and slack-jawed, as flames consumed the trailer. A thick cloud of black smoke rose into the already contaminated air.

Smith leaned forward, gasping for air that stank of cat urine.

"I... hate... it... here," he sputtered between breaths.

The only movie little Eddie had ever seen was *The Wiz*, and this explosion outdid that. "That was... so cool!"

"Uh huh..." Smith ignored the child's excitement. "How... far is... Biscuit Bucket?"

Eddie pointed, grinning.

Smith turned to see half of a peeled billboard—now illuminated by the trailer fire:

BISCUIT BUCKET: ONLY 3KM AWAY!
EXIT 5, TURN LEFT

Smith groaned, and not just because he didn't understand the metric system. It would have been nice if the answer to his question hadn't required a meth lab explosion.

If there were other men, monsters, or mutants out there in the wasteland, the blaze would definitely grab their attention.

He pulled off his already loose tie and wrapped it around his burned hand. Then he reached for the base of his neck and pulled out a modest shard of glass. He couldn't stand to leave it in, even knowing he should. A thin trickle of blood began to gush. He pressed his pocket square against it, hard, and knelt down.

"Come on..."

Smith let the boy back on his shoulders, feeling a little woozy as he stood back up.

He'd get over it.

He didn't really have a choice.

19 / SEPARATION ANXIETY

Leslie and Phil Smith sat—wigs in hand—on a busted couch, facing the now-closed entrance to this universe. Brooks, who had assured them it was fine to let their scalps breathe for a while, stood before them, bending Phil's cane back into shape following his outburst.

On one hand, Brooks was glad Smith wasn't there to meet another version of his abusive parents. On the other, much larger hand, he was beside himself with worry. His husband was trapped in some nightmare world, while he was stuck in this one. He needed to know everything there was to know about everything, and fast.

"So, portals. Spill," he said, getting right to the crux. He handed over the cane, which was a little wonkier than before. "Sorry, by the way."

"Uh... good as new," lied Phil.

Leslie scoffed. "Spill what? We're figuring it out as we go along."

Brooks reacted to her attitude the same way he always responded to his Smith's sass—with an unflinching, deadpan stare. "Then spill *what* you've figured out."

Phil fidgeted with his wig. "It's like this... every so often, a portal between your universe and ours opens in one direction or the other. Leslie and I have spent years trying to figure out the pattern. There isn't one. We've pinpointed fifteen spots where the portals open up so far, but it seems totally random. You could park yourself in one of those spots for years and never see one."

"We've been doing that in Clarksville," Leslie added.

Brooks was stunned. "You've been waiting? For years?"

"No, six years." Leslie snickered at her own joke.

Brooks stared right through her.

"A few months back," Phil continued, "we met a fellow from Akron who tipped us off about a portal here. Said he'd seen something at another mall. This is what we found when we got there." He motioned to his wife.

Leslie stood up from the couch, pulled a folded piece of paper from her pocket, and handed it to Brooks.

April 84 / 18

Date			Date		
4/1	1	B	4/16	13	B
4/2	14	B	4/17	–	–
4/3	9	A	4/18	7	B
4/4	–	–	4/19	–	–
4/5	–	–	4/20	–	–
4/6	1	B	4/21	–	–
4/7	2	A	4/22	–	–
4/8	1	B	4/23	–	–
4/9	–	–	4/24	–	–
4/10	–	–	4/25	–	–
4/11	9	B	4/26	–	–
4/12	–	–	4/27	2	A
4/13	–	–	4/28	12	B
4/14	–	–	4/29	13	B
4/15	2	B	4/30	9	A

None of it meant anything to him, except the company letterhead at the top of the page: Shoppli.

"*God.* They own everything in *every* universe!"

"We knew 84 was a year," Leslie explained, "but we figured 18 was a page number or something. Turns out it's a year too. Your year."

"What are the numbers?" Brooks asked.

"Locations. We still don't know where all of them are." Leslie pointed. "We know two is Akron, and one is..."

"Clarksville," Brooks said. "That's where Eddie got sucked in. So... since the April 6th event in Clarksville is labeled B, but the April 7th event in Akron is labeled A, I'm guessing the letters are directions?"

Leslie's voice boomed. "*Tell him what he's won, Johnny.*"

Phil smiled and wagged his forefinger. "Our son married a smart one."

"Uh huh." Brooks blinked a few times before handing the sheet back to Leslie. "So, you expect me to believe... that you just happened to find this spreadsheet with the exact information you needed to hop from one universe to the other and back... just lying around?"

"It was in a dumpster." Phil channeled his disarming folksiness. "Look, I know it seems a might suspicious, but it's the God's honest truth."

"It's more than a *might* suspicious," said Brooks. "Especially when Eddie *just* disappeared."

"Can you tell us about him?" Leslie asked.

Brooks was in no mood for reminiscing. "I'd rather talk about the portals, if you don't mind."

Phil pointed out a fact. "Next portal back ain't opening 'til tomorrow."

"... in Clarksville," Brooks realized. "It's five hours from here, and... I left my car there. Shit. Lemon's going to be *pissed.*"

"You just abandoned your car?" Leslie wondered.

"With a lemon?" Phil added.

Brooks ran a hand through his hair. "Ugh, yes! I mean... no. I mean... I hitched a ride here on a time machine and now I'm gonna have to call the girls back."

Phil and Leslie looked at him as if he'd grown a second head.

"Speak English," Phil said, in the nicest, least racist tone anyone had ever used saying that to Brooks.

"Um... so... Eddie and I," he began to explain, "we adopted two girls from... two different spots in time. They travel around in a time machine."

"What on earth do you do for a living?" Phil asked, scratching his head.

"We're paranormal detectives."

"Ohhh," Leslie and Phil said simultaneously.

"Real live dicks!" Phil added. He meant it in the detective sense, but Brooks nevertheless shot him a sideways glance.

"How'd you get into that line of work?" Leslie asked.

"My whole family was murdered by wraiths at a music festival. Then, Eddie saved my life and recruited me to work for a secret organization that fights monsters."

Their silence spoke volumes.

"Should... you be telling us that?" Leslie finally asked.

Brooks brushed the question off. "Oh, yeah, it's fine. They don't exist anymore. We're freelance now."

"Small business owners!" said Phil, but his excitement quickly turned to fear. "Wait... then how did Eddie get into that line of work? Did we... I mean, was his family...?"

Brooks shook his head. "No. I mean... they *are* dead, but that's not how he got into the business. Just your run-of-the-mill vampire encounter."

"Run of the..." Leslie trailed off.

"So, what's our son like?" questioned Phil.

"Um—" Brooks stretched that note like a diva singing the "Star Spangled Banner" before a football game.

Leslie and Phil stared at him in anticipation.

"He's... the love of my life."

"We kinda gathered that from the marriage," Phil said.

There were silent stares in both directions. Brooks had hoped that would be enough.

"Um..." Brooks didn't stop himself from sharing. "Eddie is... complicated. When he wants to be, he's the most charming person in the world. Spontaneous. Fun. Full of jokes. He's thoughtful and loving and supportive."

"And when he doesn't want to be?" Phil asked, raising an eyebrow.

Brooks wasn't inclined to badmouth his husband to anyone—least of all some random version of the man's parents—but he was inclined to connect with the Smiths. In-laws were a concept he thought he'd never encounter.

He paused to consider his words, but ultimately let them flow. "Eddie's been through a lot, and... he'll help anyone, any time. No question. But he thinks his problems are a burden, so he'll just let things eat at him."

Phil nudged Leslie. "I know someone who does that."

Leslie nudged him back.

"So, what else?" Phil asked. "Is he happy?"

"Uh..." Brooks stopped. Ever the detective, he'd noticed something strange. "You said 'our son' before."

"What?" Leslie played stupid.

He looked at Phil with an accusatory stare. "You said 'tell us about our son.' That's not normal. I wouldn't say 'my husband' if I were asking you about your kid."

Leslie and Phil both avoided eye contact.

"Why are you so eager to know about my Eddie?"

The Smiths kept silent and exchanged nervous glances.

"Don't make me bend the cane again..."

Phil waved his hands in the air in protest. "Okay... okay, fine. This is our universe. It's not a new home we're looking for, it's our original one."

"What?" Brooks balled his fists—an unnecessarily threatening gesture, but he'd had enough. "Explain. Now."

Phil leaned back into the couch. "Okay! About six years ago from our perspective... apparently a lot longer than that here... we were shopping at the Green River Mall and... there was this portal. Glowing, red thing. Eddie went in..."—he snapped his fingers—"Bam. Gone. We had no choice but to follow. On the other side, we met the other versions of us. They promised to get us home, but... they stranded us and took our places here."

"They *took our son*." Leslie's hand covered her mouth.

"Why would they... why would anybody do that?" Brooks asked.

"We don't know," Leslie professed. "It could have been

an honest mistake or it could have been... we don't know."

"We've been raising Eddie—the other Eddie—for the last six years because it's the right thing to do, you know? Heck, he's our son too... in a way. As far as he knows, we're the only parents he's ever had."

"*Híjole*," Brooks cursed to himself.

"*Gesundheit*," Phil said.

Brooks's throat tightened. In his mind, he googled 'how to tell your spouse their parents aren't their real parents,' 'alternate universe body swap?' and 'real life consequences of the parent trap.'* Nothing useful came of it.

He parked himself on the couch, stealing Leslie's seat. Phil took the space next to him.

"Can I ask you something?"

"Sure," sighed Brooks.

"The other version of Leslie and me... the ones that raised your Eddie... I'm getting the feeling they weren't any better to you two than they were to us."

"I never met them," Brooks said. "They died in the '80s."

"But you already had a negative impression when you met us. What'd they do?"

"That's not my story to tell."

Phil shuffled around a little in discomfort. "I see."

Brooks sighed and rose from his seat. It was time to face the music—or at least the rage of a former musician.

"Dead. Dead. Dead. Dead. Dead. Dead."

Leslie squinted. "What are you—"

Bright green light illuminated her face as the time machine answered her unfinished question. This time it landed a little further right, with one of its fins fully lodged in a pothole, leaving the whole thing tilted twenty degrees or so.

Phil leapt from the couch and grabbed his awestruck wife

---

* Just because he had 24/7 access to the internet didn't mean he was very good at formulating search queries.

by the arm. Neither of them had ever seen a time machine before, and they stood in wonder, unsure whether to approach.

Lemon—now in a silver jumpsuit with shiba inu patches on the sleeves—stormed out before they could make a decision.

"You gotta be florping kidding me!"

Patience followed close behind, holding her frock high above the ground. Toil was great and all, but she'd just repaired the last tear, and she wasn't yearning for another round of sewing.

Lemon jabbed a finger at her father. "Are you *trying* to ruin my life?"

"Sorry. This is kind of important."

"More important than touring the Martian Royal Palace?"

"If you care about getting your other dad back, yes."

Lemon crossed her arms. "He didn't kill himself again, did he?"

"*WHAT*?" gasped Leslie and Phil.

Lemon rolled her eyes. "He got better!" she said, before registering the two strangers. "Wait. Who are you?"

Brooks stood between the two groups, wishing he were the one who'd been trapped in another universe. "Girls, these are Eddie's parents. Leslie, Phil... Patience and Lemon."

Leslie approached, hesitant at first. "I always wanted granddaughters. I didn't expect to be so close to their age, but—"

Lemon took a step back from her, and looked toward Brooks. "Uh, it's hard to keep track, but aren't the Smiths some of the bad parents? And dead?"

Phil mumbled to himself. "Some of the...?"

"Alternate universe," Brooks explained.

"Gotcha," Lemon said.

Patience offered a hand to Leslie. "It's a pleasure to meet

you."

"So, what's the deal?" Lemon asked.

Brooks explained. "The portals only work one way. These two came from the universe where Eddie's trapped. We need a ride to Clarksville tomorrow so we can go in and find him."

"If I'm gonna have to keep giving you rides, I want gas money."

"That thing doesn't even run on gas," said Brooks. "It runs on nuclear power."

Leslie and Phil took a few steps back.

"It's fine." Brooks stepped toward the machine and motioned for them to follow.

The Smiths didn't budge.

"Come on," Brooks said. "Really. I promise. No worse than getting an X-ray."

Phil looked at his wife, and then to Brooks. "If we have time before we head to uh... tomorrow, what say we have ourselves a nice family dinner?"

Brooks repeated the last two words under his breath. "...What."

"I'm starving," Phil added.

"We haven't had good food in years," pleaded Leslie.

Brooks couldn't see any harm. With Lemon and Patience here, he had all the time in the world, quite literally.

"Um... sure. I guess. Girls?"

"I am unopposed," Patience said.

Lemon shrugged in agreement. "I'm never winning X over at this point anyway."

Phil pumped his fist. "Great! Is Biscuit Bucket still around in this universe?"

Brooks buried his contempt for that question deep inside, next to a catalog of horrific crime scenes and his memories of a one-night stand with a demon named Percival.

⁂

Not long after, the five sat at a table for six, under a retro tin sign advertising seed packets. Dinner with in-laws is awkward enough under normal circumstances, and these—with Smith not being present and the in-laws being from an alternate universe—were immensely uncomfortable circumstances. Brooks decided the best way through was to keep the Smiths busy talking about their universe so they wouldn't ask too many questions about his, and to take full advantage of Biscuit Bucket's bottomless mimosas.

For a while, it worked, as the Smiths brought them up to speed with a brief history of their foster universe. In summary, the Cold War became a Hot War. Bombs dropped. Crops failed. The Northeast and Midwest were the hardest hit, and soon thousands of miniature civilizations rose up in replacement, with thousands of ideologies maintaining them—each living its own reality.

Those who didn't adjust defaulted to burying their heads in the sand. If they pretended things were fine, things were fine. For some tubular citizens of the 1980s, shopping malls represented normality, so they flocked to them—window-shopping aimlessly, forever. These mall occupants didn't buy anything, as there was no way to restock, and having no stock would have quickly killed the vibe. But walking the same halls, browsing the same goods, and watching the same movies over and over was a comforting, easy existence.

"You people live in an abandoned mall?" Brooks asked.

"Sure. There's employee bathrooms and showers with recycled water. Plenty of space too. Most people sleep in their cars, but we built ourselves a little underground nest next to the sewer tunnels," Phil said.

"You have water? How? What about heating? Electricity? What about the power grid?"

"Shoppli takes care of it."

"What, out of the goodness of their hearts?" Brooks doubted that, since Shoppli hadn't even been willing to refund a broken gravy boat.

"Children," Phil said. "It costs children."

Brooks blinked. "*What?*"

"Any babies born in the mall must be surrendered to Shoppli."

"So... you're telling me... people are willing to give up their kids to live in... a mall?"

"Beats a lot of the alternatives," Leslie said coldly.

Phil realized how that made them seem, and jumped to defend their honor. "We haven't given any up! We always use protection! And we keep our Eddie hidden. We just wanted to set up near the portal, in case another one home opened up, or someone came over who knew something."

"Yuh huh," said Lemon, unconvinced.

"But enough about us," said Phil, changing the subject.

Leslie nodded. "Yeah. Who cares about the craphole we just came from? We want to know about here... what it's been like since we left. We beat the Soviets?"

"Kind of, I guess," Brooks said. "Now they just radicalize teenagers on the internet."

"The what?"

Lemon gasped. "Ohhhhh. Y'all don't have the internet!"

She hopped out of her chair, moved into an empty one next to Leslie, and began showing off her Zanephone.

"It can do *anything*. You wanna do math? Calculator! You wanna talk to someone? Chat! You wanna send a letter? Email! You wanna rage-tweet at Orlando Bloom? Gotcha. You're gonna love—"

"*Este pinche lugar.*" Brooks hit the bottom of another mimosa.

"You wanna translate that? No problem!" Lemon tapped a button.

A robotic female voice responded. "This. Lousy. Place."

'Lousy' was a kind interpretation, but Brooks let it slide.

"Well, heck." Phil pointed at the phone. "Does it have any

pictures? I wanna see my boy and his family."

"Yup!"

Lemon pulled her phone close to her face so she could scroll through her photo gallery in privacy. After a moment, she found what she was looking for and presented the Smiths with a picture of the whole family celebrating Patience's graduation from the Little Achievers Academy—New York City's least prestigious private school that was also least likely to ask questions. In the center, the Puritan wore a black cap, a gown, and an exasperated frown as she held a diploma rolled up so tightly that no one could tell it was signed in crayon. Brooks, Smith, and Lemon stood around her, smiling proudly.

Leslie turned to Patience. "You don't look too happy about that diploma."

"Hmm?" Patience glanced at the phone. "'Twasn't a reaction to the diploma. I simply have an aversion to photography."

Phil chuckled. "This kid's weird. I love it. Lemme see that thing."

Lemon handed the phone over. "If you wanna zoom, you can pinch the screen like this." She demonstrated.

"Look at that," Phil said. "Our boy grew up to look just like—"

"—*you*," Leslie finished, and the couple chuckled.

"What happens if I—"

"Noooo—" Lemon grimaced.

Phil committed a modern-day cardinal sin. He swiped.

The next picture over was a selfie, taken at the dinner after the graduation ceremony. In the foreground, Lemon posed with a massive grin for her followers. In the background, Brooks and Smith performed an exaggerated makeout session—a well-timed photobomb meant to make their daughter cringe.

Phil handed the phone back and squirmed a little in his

seat.

From his vantage point, Brooks couldn't see the photo. "He didn't swipe to one of Duke's dick pics, did he?"

"I did *not* keep those," gasped Lemon, taking offense.

Phil's nervous chuckle fell into a ramble in his desperation not to offend. "Oh, it's nothing. Cultural differences. You know... I just... expected private dicks to be a little more private."

Brooks frowned.

"It's not my business. Really. You live your life however makes you happy..."

Brooks took a sip of his newly replenished drink. "You say that, but you don't mean it. You wish you had a normal son, right? That's what my dad said at first. He didn't start coming around until right before he died..."

An awkward silence descended.

"I didn't mean anything of the sort," Phil said.

Brooks, drunk on mimosas, cackled to lift the mood. "I'm messing with you."

There was a collective sigh of relief.

"Can we talk more about you being a *private dick*?" Lemon asked.

"Not if you want that gas money."

They all laughed, except Patience, who ever so slightly raised the left corner of her mouth.

"I've missed you two," Brooks said, smiling at his daughters. "I've missed this."

It wasn't just the mimosas talking and, at that moment, the girls felt the pangs of something that rhymes with quilt.

Guilt. It was guilt.

20 / MAKE BISCUITS NOT WAR

Smith spotted some sort of barricade in the distance. The closer he and Eddie got, the clearer it became that it had been hastily thrown together from whatever was available. Pieces of spiky wooden fencing and tree branches shot out from a rusted ladder tilted on its side, and an inverted couch had been skinned of its covering and adorned with barbed wire. Behind the barricade, a shadowy figure paced with something in hand, their form becoming clearer as they passed into the glow of several fires burning behind them.

"Is that an armed guard?" Smith removed pressure from his neck wound for a moment to stare at the blood that had seeped through to his hand, and to think about how much he didn't want to be shot on top of being burned and pierced with broken glass.

Eddie chirped. "They're good guys. My mom and dad say so."

"Oh, well I definitely trust *them*."

Eddie once again failed to recognize the sarcasm.

"You wait here," Smith directed.

"What if those guys come back?"

Smith wanted to say something about how their brains were now aerosolized, but he thought better of it.

"They won't," he said.

Smith—with nothing to lose but his life—continued his approach. Anything that could be shoved into the barricade had been: exercise bikes, wooden pallets, dining chairs, rolling pins, large seashells... all of it secured a cemented area tagged with the letters BBAZ in black spray paint. Pronounced "bee bazz," the letters stood for Biscuit Bucket Autonomous Zone—one of the thousands of miniature civilizations that had sprung up in the aftermath of nuclear devastation. BBAZ, which spread over two square miles, had no leader, just a simple concept that its hundreds of residents agreed upon: Biscuits Good, Crime Bad. They'd gathered enough of this universe's sparse weaponry to enforce that.

The patrolwoman wore a Colts jersey and helmet, and pointed her rifle at Smith.

"What're you here for?"

Smith hesitated. "Biscuit Bucket...?"

She responded with almost no emotion. "Hand over any weapons."

"Sure." Smith pulled the nonfunctioning Chekhov from his waist and deposited it into a large, festive red and green storage container filled with guns and knives.

She looked unimpressed. "That all?"

Smith removed a small pocketknife from his pocket and tossed it in. He pulled a skull-shaped lighter from another pocket and tossed it in as well. For good measure, he mimicked his husband at LaGuardia and turned his pockets inside out.

The guard lowered her gun and waved him in between the ladder and couch.

"Enjoy your biscuits."

Smith, in turn, waved for Eddie to follow. The prospect of biscuits gave the boy a second wind, and he sprinted toward the BBAZ encampment before skidding to a stop, his nose inches from the guard's rifle.

"Weapons."

Eddie deposited his wagon handle. The guard didn't budge or say a word.

"Um..." The child searched his pockets and came up with two dried gummy bears covered in pocket lint, a small rock, and a rusted key he'd found on the ground.

That was good enough for admission.

"Enjoy your biscuits."

The autonomous zone didn't look much different from the

wasteland that surrounded it. Once a suburban business district, all that remained were rubble and parking lots, dotted with tents and lit by lanternlight and campfires. At the center of it all was their destination: Biscuit Bucket. It was a little worse for the wear, but its yellow façade was just the same in this universe, minus the patriotic bunting. The building shone blindingly bright—the only facility with electricity for miles. The generator providing the power whirred, hummed, and occasionally sputtered.

With plenty of his newfound energy to spare, Eddie broke into another sprint while Smith—still out of shape and covered in blood—lumbered after him. He didn't remember having as much energy or enthusiasm when he was Eddie's age, but then again, he did have a worse childhood experience than just about anyone outside of Hollywood.

When Smith finally made it to the building's entrance, Eddie was already in the foyer, tapping an imaginary watch on his wrist.

"Come on!"

Smith heard the shout through the chipped glass, and made his way inside. The bell above the door let out a little jingle. There was no gift shop full of tchotchkes; that part of the building had been trashed at some point, and all that remained were tipped over shelves and scattered bags of black licorice.*

No host greeted them. A cardboard sign taped to the host stand told the pair to seat themselves. The lights above flickered as they entered the dining room, and the three parties already present—also covered in grime and wounds—glanced at the newcomers before determining they were of little interest. That was a marked improvement from the staring and gossiping at the mall, and from the baseball bat wielding thugs outside.

---

* Even in a wasteland, people had *some* sense of taste.

Eddie hopped into a window booth, and Smith slid into the other side. The table pressed into his stomach. Even in this universe, Biscuit Bucket couldn't figure out proper spacing. As he had in his home world, he tried giving the table a little shove forward, to no avail.

"You wanna switch sides?" he asked.

Eddie giggled at his struggling counterpart. "No."

"Will you anyway? I did get stabbed and burned getting you here."

Eddie's face scrunched as he considered the request. "I guess."

They swapped. Their server arrived almost immediately, and though her jeans and a leather jacket were far out of spec for Biscuit Bucket employees, Smith couldn't fault the speedy service. She set two glasses of water on the table, then reached into her pocket and pulled out two sticky notes. She pasted one to the table in front of Eddie, and one in front of Smith.

"Can I get you anything else to drink?" she asked.

"Yeah. The highest proof liquor you have," Smith said.

She eyed the boy. "And you?"

"Banana pop!"

"Got it. I'll give you two a minute to look at the rest of the menu." With that, she disappeared into the kitchen.

"The rest of the..." Smith scanned the post-it note. There were two options: Meaty Tenders and Simply Salad. Both came with a biscuit. "Jesus Christ."

Smith took one sip of his water, determined it wasn't sewage runoff, and drizzled some over his neck wound.

"What are you doing?" Eddie asked.

"Trying not to get gangrene."

Smith heard the kitchen door swing open, and set his water down. The server returned with a mustard-colored soda for Eddie, and a tumbler of something that smelled like rubbing alcohol for Smith.

"You have any questions, or are you ready to order?"

"What's the meat in the meaty tenders?" Smith asked.

"I'd have to check in the back. Usually big rat, but it depends on—"

"I'll do the salad."

"Me too," said Eddie. He preferred the tenders, but after the most exciting (and only) explosion he'd ever seen, he would have ordered whatever 'Mr. Brooks' had.

With the server again out of sight, Smith splashed a bit of the alcohol on his hands, using it as makeshift sanitizer. He drizzled a little more water on his neck, brushed some clotting away, and clenched his jaw.

Gross as it smelled, the alcohol was enticing. Smith gave it a wistful look before pouring it onto his reopened wound. He somehow managed to keep the cursing to a minimum and mostly under his breath. When the tumbler had run dry, he raised the cloth napkin to his neck and pressed down as hard as he could.

"What did those guys want with you?" he asked, hoping conversation might distract from the searing pain.

"I dunno. My parents don't tell me anything," Eddie moaned.

"Are they..." Smith wanted to finish with "total pieces of shit," but toned it down for his eight-year-old audience. "Do your parents ever hurt you?"

"Um... one time I ate a candy bar that had almonds in it. Then they stabbed me with some medicine so I wouldn't die. That hurt."

"Yeah, I didn't mean epi-pens. I mean... do they beat you or—"

"They beat me at board games all the time."

"I'll take that as a no."

Evidently, the smaller Eddie had stupid parents, not evil ones. Smith felt the slightest pangs of jealousy, but they dissipated once the waiter returned and set a wide-rimmed bowl in front of him.

This Biscuit Bucket's idea of a salad was a heap of dried corn husks, topped with raisins, craisins, and some other dehydrated fruit that was beige in color. For protein, a handful of cicadas had been piled in the middle of the bowl. The dressing, provided in a tasteful sidecar, smelled exactly like the beverage Smith had poured all over himself, but it was slightly more viscous and contained little flakes of dried herbs.

Before he could react, a plate hit the table next to the bowl. On it were two perfect-looking buttermilk biscuits—round and golden—and some surprisingly normal-looking packets of butter and jam.

Smith tilted his head and eyed the salad with revulsion. Eddie didn't see a problem with the food. He dove right in.

The crunching and popping sounds of the child devouring a locust bowl were all Smith needed to hear, and he shoved his bowl to the middle of the table. He kept the biscuit plate, though. He doubted even this shitshow of a universe could mess up biscuits.

21 / MALLS TO THE WALL

In the other Clarksville, Brooks stood between the Smiths and the dimensional gateway. He'd stopped to inventory the supplies in his backpack—the results of a last-minute, hangover-fueled Costco run. Water filter? Check. First aid kit? Check. Matches. Compass. Mask. Hand sanitizer. Emergency blanket. Plenty of granola bars.

"That should cover it," Brooks said, satisfied.

"No weapons?" asked Phil.

A glimmer came across Brooks's eyes.

"I am the weapon," he said, seizing the opportunity to throw out some B-grade action movie dialogue.

Leslie rolled her eyes in response.

Phil shrugged. "Fair enough."

"Before we go in..." Brooks struggled to find the words. "I mean... once we get there, I need you to let me talk to Eddie first. If you could not..."

"Run up to a complete stranger and tell him I'm his father?"

"Exactly. I don't know how he's going to react to all of this, so..."

Leslie nodded. "We get it."

They really didn't. Brooks wanted to tell them that, but he kept his mouth shut. He may have been a dick, but he wasn't a *dick*.

"Let's get rollin' then," Phil said.

The three linked hands. This, the Smiths had explained, was the only way to ensure they arrived at the exact same time and location. Joining hands turned them into one body, as far as the stupid portal was concerned.

There's no universal way to determine whether someone is lying. Fidgeting, avoiding eye contact, using filler words, and profuse sweating are tell-tale signs, but the only way to know for sure is to know someone's baseline when they aren't lying, then look for changes in behavior.

Brooks lamented this fact as he gripped Leslie and Phil's clammy hands. They could be leading him anywhere, including into a trap. All he had to go on was their word, and the spoiler-free assurances of his far-flung daughters.

Brooks and the Smiths—which could have made an excellent Morrissey collaboration, were there anyone capable of tolerating Morrissey for more than an hour—moved toward the portal, as one. The closer they got, the stronger its pull became.

For the briefest moment, Brooks felt like he was shrinking, then growing back to his original size. It was over almost as soon as it began.

They emerged in the more hellish universe, hands still linked. The mall towered over them, its windows still aglow. Heavy snow had settled on the parking lot, covering the hundreds of parked cars. Inside many of them, mall residents huddled in sleeping bags and under blankets. Some gathered outside, around makeshift campfires.

"Why don't they sleep in the mall?" Brooks asked.

"Mall closes at ten PM," Phil said.

"It doesn't *have to*." Brooks had been in this world for mere seconds, and was already filled with contempt for its occupants.

"Makes it feel like normal, though, right?" Phil said. "You got that flashlight?"

Brooks removed it from the backpack and handed it over. Phil—flashlight in hand—led the group away from the mall, toward the sewer entrance. Each step was darker than the one before it, not that it mattered to Brooks with his night vision. Soon, the flashlight beam illuminated a large, open pipe behind a turned-over, rusted car frame—the Smiths' front door. As they entered, their footsteps on the bone-dry metal caused faint clanging sounds to echo throughout the sewer system.

Brooks's foot landed with a CRUNCH. He looked down to see the remnants of a rat skeleton he'd just obliterated.

"Oh, crap," said Leslie, spotting a light in the distance. Someone had left the door open, and the glow of her fruity candles had revealed their hideaway to the world.

"Oh *crap*," she said again.

The group rushed toward the door, and Phil and Brooks called out at the same time.

"*Eddie!?*"

The place had been completely ransacked. Gone were the sleeping bags and jugs of water. The wig box had been toppled; its contents were scattered across the floor. One hairpiece—now a melted, blackened puddle—had landed on a candle and caught fire, adding a toxic chemical quality to the ambient fruit scent.

"At least they left the Mutant-B-Nots," Phil said, glancing at a crate. Too many wastelanders were happy to grow additional limbs.

Leslie shot Phil a worried glance. "You think marauders got them?"

"Marauders?" Brooks wondered.

"Groups of dickhea—" Leslie began, but caught her husband's judgmental stare, "—jerks roaming the wasteland, looking for anything they can trade. Weapons. Gold. Kids. Little Eddie would fetch a good price."

On the ground, next to a discarded Almond Joy wrapper, sat a Biscuit Bucket rewards card, deliberately placed. In pen, hastily jotted across it, were an arrow pointing at the restaurant's logo and the words: 'Not dead.'

"There!" Brooks grinned. "Eddie found Eddie, and they went to a Biscuit Bucket."

Phil didn't seem too happy about that. "The BBAZ? That's four kilometers away."

"Through the wasteland," Leslie added.

Brooks noted the panic on their faces.

"If they went without a vehicle..." Phil tapered off in fear.

"There's all kinds of sick bastards out there," Leslie said. "Not just marauders. I've heard about people running into cannibals, mutants... and the rats. Big rats can grow to the size of ponies."

"I'm sure Eddie can handle it."

Leslie and Phil's worried looks said otherwise.

"We need to find them, quick-like," Phil said.

"Do you have a car?" Brooks asked, skeptical about the logistics of carrying two fully-grown adults on his back at once.

"No, our scooter's in Akron," Phil said.

"But we can get one," said Leslie, with a grin.

Phil eyed her with suspicion. "We can?"

"Gus owes me a favor."

"Gus?" Brooks wondered.

Phil explained, with a downcast face. "He works at the Broccoli Julius. He's a loner sort. Kind of fella who—"

Leslie cut in. "I let him take artistic nudes of me, in exchange for information on what goes on in the Food Court."

"I don't like it," said Phil, "but a good deal's a good deal."

"But why would he lend you his car?" asked Brooks.

Leslie smirked. "The pictures are that good."

"She ain't lyin'." Phil gave his wife's rear a quick tap.

Brooks recalled the many times he'd told Smith "you are not your parents," and decided that he may have judged too soon.

22 / TOO MANY BISCUITS FOR ONE PLATE

Inside the BBAZ, Biscuit Bucket was open all day, every day. At first, it caused a bit of a stir because Hieronymus Hardtack—even in this dimension—had always insisted his employees have Sundays off. Many thought the principle should continue, but after the fall of civilization, no one really kept track of the days of the week. After a few accidental Sunday openings, BBAZers discarded the concept of days altogether. Every day was Biscuit Day.

Smith, downing his eighth cup of coffee, vibrated with energy. Without anywhere to direct it, he simply sat upright in the booth, fingers trembling and feet tapping.

Eddie's three banana sodas had also taken effect. He bounced up and down in his seat.

"Can we go to Happy World Fun Park?"

"No. I don't know what that is, but no."

"*Come onnnn.*"

Smith pressed a shaking hand to his temple. "Kid, I have more coffee than blood in me right now. I also *don't* have whatever currency these biscuit people take, so I'm kinda stalling for time here."

"Yeah, you do," said Eddie, pointing at Smith's poorly bandaged hand.

"My tie?" Smith asked.

Eddie laughed. "No."

"My... hand?"

"No!" More laughter.

"Just tell me before I die of blood loss."

Eddie gestured at the wedding band on Smith's finger and the detective couldn't censor his reaction. "What the fuck does anyone need gold for in a goddamn wasteland?"

If Brooks had been there, he'd have told Smith about the metal's numerous electronics and aerospace applications—about how it's conductive, nonoxidizing, noncorroding, and can act as a heat shield. He might have even mentioned that gold was abundant in his cybernetic components.

But Brooks wasn't there, and Eddie didn't know anything about gold.

"I dunno. My mom and dad—"

"—don't tell you anything. Yeah, I know."

"So, can we go now?" the child whined.

"To Happy Park Fun Land? I don't think so."

"It's *Happy World Fun Park*."

"Whatever. No. This ring means more to me than you do, so I'm gonna keep stalling and hope Broo—*the other* Mr. Brooks gets here soon."

Eddie folded his arms, scooched back in his seat, and let out a dramatic huff.

Smith rolled his eyes. "Sorry. That was rude. But we're still waiting here."

He didn't have to wait for long. The next time the bell above the entrance jingled, Smith discovered that his Biscuit Bucket rewards card lure had worked.

He bolted across the dining room toward Brooks, ignoring his husband's other companions, and his general pissiness melted away. Things always ended horribly, in Smith's view, but at least this time they wouldn't end with him stuck in Hell World without his husband. His heart—already racing from the caffeine—raced harder.

He'd stood up too quickly. Smith's emotions were overtaken by physical agony. He swayed with dizziness, and his knees buckled.

Brooks caught him mid-fall and pulled him close.

"Hey..."

"Sorry, Secretariat... I don't have any hay..."

Brooks shook his head at the lame joke, and then at his partner's pathetic appearance. "I can't leave you alone for five minutes..."

Smith let out a faint half-laugh as Leslie scurried toward the booth where her caffeinated son sat. She wrapped him in a big hug, then scolded him for losing his wig. Phil hobbled slowly behind, thanks to the armed guard at the gate having confiscated his cane.

Smith put a hand on Brooks's shoulder and steadied himself.

"Are you okay?" Brooks asked. "You—"

"Look like an unmade bed?"

"Well... yeah." Brooks gave the air a concerned sniff. "And you smell like moonshine."

Smith pointed at his neck. The bleeding had slowed to a small trickle. "Disinfectant. Not off the wagon..."

"Oh!" Brooks pulled his backpack around to his front and poked around inside until he found the first aid kit. "They took the scissors, but—"

Smith wobbled a little. "I'm gonna sit down."

"Here." Brooks guided Smith to the floor, and readied the supplies.

In Hell World, it was perfectly normal to treat wounds on the floor of Biscuit Bucket. No one in the dining room gave them a first thought, let alone a second.

Brooks rubbed the wound with a styptic pencil, then squirted a gob of antibacterial ointment over the area. "What happened?"

Smith looked toward little Eddie. "Saving the kid from cannibals... I think."

Brooks pasted a large bandage onto Smith's neck and applied pressure. "You think you were saving him or you think they were cannibals?"

"I'm bleeding to death and you're correcting my grammar."

Brooks rolled his eyes. "You're not dying anytime soon. They were probably marauders looking to trade the kid. That's a thing here."

"And you know that because...?"

Brooks glanced across the dining room. "I got the guided tour."

"Great." Smith unwrapped his swollen, reddish purple left hand. "Got anything for burns?"

"*Mierda*. Yeah."

Brooks sprayed the blistering hand with analgesic and wrapped it with fresh bandages before tucking the supplies back into his bag.

"Thanks..." said Smith.

"Don't ever wander into a portal again." Brooks planted a soft kiss on his husband's dry, coffee-scented lips.

"I'll try not to."

The Smiths—watching from the booth—averted their eyes and focused on their other son. And on taking away his soda. The bouncing boy needed a detox, stat.

Smith took his husband's arm and stood, steadying himself against the wall. He exhaled.

"This place sucks."

"But if there's a way in, there's a way out," said Brooks optimistically.

"Not true for Scientology."

Brooks laughed. "Shut up. I know there's a way out. My, uh... tour guides came through the other side..."

He gestured toward Leslie and Phil, then got quiet. "Um..."

Smith stared at him.

"I... um..."

"You're being weird," Smith said. "What's wrong?"

"I have to tell you something."

Smith squinted. "So tell."

Brooks looked at Smith's blood-stained shirt and newly bandaged hand. "Now's not a good time. You're not well."

"Always the case, babe," said Smith with a wry smile. "Spill."

Brooks swallowed. "That kid you were hanging out with is..."

"Me. Yeah. I know."

"Oh." Brooks blinked rapidly. "Right. And those two are—"

"Let me guess. The mirror universe versions of my deadbeat parents? Yeah. I remember what they looked like. Way ahead of you."

Brooks had been prepared for an outburst, and Smith's demeanor caught him off guard.

"I know how alternate universes work," Smith said, then corrected himself. "Well... no... I don't, but I know you can't blame Spock for what Mirror Spock does. I get it. You don't need to tiptoe around it. I'm fine."

This was a shockingly mature outlook, and Brooks knew he was about to ruin it. He shut his eyes and took a deep breath before speaking. "Time flows differently here."

Smith shot him a look of amusement. "Kinda figured that out from it being the '80s. Did that portal scramble your wires? You got an electronics repair kit in that bag?"

Brooks's face remained serious. "It's 1984 here, and it's 2018 back home."

"Okay..." said Smith, still not following.

"But when it was 1978 here, it wasn't 2012 in our world. It was 1978 in both places."

"Brooksy... you're being stupid and it's freaking me out."

"Six years ago here was almost forty years ago back home."

"Yeah. I get the basic concept of time." Smith put a hand on Brooks's shoulder. "Why am I the one with the doppelganger and the living dead parents, but you're the one being touchy about it?"

"Because those aren't his parents, they're *yours*." Brooks paused as Smith slowly processed what he'd said, then continued, the words falling out of his mouth before he could consider them. "Your parents portal hopped with you when you were two years old. You made it back home. They didn't." He tilted his head toward the Smiths. "That's them."

Smith stared at him, slack-jawed. It wasn't clear to Brooks whether his husband was upset or merely confused. The next word out of Smith's mouth didn't clarify the matter.

"Huh?"

23 / LONE STALL STATE

Smith glanced over his shoulder to the booth, where little Eddie now sat across from his parents. *His* parents. The boy stared in awe as they unfolded an enormous Biscuit Bucket menu they'd collected while universe hopping.

"Walk me through this again," Smith said.

Brooks explained what he knew about the portals and how the Smiths had encountered their alternate universe selves. He spoke softly as he elaborated. "Forty... or six... years ago, I guess, the Leslie and Phil from this world escaped and took the place of the Leslie and Phil in our world. But they grabbed the wrong kid. You."

Smith looked back again as Leslie was wiping some cicada smudge from the side of Eddie's mouth. He gritted his teeth. "So... my parents—er, *the assholes* I remember—fucked up and left their kid in this shithole, then treated me like garbage for their mistake once we got back—"

"That, or just because they were assholes from a nightmare world."

"—meanwhile this little shit is here..." Smith bit his tongue.

"It's not his fault."

Smith took a deep breath. "Yeah, I know. Bearded Spock."

"It's not."

"*I know.* I know. I'm not gonna take it out on the kid, okay? He's cool, other than the thing with the wigs..."

"Yeah, they all do that..."

Brooks looked his husband over for signs that he was going to snap.

"Do they know who I am?" Smith asked coldly.

Brooks took another deep breath. "Yeah. I told them to let me talk to you first."

"Good. Then I'll just keep talking to you and not have to deal with it right now." That was self-awareness.

"Did you tell the kid—"

"That he's me?" Smith shook his head. "No. I didn't see any reason to freak him out."

"Okay." Brooks looked deep into Smith's eyes. "Eddie... we can handle this any way you want. If you want me to give you some space with them for a while, or you want me to tell them to leave you alone... If you just want to leave, we can. I don't think that's a good idea since they have a whole spreadsheet about portals, but we can find another way home. Just... tell me what you want to do."

That was a lot of words, at least one of which was "spreadsheet," and Smith didn't have the energy to process any of them.

"I want... to take a leak..."

He took a deep breath and pushed himself off the wall.

"Eddie—" Brooks called out, but made no effort to stop him. "Sure. Wander off again," he muttered to himself once his husband was out of earshot.

Smith stumbled toward a hallway with a large, glowing 'RESTROOMS' sign hanging in front of it, dangling by a single electric wire. He pushed open a door labeled 'Cowboys' and made his way into the lone stall. Miraculously, it still had a door—mint green where it wasn't chipped or covered in graffiti—and Smith jiggled the latch until he found the angle at which it would lock. A frigid breeze whipped around him as he observed the facilities.

It was a corner stall, and against one wall, a grimy toilet beckoned. The other wall wasn't a wall at all, but a pile of bricks that opened out into the snowy wasteland of the BBAZ.

"Whatever," Smith huffed.

The most pressing thing was to keep Brooks from following. If a roving pack of cannibals yanked him out into the wasteland, well... that was just fine. At least he wouldn't have to face his birth parents.

Smith dropped to his knees in front of the toilet. For a long moment, he stared at the floor. Where there was still flooring, it consisted of thickly grouted, one-inch hexagonal tiles. At some point, both the tiles and grout were white. Now they were a dark, greyish brown. Smith had never paid attention to tile flooring before, but it provided something to focus on. His stomach processed his feelings before his brain did, and it sent him lurching forward to spew the contents of his stomach. He mostly missed the bowl, but the mess didn't change the character of the room.

When the nausea subsided, Smith rose to his feet, unsteady once more. He reached up to wipe his mouth with his sleeve and found that his skin was clammy and cold. He stepped over the rubble and walked a few paces from the restaurant, breathing in the frozen air. He doubled over, and somehow his stomach found something beyond coffee and biscuits to expel.

Smith became aware of footsteps approaching, but he was in no position to react.

"Eddie..."

He didn't react to his husband's voice either.

Brooks knelt down beside him and put an arm under his chest. He raised Smith to a seated position and steadied him there.

"I'm fine," Smith slurred.

Brooks squinted in disbelief. "You sure?"

"It's the Biscuit Bucket. Bad biscuits... Not having a mental breakdown at all."

It was a definitely a bit of both. Smith feigned a smile.

Brooks eyed him like the liar he was. "It's going to be okay. This doesn't change anything about your life."

Smith laughed. "Like hell it doesn't."

"It's just one more possibility that could have been but

isn't. We went through this with the genie, remember? If you worry about all the things that could have been, it'll drive you crazy and you'll end up murdering a venture capitalist or—"

"That's you. I'm not worried about *all the things* that could have been. Just one."

"Look around you..." Brooks gestured at the wasteland.

From the distance—somewhere near the entrance to BBAZ—came sounds of automatic gunfire. Nearer, a Biscuit Bucket employee wrestled a mutated rat that was bigger than a golden retriever, armed only with a spatula.

"Would you rather have been here your entire life?"

"You're asking me... would I rather be a sheltered eight-year-old with loving parents right now? With my only problem being finding the right wig to wear? Yeah. That's not really up for debate."

"So, you'd rather live in a dystopian hellscape than be with me and the girls. Okay." Brooks looked genuinely hurt.

Smith glowered in response. "Oh, a guilt trip. You know I love those. Brooksy, you've spent the last *decade and a half* trying to recreate your happy little family with your Christmas dinners and... piss bottle road trips. Tell me: If we ended up in some dimension where *your* parents and sister were still alive, you wouldn't rather have grown up there?"

Brooks didn't have an answer.

"Yeah." Smith averted eye contact. "That wouldn't have anything to do with me, and this doesn't have anything to do with you."

"Okay. Fine. What do you want to do?"

"I don't know."

"What do you need from me?"

"I. Don't. Know," said Smith, struggling to rein in his temper. "Christ. What do *you* need from *me* since you're the one who won't stop talking?"

Appalled at himself, he shook his head. "Sorry."

The attitude wasn't what concerned Brooks. "I need to

know you're going to be fine."

"Well, I can't predict the future." Smith hazarded a guess. "I'll *probably* be fine, as long as those biscuits weren't laced with rat poison."

It was a possibility, judging from his stomach's reaction.

"You've overcome a lot worse," Brooks said.

"No. I haven't."

"You were *literally dead.*"

"I haven't overcome anything." Smith pushed Brooks away and dropped back to sit on the ground. "I'm a liar."

Brooks sat facing him. "What are you talking about?"

"I'm a liar. A big fat fucking liar, okay? Every day, I lie to you. I lie to the girls. I lie to everyone. I say I'm fine when I'm not. I'm just getting better at faking it because that's what I'm supposed to do." He tossed up some air quotes. "I'm *self-aware.*"

"You're not that good at faking it," admitted Brooks.

"Am so," Smith griped. "You... you think you see me at my lowest. Like back in Clarksville, at the river. You think it's an exception, and I'm okay the rest of the time. It's not. I'm not."

"I don't understand," said Brooks. "You've made so much progress with your therapists."

"And *how many have I been to*? Open your eyes. I tell you they moved or they quit practicing or they don't take our insurance anymore so maybe... maybe the next one will be the one. And I try all the stupid shit they tell me to do. I kept a journal. I did yoga, for fuck's sake. I tried antidepressants and all they did was kill my boner and make me want drugs that actually do something. Nothing ever helps, so... I just started pretending it did. 'Cause I wanted something to work. Maybe I could fake it 'til I make it."

"Eddie, breathe."

Smith took a deep breath, and continued. "So, every day, I lie. And it's... it's nothing against you or the girls or anyone.

I love you all, but... I can have the best day of my life, and it doesn't matter. It could be a Hallmark movie with cookies and rainbows and... at the end of the day, when I go to bed, it's doom and gloom and this little cocksucker of a voice in my head telling me nothing good can ever happen. That I'm just... teetering on a ledge waiting to fall into a shark pit or something. Then I feel like a piece of shit because if I can't be happy at the end of the perfect day... then I guess I just can't. Ever. That's just my life."

"You've seen a lot. You're allowed to be overwhelmed."

"*Every day?*" Smith's voice cracked. "Shit."

Brooks threw his arms around Smith and pulled him in close. His husband looked empty-eyed toward the Biscuit Bucket, where the other Smiths sat staring at him from their booth. *His parents.*

Smith pulled away. "It's fine. I made my peace with it. I really did. But now you're telling me that all of it—the whole shitshow that is my life—was a fucking *clerical error?* That I was supposed to have a normal family? That the kid over there is me, and I'm him... but we're different. So, then everything we are is our history and our upbringing—"

"Breathe."

Smith couldn't. "—and if that kid was supposed to be me, it means..."

"It means what?"

"It means... I didn't have to be me. It means... I could have been happy, and it means... I could have been good."

He buried his head in his hands.

24 / THE GOOD SON

Back in the spring of 2005, Edward Smith heard knocking on the door of his third-floor walkup. He set his beer down next to a handful of empty bottles and rose, annoyed, from the only piece of furniture in his living room: a beige La-Z-Boy recliner with a few suspicious stains. He didn't know how lucky he was that someone had come to interrupt him during the series finale of *Star Trek: Enterprise.*

Smith briefly considered putting on a shirt, but didn't bother; whoever it was could deal with his grey flannel pajamas, or they could get fucked. He walked over to the door and pulled it open just as another knock was about to land.

In the doorway, Arturo Brooks awkwardly pulled his hand back. "Hi."

"Can I help you?" Smith asked, in a huff.

It took every bit of Brooks's willpower to avoid mentioning the dragon tattoo peeking out of Smith's pajamas. He introduced himself.

"I don't know if you remember me, but—"

"Willowbrook Park."

"—um. Yeah. My name is Arturo Brooks..."

"I remember. Come in."

Smith glanced at the TV, where his least favorite show was busy being even more horrible than usual, and he shook his head.

Brooks eyed the screen. "I can come back later..."

"It's fine. This sucks anyway." Smith grabbed the remote and turned it off. "How'd you find me and what do you want?"

Smith half-sat on the arm of his recliner as Brooks explained.

"I only know two people who work for the Reticent,

and—"

"You don't know me," Smith corrected. "We've met once."

"Right," continued Brooks, "well, Agent Burroughs wouldn't help me. But I did get her to tell me where you live."

"Uh huh. And if she wouldn't help, what makes you think I would?"

"You seem less... by the book?" said Brooks, trying to phrase his answer with tact.

"Shady, you mean?"

"Kind of. Yeah, I guess."

"Like a real piece of shit?"

"I didn't say—"

Smith shrugged and cut him off. "What do you want?"

Brooks got to the point. "I failed the entrance exam," he admitted. "Twice."

"For the Reticent?"

Brooks nodded.

"Lucky for you, then." Smith took a sip from his beer.

"No, it's not," said Brooks, a bit desperately. "I only get one more chance and I really want to do this. I've never failed a test before in my life. I can't figure out what I'm doing wrong."

Smith stared at him. "It's a personality assessment. You don't have the personality."

"And you do?"

"I passed the test, didn't I?" Smith smiled, then took another long sip.

"Exactly." Brooks pulled a folded booklet from his jacket. "So, I thought maybe we could run through some of the questions and see how you would answer them."

Smith raised his brow. "Where'd you get that?"

The entrance exam was proctored, and there should have been no way of sneaking out of the testing room with an extra copy.

"Don't worry about it," said Brooks.

Smith smirked. "You're not as big a dork as I thought."

"You were watching *some space show* when I walked in!"

"Yeah, but I'd never come to someone for help on a test," Smith said.

"Ugh. Whatever. Will you help me?"

Smith took another sip while he thought about it. It didn't take long. "I guess."

Brooks's eyes lit up.* "Thank yo—"

Smith cut him off mid-sentence. "On one condition."

"What?" Brooks raised an eyebrow.

"You gotta blow me first."

Brooks took about five milliseconds to consider. "Okay," he said, taking a step forward.

"Whoa." Smith put up his hands, in a do-not-step-closer-and-blow-me gesture. "I was joking. That was a joke!"

Brooks's cheeks flushed.

"Jesus fucking Christ, dude." Smith shook his head and walked over to his fridge, grabbed a new drink, and popped the cap. "You want anything? A sense of shame maybe?"

"I'm... good," replied Brooks.

"Dunno about that." Smith leaned against the only three-foot patch of countertop in his kitchenette.

Brooks pushed through his embarrassment, cleared his throat, and began.

"Question one. Would you enjoy building kitchen cabinets?"

"Is that really one of the questions?"

"Yes."

"I don't know," Smith said. "Never tried."

"But how did you answer the question?" asked Brooks.

Smith shrugged. "I don't remember."

---

* Metaphorically. He wasn't a cyborg yet.

"Okay... number two, then. Are you highly competitive in sport?"

"I don't know," Smith said. "Never played any."

"But do you remember how you answered that one?"

"Not really. No."

Brooks emitted a drawn-out sigh. "Fine... question three. Stu, Diane, Vince, and Holly work for the same employer. Stu is in Diane's office. Diane is in Holly's office. Holly is in Vince's office. Vince is in Stu's office. Which of the following is not possible: A) Only one of the statements is true, B) Two of the statements are true, C) Three of the statements are true, or D) All of the statements are true?"

"C."

"I'm pretty sure that's wrong."

Smith shook his head. "Sorry, I zoned out around the second sentence, but I heard someone say once if you don't know you should just pick C, and... it worked when I got my GED."

Brooks tossed the booklet to the ground in frustration. "*¡Que carajo!* You didn't even care about taking this stupid test and you aced it. Meanwhile I've never wanted anything more in my life—"

"You ever think that might be why you keep failing?"

"What?"

"Because you care too much?"

"That doesn't make any sense," said Brooks. "Why would you hire a bunch of sociopaths who don't care about people for a job that's about helping people?"

"Because the job's not about helping people. It's about stopping monsters. They don't want someone who's gonna overthink whether to stake a vampire or not. You just have to react. I don't know what my answers were on the test because I just picked whatever, but I made a decision."

"It's timed..." Brooks was on the cusp of a realization. "How long did the test take you?"

"I don't know. Fifteen minutes, maybe?"

Brooks had been taking advantage of every second of the hour allotted for the exam. He beamed. "I just have to pick quickly! Thank you!"

"I didn't do anything..."

Brooks cut off Smith's sentence with a big, obnoxious hug. The agent tensed, and Brooks released him. "Sorry. I'll leave you to your space show. Just... thank you for not caring."

That statement stung a little, and Smith chugged the rest of his drink.

Brooks bent down to grab the discarded exam and bounded toward the door, a new spring in his step. As he was about to leave, Smith called out to him.

"Sixty-three people died."

Brooks turned around. "What?"

Smith took a few steps toward him. "In Willowbrook Park last August. Your dad and your sister were two of *sixty-three people*. Last week, goblins got four kids in Park Slope. The full moon is in... ten days. You can bet on werewolves picking off at least half a dozen then. What I'm saying... you've gotta be ready for... I mean... we lose at least as many as we save. Probably more."

Brooks absorbed all that. "You do care."

Smith didn't answer with his words. He simply stared at the younger man, his striking green eyes failing to hide the hurt behind them.

Back in the 1980s Hell World, those same eyes regarded Brooks with the same expression. Smith hadn't left his spot on the frozen ground. No longer a hot mess but a cold one, he'd remained still so long that his hair and jacket were covered in a light coating of snow.

"We should go inside," Brooks suggested.

"Good idea..." Smith said, as he stood and eyed the restaurant. "I need a drink. Some of that rubbing alcohol or whatever the fuck it is."

"*Eddie*." Brooks stood and grabbed him by the shoulder.

"Don't *Eddie* me," Smith snapped back. "We're trapped in a *parallel universe*. I'm out of cigarettes and I'm out of patience. Do you see a therapist I can lie to right now to score some Xanax? Do you see a *stress ball?*"

Brooks raised his voice. "You were just telling me that you want to get better. Drowning yourself in a Biscuit Bucket Beer Bucket is going the opposite direction."

"Try listening. I told you *there is no getting better.*"

"*Las cosas que soporto por eso salchichón...* you're infuriating! When we get back to our world—"

"*If.*"

"*When* we get back... if you've even looked at a drink the wrong way, I will drag you to rehab and throw your ass through the door."

Smith mumbled something under his breath and kicked at the snow-covered dirt.

"What was that?"

"You're right, okay?" Smith repeated, louder.

"I am?" Brooks grew suspicious.

"I don't want to drink," Smith said. "I don't know what I want to do. I don't *ever* know what I want to do. I just... do things, and then I wake up the next day... and I guess they worked because *I'm still here.*" He didn't exactly seem thrilled about it.

Brooks wasn't sure how to respond. "I—"

"What should I do?" Smith's voice became soft and pleading.

"That you're even asking me means you've gotten better, whether you believe it or not. But I can't tell you what you should do. This is *your* family," said Brooks.

"What would you do?" Smith asked.

"I'd stop lying."

Smith paused. "You don't want me to do that."

"I really do."

Smith shook his head. "You *really* don't. Any time I say the smallest thing that makes you uncomfortable, you give me this look..."

"What look?"

"*That look*. Like you're googling emotions. Pretending you're listening but not really because you wish I'd just shut the fuck up."

Brooks snapped. "You *don't know* what I'm thinking."

"Why don't you enlighten me, then?"

"I'm thinking about what I'm going to do *when you're gone*, Eddie. Because I'm afraid that one day I'm going to wake up and find you lying on the bathroom floor next to an empty pill bottle, or with a bullet through your head. So... *I'm sorry* if my focus wanders a little sometimes!"

Smith looked him in the eyes, serious. "I'm not gonna kill myself."

"You just told me you lie about everything!"

Smith raised a fist to his chin. "Shit."

Both men broke into something halfway between laughter and sobbing. Brooks was right. Smith needed to start telling the truth.

25 / WHAT DIFFERENCE DOES IT MAKE?

It was nearly midnight, and the BBAZ Biscuit Bucket was busier than ever. With snow coming down hard, tent dwellers had gathered to enjoy the building's relative warmth. Leslie, Phil, and little Eddie remained in their booth, tucked among them.

Brooks and Smith entered, stomped their feet on the decaying rubber floor mat, and brushed the snow from their jackets. With eyes still red from the winter air, they surveyed the family from across the dining room.

"Are you sure about this?" Brooks asked.

"I've never been sure about anything. 'Cept you."

"That's flattering *and* terrifying."

Smith stood near the abandoned host stand while Brooks went over to the Smiths. After a few words, he pulled Eddie aside and drew the child's attention to a display on the opposite side of the diner—some assorted Hot War era propaganda.

Smith had no idea what he might say to his parents, but he had enough sense to make sure the boy wouldn't hear it. The kid had been sheltered from the madness this long—might as well let him stay that way a while longer.

Leslie and Phil waved enthusiastically for Smith to come join them.

This is stupid, Smith thought. If the thought of introducing himself to his parents was stupid, his legs were even stupider since they moved him to do it. Soon, he stood at their booth and offered a weak wave as he absorbed how bonkers it was to be a forty-one-year-old man talking to a mother and father who were in their late twenties. He wanted to say something funny, but copped out.

"Hi..."

"Hi," Leslie and Phil said together.

"Go ahead and sit down," Phil added.

Smith squeezed into the side of the booth across from them, where, as expected, the table pressed hard into his abdomen.

"You look like you've had a heck of a time. There's plenty of water if—"

Smith raised his palm. "I'm gonna talk and I need you to just listen, 'cause if I stop, I'm probably gonna lose it."

Leslie and Phil nodded, the latter adding a hokey mouth-zipping gesture.

Smith spoke with no emotion. "I guess you already know... my name is Edward Smith. As far as I know, I was born December 4, 1976 in Clarksville. My parents were Leslie and Phil Smith—the other ones—and they were dogshit. They beat me and berated me and... you look exactly like them." He swallowed. "So, when I came here... finding another version of myself traipsing around this universe didn't exactly make me feel warm and fuzzy. I mean, another me dealing with... honestly... I thought I was gonna have to rescue the kid from *his* shitty, abusive parents..."

Smith shook his head and got back on track, as much as he had a track. "Anyway, they died when I was eight, which set off this whole chain of events that... *sucked*."

From there, Smith narrated his whole shitty life story. If everything he said were included in this book, it would take up about six pages with nothing but dialogue, and the editor would suffer a stroke. But, needless to say, he covered his time in foster care, his substance abuse problems, his recruitment into the Reticent, his multiple brushes with death...

All of it presented the picture of a broken man.

Eventually, he came to the crux of his issue. "When I found out that my whole life—all of that bullshit—happened because I was taken from you... that it could have been better..." Smith glanced at little Eddie and shook his head. "Part of me wants *him* to pay for stealing my life. Part of me wanted to come over here and scream at you and ask how you could let anyone take your son away. But that's not fair. Shit happens. I mean, fuck... I mentioned the genie thing, right? And I don't know anything about either of you, so... I don't know. I guess I just needed to lay all that out there and get it over with, so I don't have to spend the rest of my time here answering questions about myself."

He paused to breathe. "I know that you've probably imagined who your son might grow up to be, and I'm not him. Believe me, no one's more disappointed in me than I am. But that's that. I got it over with. Now we can focus on getting the hell out of here..."

Leslie and Phil both began to sob openly.

Smith cringed. "Can we *not*?"

"You're not a disappointment, Eddie. You're a darned hero," Phil said.

"Really not."

"He's not asking," Leslie agreed.

"The *alternative lifestyle* threw me for a bit of a loop, if I'm being honest," Phil said. "But you're alive and well. That's what matters."

"Yeah," Smith lied. "I am."

"And we're gonna get you home and keep it that way."

Phil slid out of the booth and leaned on the table. Leslie slid out after him. Smith freed himself from the booth and viewed his parents with apprehensive eyes.

"Come on. Hug time," said Phil, extending his arms. "Get your butt over here."

Smith extended a hand, hoping for a shake. "I'm not much of a—"

Phil grabbed his son's hand and pulled him into a hug, which Leslie joined.

Smith's mind recalled the sad instrumental from the sea bream movie, and had the same thought it had when Tiffany sacrificed herself.

This is annoying.

26 / CUE HIERONYMUS

Looking for an escape from never-ending human contact, Smith beckoned his husband over. Brooks, who'd been half-listening to the younger Eddie's enthusiastic explanation of how magnets worked, caught the signal in the corner of his eye and escorted the child back across the room.

Smith wormed out of his parents' arms, and Eddie slid in to replace him.

"Heck," Phil said. "This booth isn't big enough for all of us. We gotta find a table..."

"You do that," said Smith, grabbing his husband's arm. "We'll catch up."

As Phil, Leslie, and Eddie wandered off to find a table for five, Smith snatched his mother's glass from the table and chugged what water remained.

"How'd it go?" Brooks asked.

Smith set the glass down. "They loved hearing about my miserable life. How's the kid?"

"Good. I was just telling Eddito about—"

"*Eddito*?" Smith said, in disbelief.

"I need some way to differentiate."

"Yeah, but... he's white."

"Well... when we meet my doppelganger, I'll let you name him."

Smith considered the possibility. "Turo Two. No. Two-ro. Twoturo?"

"*Anyway*," said Brooks, "before he wandered off on a tangent about magnets... I was telling him all about our world, right?"

"Sure..."

"When I mentioned Shoppli, he was terrified."

"Okay?" said Smith. "What's your point?"

"Your parents told me that Shoppli runs the malls in exchange for people's kids. I figured it was either trafficking them through Adopt Shop, or some gross Epstein kind of thing. But Eddito is under the impression they'll take *his parents* away. He really believes that."

"So, either he's wrong, or Shoppli is collecting kids *and* adults. Wouldn't be the first human trafficking scheme we've seen..."

"It wouldn't be," Brooks said. "He also asked if I'd take care of him if you and your parents were all taken away."

"'Cause you're a cyborg they can't capture?"

"Because I'm not blond..."

Smith's eyes widened as he made loose connections. "Tape World... the wigs... those marauders were super happy to find out other me was blond... Mirror Hitler!"

"...What?"

"Mirror Hitler's trying to exterminate blonds. Case closed," said Smith. This was far from the case.

"I love you," Brooks said stiffly.

"I love you too?" Smith replied.

"I'm just reminding myself," Brooks said.

Smith rolled his eyes. "Yeah, okay. So, human trafficking..."

"*Cross-universe* human trafficking. Remember how many of the kids on that app were blond?"

"Yeah, that was weird. But what do they want with the adults?"

"Remember our NDAs?" Brooks asked.

"They were like forty pages long, babe," Smith said. "I skimmed."

"There was a part about identity protection..."

Smith grasped where his partner was headed. "Take the kids, then exterminate anyone who could identify the kids... so you don't have a situation like the one we're in with people trying to hop universes and get 'em back."

"Exactly."

From a short distance over, Leslie and Phil waved for Brooks and Smith to join them at a table for six.

"Well," said Smith as he was tugged toward the table, "the good news is, it's probably easier to break into Adopt Shop in this shithole than it is back home."

They each took a seat and Brooks began. "So. Plans."

Phil unfolded his spreadsheet and slid it across the table. "The next portal back to your world is in Akron. That's bad. For two reasons. One: Akron is full of cannibals. We barely made it out of there last time."

"It's a sh—"—Leslie censored herself—"craphole."

"And the other?" Smith asked.

"According to the chart, it's not for another twenty-three days."

"According to your—"

Phil pointed at the wrinkled sheet.

Smith took a cursory look. "None of this means anything to me, but I've waited longer for stupider."

Phil's face was stoic. "That's fine in principle," he said, "but remember time passes differently back home. You've been here for, what, half a day? That's at least a few days there. If you're here for three more weeks, that's... I'm not sure, but it's a heck of a lot."

Brooks did the math in his head. "196 days, which is... 28 weeks."

Smith shook his head. "If we want to still have a house when we get back, we're gonna need to figure something else out."

Brooks turned to the Smiths. "Do you have Adopt Shop in this world?"

Leslie shook her head, almost too quickly.

"Never heard of it," Phil said.

"Okay," said Brooks, pushing on. "Any idea where to find Shoppli HQ?"

Phil shuffled a little. "Why?"

"Well," said Brooks, pointing at the paper, "your little spreadsheet has a Shoppli header. If they're keeping records of the portals, they might know about more of them."

"It's in Pennsylvania..." Phil said in a dissuasive tone. "...in Allentown."

That was about as far from them as a town in Pennsylvania could be, aside from East Centralia, which existed in an inaccessible pocket dimension.

"*Great*," Brooks said.

Smith smirked. "We're gonna go, right? You... me... stagflated nightmare world..."

"Of course we are."

Smith planted a quick peck on his cheek. "Never stop dating your spouse."

"Get out of my restaurant!" boomed an irate voice, from near the entrance.

Brooks tilted his head. "Is that..."

Before them stood Hieronymus Hardtack—alive, well, and still a member of the Church of Smite. With its sweaty, homophobic founder still around, this universe's Biscuit Bucket wasn't 'doing better.'

The short, mustachioed man adjusted his suspenders, then pointed at the door. "Out."

"We didn't do any—"

"Out." Hieronymus repeated. The BBAZ was leaderless, but he still lorded total authority over his restaurant. He pulled Eddito's chair out from under him, dumping the boy to the floor.

"Out."

"*We heard you*," Smith said, pushing back in his chair so that its legs screeched across the floor.

He rose, along with the others, and they made their way toward the exit.

"Out!"

Brooks sneered at him before they stepped outside. "I hope you get eaten by cannibals."

Out in the snow, a cold wind battered the group as they pondered their next move.

"Aww, man," complained Eddito, "I wanted another banana pop." He crossed his arms at Smith. "What'd you have to be gay for?"

Smith grinned a little. "You'll find out in about..."—he counted on his fingers—"five years."

Eddito's face scrunched as he tried to figure out what that meant.

27 / THE FAMILY TRUCKSTER

Having dumped both a heap of emotional baggage and the contents of his stomach all over the BBAZ, Smith was ready to get the hell out. He and his dimension-hopping family approached the check-in point to retrieve their 'weapons.'

Eddito glanced into the container and didn't see his gummy bears. "Aww, man."

Smith's reaction to his missing Chekhov was less polite.

"Wasn't it broken anyway?" Brooks wondered as he retrieved his scissors.

"Yeah, but it was still *mine.*"

Smith collected the rest of his belongings, and the other Smiths directed him to their borrowed ride.

"There she is," Phil said.

"You didn't say you had a car," Smith said to his younger self, miffed that his burnt hand and wounded neck hadn't been necessary.

Eddito's face scrunched. "We don't..."

Leslie hushed him.

Brooks mouthed "you don't want to know" at his husband, who seemed to understand.

Parked just outside the BBAZ was a diesel-powered, brown station wagon with wood paneling along its bottom half and windows riddled with bullet holes. A relic of the 1970s, it had three rows: a normal front seat, a normal back seat, and a combination cargo/passenger area with a rear-facing seat.

"We'll drive," Phil said, "since we know the way around here."

Brooks eyed Smith warily. "I hope you're better drivers than he is."

"*One fender bender,*" Smith said, as he opened a door and slid across the middle row to the driver's side. Brooks slid in beside him.

Miraculously, the thing had seat belts. Brooks fastened his. Smith, of course, did not.

"I get to ride in the back? Yes!" Eddito ran to the wagon's rear, pulled the latch, and leapt in. The compartment wasn't very safe, but then again, neither was anything else in this universe.

Brooks put a hand to his chin. "I wish my GPS worked here..."

"You don't need it," Smith said.

"No, but it would make me feel a lot better."

Phil took the driver's seat and turned the beater's engine. It started with a piercing screech, then settled into a sound like a film reel reaching its end and flapping against itself. A pathetic burst of heat puffed from the vents.

"You fellas sure you wanna go to Shoppli?" Phil asked.

Smith nodded. "Let's get moving."

"Okie doke." Phil turned the high beams on, put the car in drive, and started east, over rough terrain. The station wagon shook and complained, but it was a trooper.

Smith smirked, then broke into a full grin. Brooks squinted at him, unsure what dumb fuckery was on his husband's mind. "Why are you..."

Smith softly sang to himself—the opening lines of Lindsey Buckingham's "Holiday Road." The lyrics can be found online, but not in this book because copyright laws are real.

"No one knows that song," Brooks said. "It would have come out after the nukes fell."

"And that stops *you* from joining in because...?"

Brooks simultaneously smiled and rolled his eyes.

He joined in for the chorus. "Holiday roooo—"

The Smiths didn't get it, at all.

28 / WEST END GIRLS

Back in the other universe, no one was singing. The pothole in Akron had caused more damage than Patience or Lemon had initially thought. That is, more than Lemon thought. Patience never really considered time machine mechanics, as she was too busy reading up on alien abductions.

The time machine had survived one brief jaunt back to the Victorian Era, but as soon as they brought it home to check whether their adopted parents had returned, one of the lower fins detached with a loud CLONK. The girls had stepped out just in time, as the entire machine—all three thousand pounds of it—toppled onto its side, before crashing through the upper floor of the Brownstone and into the living room. All fourteen of the Brownstone's building code-mandated smoke alarms rang out at once.

Lemon ran to the kitchen, grabbed a fire extinguisher, and coated the machine (and a good portion of the living room) in foam. She brushed the sweat from her forehead.

"*Brannon Braga*! That was close."

"Hmm." Patience knelt down and rifled through a large pile of envelopes beneath the mail slot. "It would appear Edward and Arturo haven't returned home in some time."

Lemon grabbed a bright yellow envelope with NOTICE: PAST DUE stamped on the front. "Hoo boy. That's no good."

Erin Burroughs—former Reticent agent, former paramour to Edward Smith, and former band manager for Pop Tart & the Activation Energy—had been dogsitting Widget for two weeks. Burroughs wasn't a dog person to begin with, and

Widget's unrelenting energy had pushed her to her limits. Though she now worked from home, she hadn't been able to stop the tiny Norfolk Terrier from ruining the carpet beneath her favorite chair. Tending to the dog's needs had severely cut into time she needed for important things like organizing 3D printer filament, and she was over it.

When Patience and Lemon appeared on her doorstep, Burroughs breathed a sigh of relief, then shot the yapping dog a fierce stare.

"Where are your fathers?" she asked the girls.

Lemon stepped through the doorway first, and knelt down to accept kisses from Widget. "Dunno. That's why we're here. Thought you might've heard something."

Burroughs sighed. "I've been texting them for two weeks about taking this dog back, and I haven't heard anything. I'm starting to think they're dead."

"They're probs not dead," Lemon said.

Patience agreed. "They are actually quite difficult to kill."

Burroughs ran a hand across her scalp and down through her long, dark brown hair. "Probably...?"

"Edward and Arturo have done something most concerning—" Patience started to explain.

"—They hopped through a portal into another world," said Lemon, cutting to the chase.

"Is that all? Meh." Burroughs had expected worse. "Anything else?"

"We know Eddie hopped through one, then Turo went in after him. We were gonna hop around time some more and look for them, but our time machine plorped out."

"There are numerous unpaid invoices in our foyer, as well," Patience added.

"What are we supposed to do?" Lemon wondered aloud, hoping her big, puppy dog eyes might inspire the older woman to make a donation.

Burroughs—not a puppy dog person—donated only a

suggestion. "Get a job?"

That wouldn't do.

A twinkle appeared in Lemon's eye as she began formulating a different plan. She grabbed Patience by the arm and pulled her toward the door.

"Come on," she said.

Burroughs moved to follow. "Are you going to take—"

But the girls were gone. Burroughs looked down at the excited, panting pup and sighed.

29 / ON THE ROAD AGAIN

In Brooks and Smith's normal universe, the drive from BBAZ to Shoppli HQ in Allentown would only have taken around ten hours. It could have been done in one night. But in Hell World, back roads were the name of the game.

Highways could be collapsed, covered in broken-down vehicles, overrun by gangs, claimed by K-Mart, or otherwise rendered unusable. Rural roads weren't traversed enough to be full of wrecked cars, and they weren't worth the effort it would take for marauders to patrol them. They were safe, dystopia-wise.

In three hours, the station wagon had made it as far as Falmouth, Kentucky. Former Population: 2100. Current Population: 0. It was one of many towns depopulated by a hundred megaton blast over Cincinnati. Those who hadn't perished in the impact or succumbed to radiation sickness were left incapacitated, unable to feed themselves or escape the wasteland that remained. No one came to help because there was no one left to do the helping. The area was an atomic ghost town.

Modern diesel has low sulfur levels and degrades after a year or so, but 1980s diesel didn't give a shit about the environment. It could remain viable for years. Accordingly, Phil pulled the puttering wagon into an abandoned service station.

While Eddito slept in the deep way that only cats and children can, the adults all filed out of the vehicle to stretch their legs. Brooks had night vision, but he pulled the flashlight from his backpack and pointed it at the pump for everyone else's benefit, allowing Phil to fill the tank, along with two metal fuel cans he stored in the back next to his son.

"It's about time we got some sleep, don't you think?"

Leslie suggested, pointing to a former roadside motel that stood across the street.

Brooks redirected his flashlight to its formerly neon sign. The lights had all burst long ago, and all that remained was faded paint spelling the words 'Periwinkle Motel.' Like the lights, the hotel's windows were busted, but its one-story brick structure had remained intact. So had the green metal roof and bubblegum pink doors, though they were chipped and worn.

"We've been sleeping in a bunker for four years," she pleaded. "I wouldn't say no to a real bed."

"Not gonna be very warm," Smith warned.

"Neither is the station wagon," said Brooks, eyeing the bullet holes in the bodywork.

Phil thought on it for a moment. "Well, I'm sure we won't be intruding on anyone. If it's safe and you boys are all right with it..."

Smith looked to Brooks, and shrugged. "What's a few hours?"

Phil pulled the station wagon in front of the motel while the others walked over.

There were six potential rooms. Brooks scanned the complex for signs of life and found none. He pulled open the door to Room 1.

On the bed were two skeletons in a compromising position.

Smith snickered. "They're *boning.*"

Brooks elbowed his husband and quickly shut the door before Leslie could see.

"Let's see what's behind door number two," Brooks said.

He forced the door open to find another skeleton. This one had been sitting in a chair, facing the television, with his hand at his crotch.

"Does anyone actually *sleep* in hotels?" Brooks wondered aloud.

Leslie wedged between the men to see.

"That's a *stroke* of bad luck," she said, catching an eyeful.

Smith grinned. "He fell on *hard* times."

"*Por favor...*" Brooks moaned. "If either of you makes a pun about whatever's in the next room, I'm leaving."

Lucky for Brooks, the next two rooms contained no skeletons. Sure, they were worse for the wear—what with the nuclear holocaust and all—but peeling paint, collapsing popcorn ceilings, and what might have been black mold near the windows weren't dealbreakers for a few hours' stay. Two rooms, each with two full-sized beds, and they were dry.

Phil approached, dragging a groggy Eddito by the hand. The boy yawned and drooped, swaying as he stood. His father stalled for a moment, then spoke up.

"Will... do you two mind watching Eddie for the night?"

Smith squinted suspiciously. "Why? Worried we're gonna do gay shit?"

"If anything attacks, I'd feel a lot better with a cyborg protecting him," Phil explained.

Leslie tilted her head. "And... we haven't had a night alone in *years*."

"Oh. Gross," Smith said. "Do *not* make another me!"

Brooks nodded at the Smiths. "We'll watch him."

Once they were settled, it wasn't long before the boy developed a newfound burst of energy.

"Are we gonna play more games?"

"It's three in the morning," Smith said.

"Morning means I'm supposed to be awake."

"He's precocious," Brooks said, in the kid's defense.

"Think he knows just what it takes to make a pro blush?" Eddito scratched his head.

"It's funny if you're in your forties and from our universe," Smith said.

Brooks swayed his hand in a so-so gesture.

Smith turned to his younger self. "So... games... do you

have friends? Wait... have you ever even met another child?"

"Umm..." Eddito thought on it, then shook his head.

"That's so sad," Brooks said. "You never got to be a kid."

Smith walked over to the window and peered out into the falling snow. It was très mélodramatique. "Guess some things are the same in this universe."

Eddito still hadn't caught on that he and Smith were the same person. "What do kids do?"

"Um..." Brooks struggled to explain. "They're sort of un-predicta—"

SPIFF. A large snowball smashed into the side of Brooks's face, cutting him off.

"Like that," Smith said with an impish smile.

Eddito burst into a fit of laughter.

Brooks wiped the side of his face.

"*Really?*"

"Do another!" Eddito cheered, but Smith shook his head.

"Nah," he said as he approached Eddito's bed. "I'm gonna teach you something different. Two magical words."

The child tilted his head in confusion, and Smith whispered something into his ear.

Brooks—with his cyborg hearing—knew exactly what was coming. He let it happen anyway.

"Pillow fight!" Eddito screamed as he leapt into the air.

So began the legendary bedding war at Room 3 of the Periwinkle Motel—a skirmish so epic that bards would have sung about it for centuries, had there been any around.

It was a pillow battle for the ages, but eventually, the two Edward Smiths got tired of annoying Brooks. It was late and being irritating was exhausting. They each took a bed and fell asleep.

For Brooks, the fight had the opposite effect. He lay awake beside Smith, wired, wide-eyed, and missing a world with internet access.

Somewhere outside, a tree branch snapped. He got up and

stepped over to the window, then scanned the area. There were no signs of life and no further branch snaps. Just the sounds of Leslie and Phil stifling their moans for their sons' benefit.

Brooks lingered for a moment, before returning to bed. He couldn't shake the feeling he was being watched.

30 / ROAD HOUSE

In daylight, the journey was even more eerie than it had been at night. After checking themselves out of the motel, all four Smiths and Brooks continued along back roads, with Leslie taking the wheel. As expected from an already remote region that was now devastated by nukes, they never encountered another person—just a few abandoned cars that Brooks kindly pushed out of the way with his cyborg strength.

The winding roads were dotted with appalling homes. Two cabins in particular left Brooks and Smith grimacing. Nestled close together, they'd clearly been handcrafted by someone without a carpenter's bone in their body. The homes' flat, corrugated tin roofs were almost rusted through, and jagged boards had been nailed across rough window frames, except for one where a piece of blue tarp flapped loose in the wind.

The homes were connected by a six-foot-long piece of string, with dangling empty beer cans playing the role of windchimes. The leftmost cabin was festooned with stolen road signs, while the one on the right had been hand-painted with a message, in the time-honored American tradition of overzealous political commentary:

Both houses were well outside the blast radius.
To distract themselves from the desolation of the

wasteland, the family passed the time by playing road games like Twenty Questions.

It was Smith's turn.

"I'm thinking of a... thing," he said.

Eddito pulled himself up to lean over the seat.

"Is it a magnet?" he blurted out.

"No."

The boy bit his lip, looking upwards in thought. He tried again. "Is it a gay thing?"

"*No.*"

"Is it—"

"Why don't we let everyone else take a turn?"

Eddito harrumphed and sat back down. "Fine."

Brooks turned to his husband. "Is it something you personally own?"

"Yeah."

"Is it something you wear?" Phil asked, peering back from the front seat.

"No."

Eddito leaned over again and shouted. "Is it a wig!?"

"I just said it's not something I wear—"

"You don't wear a wig," Eddito noted.

Brooks snickered to himself.

"The answer's still no," Smith said, amused.

"Is it a sense of existential dread?" Brooks asked.

"So close," Smith said dryly, "but no."

"Something you can hold in your hands?" Leslie asked, still keeping her eyes on the road ahead.

"Yes."

"Is it a weapon?" Phil asked.

"No..."

"Is it the other Mr. Brooks?" called out Eddie, still unaware that he and Smith were the same person.

"I said *thing*, not *person*."

"You also don't own me," Brooks said.

"Pfft. I own that ass," Smith mumbled out the side of his mouth.

The comment slipped right by Eddito as he explained his guess. "He's not a person, though. He's a robot."

Smith spotted a glint of hurt in Brooks's eyes, but the cyborg pushed past it.

"Eddie, are you thinking of your Biscuit Bucket rewards card?"

"Bingo," Smith said.

"That was gonna be my next guess," said Phil from the front seat. "Honest to God." Leslie rolled her eyes.

"You're so obvious," Brooks said to his husband. "I knew it was gonna be either food-related or... something Eddito will understand when he's older."

Eddito crossed his arms, sank back into his seat, and huffed.

The games continued like that for some time, and what would have been a six-hour drive in another world took the entire day. As the sun began to dip, the group finally arrived in Pennsylvania—specifically, the town of Normalville. Former Population: 2250. Current Population: one lonely doomsday prepper. He'd been in his bunker inventorying canned goods when the bombs hit Pittsburgh and had remained there ever since, eventually succumbing to madness with no one but himself to talk to, and nothing but the same four books to read.*

Leslie pulled them over to the side of the road.

"Where the fuck are we?" Smith asked.

"Swear jar!" Phil pulled the notepad from his pocket and added a tally for Smith, whose checks had nearly filled an entire page.

"Roqslyde," Leslie said, gesturing out the open window at an impressive edifice.

---

* This is a subliminal message to buy more than four books.

One of David Allen Jade's earliest designs, Roqslyde was also his most famous. A mansion designed for an oil baron and his three wives, it had been converted into a tourist attraction sometime after the baron's death. Souvenir magnets and corn dogs had been enough to distract locals from the fact that there was an opulent and unoccupied mansion right next to their collapsing cabins, ripe for the taking. Tourism was good for the economy, someone once said, and the opulence would trickle down.

Of course, the only tourists now were the Smiths and Brooks. They stood in a gravel lot, staring in awe at the architectural marvel. The building was boxy, white, and four stories high. Its rear was partially embedded in a hillside, and a foot-thick square plexiglass chute bore through the center of the home and out the side of a mountain, allowing falling rocks to pass through. Thus, Roqslyde. The home had no windows, and all external light came from the central chute.

"You ever spend the night in a mansion?" Phil asked.

"Yeah," Smith said, "and I don't wanna talk about it."

They all settled in on some very uncomfortable furniture. Eddito nabbed a disheveled egg chair, Leslie and Phil took the tatty circular bed in the master bedroom, and Brooks and Smith claimed a flat, olive green... thing. It was queen-sized like a bed, but it had no pillows or bedding, like a couch. It could have been a gigantic ottoman or maybe a chez round—with artists, it's impossible to tell. Whatever it was, they were warm inside, thanks to the rock chute, which had been absorbing sunlight all day. Falling asleep was easy, for everyone. Staying asleep was another matter.

In the middle of the night, Smith's bladder betrayed him—as happens when an alcoholic replaces his preferred liquid with gallons of water.

Christ, I'm almost old enough to qualify for prostate screenings, he thought as he maneuvered off the green furniture, careful not to wake his husband.

David Allen Jade buildings never contained toilets, because the artist found them unseemly. This would have gotten him in quite a bit of trouble under the Americans with Disabilities Act, but that law wouldn't come into effect until 1990. Or ever, in this universe.

Brooks sleep-mumbled. "What're—"

"Taking a leak. Be right back."

"Oka..." Brooks passed out before finishing.

Smith stepped out the front door and onto a flat bit of concrete that passed for a porch. He tiptoed to the edge, aimed into the distance, and once again found himself alone, watering some weeds.

It is often said that there is safety in numbers. This is not the case for the number one.

Before Smith could react, a hand was on him.

He felt a pinching sensation at the back of his neck, and the world around him swirled in black.

31 / LITTLE ORPHAN EDDIE

Smith had endured quite a few hangovers in his life. This one—though not alcohol-induced—was mild. He awoke abruptly, with sweaty skin and a light headache, his body jolting into consciousness a few inches into the air and back down as the tires beneath him rumbled across bumpy terrain. He remained in place, thinking himself through the scenario.

Benzos, probably... Lot of breeze. Back of a pickup?

Way to get kidnapped, idiot.

Gotta figure out if anyone else is back here.

Don't let them know you're awake.

He listened intently, searching for anything other than ambient road noise.

No heavy breathing. No footsteps. Smith was alone in the truck bed, presumably.

He cracked his eyes open the slightest amount. If there'd been any light, he would have felt it, given the hangover. There wasn't any.

He wasn't restrained. That was bad kidnapping procedure, but good for his sanity. It also meant that whoever'd kidnapped him probably expected the drugs to last a lot longer than they had...

Using the most subtle of hand movements, he felt at the surface beneath him. Nothing but cold metal ridges. Nice and solid—they wouldn't give his movements away.

Smith rolled over to face the front of the truck. Thanks to the truck's headlights, he could just about make out two silhouettes in the cab.

Get up and jump out? No. Let's see where this thing goes.

I wish I had my gun... and ammo. If I run into Mirror Hitler and don't have anything to kill him with...

As the truck turned a corner, the whole world lit up, and

Smith's headache went from mild to searing.

Shit...

Last time I felt this rough was after Lemon's graduation party.

What a shitty night that was.

I wonder what she's up to...

32 / THE DAUGHTER, SHUN, AND HOLY RAGEBAIT

Lemon sat on the couch in the Brooks-Smith living room, leaning against the armrest, staring at her phone with intense focus.

The inventor of time travel was alive, rich, and mostly well. His name was Hudson Marrow, the philandering physicist who'd given Lemon and Patience their immortality in the first place. Originally from Staten Island, like anyone who'd found success, he left—first for Manhattan, then for parts unknown. Hudson then experienced a few rough years that included two divorces, several patent lawsuits, and the brutal murders of all the other superheroes in the team he'd founded. As a result, he'd gone into seclusion. No one knew where he was.

Lemon knew how to find out, and she was working on it.

Next to her, Patience was attempting to watch a History Channel documentary about aliens in Macedonia, but the giant, immovable time machine planted in the middle of the room wouldn't permit it. She stretched and craned her neck, but couldn't find a decent viewing angle. She relented with a soft sigh, grabbed a needle, and resumed stitching up her dress.

After a grueling day drafting and redrafting a tweet, Lemon finally sent it:

> Hudson Marrow is a mega creeper. I have receipts.
> If I knew where he was hiding I'd go give him a piece
> of my mind. #ImmoralImmortal #PervsBTFO

Lemon was internet famous, and her hundreds of thousands of followers took the bait, spreading her vague accusation far and wide. Within an hour, her DMs had blown up with dozens of Hudson sightings, all from Connecticut. But before she could pack her bag and take a train north, her cell phone began to ring.

Lemon saw the incoming caller's name, and answered with a cheerful, "Hyello?"

"Hi. I need you to take back that tweet," said Hudson Marrow. He sounded pissed.

"Do ya now?"

"Yes, I do," he said. "Because it's not true—"

Lemon grinned as he began grasping at straws.

"—If I have to, I'll sue for defamation, but I'd rather not have to go to court... again."

"Sure, I'll take it back—"

"Great."

"—I*ffffffff*..."

"If what?" Hudson sounded just the right amount of desperate.

"...if you come fix our time machine. We hit a pothole."

"You do realize it's made of aerospace-grade titanium?"

"Well, it's aerospace-grade *broken,* and I'm not retracting that tweet 'til you agree to come fix it."

The line fell silent for a few seconds.

"*Fine,*" he relented. "I can be in Brooklyn tomorrow."

Moments later, Twitter ended its quest for vengeance when a new tweet appeared:

Deleted my earlier tweet. Hudson Marrow called, turns out we had a BIG misunderstanding. Oops! #mybad

Patience absently stood up from the couch and began pacing back and forth between the living room and the kitchen. She hemmed and hawed in her normal fashion before finally presenting her objection as a question.

"Is it right to coerce the machine's repair through black-mail?"

"Already did, Paysh."

Patience frowned. "Yes, but..."

"We could always rob a bank," Lemon said with a wink, as her sister's brow furrowed further. "I know. It's not a great look, but it's either this or we find jobs. If I wanted to work, I'd have stayed on the moon and enlisted." On Luna, military service was mandatory.

"I don't think I'd mind a vocation. Assuming it's one permitted by the holy text."

"You mean the Bible?" Lemon wondered.

Patience shook her head. "I've discovered a Newer Testament online."

"A *Newer* Testament?" Lemon's eyes narrowed. "Where?"

"Somewhere called 4chan."

Having been born in 1676, Patience had never learned how to properly evaluate sources for accuracy.* She'd also never been prepared for a world in which information flowed 24/7.†

Lemon grimaced. "Hoo boy."

"I've been fuchsia-pilled. It's most intriguing."

"I'm sure."

Lemon made a mental note to talk to Patience about her internet use later, once the time machine was fixed and she was less stressed. She would absolutely forget to do so.

---

* This made her unlike the people in our world, who have uncovered the secrets to curing cancer with essential oils, interpreted the secret pedophilic messages in every piece of media ever created, and prevented Bill Gates from microchipping everyone on the planet.

† This made her unlike the people in our world, whose educations definitely prepared them for a twenty-four-hour barrage of news, non-news, and hearsay.

*
**

As soon as Hudson arrived the next day, he noticed two things. The first was that the girls were older than the last time he'd seen them, which he commented on because he was a pervert. The other thing was that the time machine was more than just broken. He pushed past Lemon and dropped to his knees in front of his precious invention.

"What have you done to my time machine?"

"I told ya. Pothole."

Hudson ran a finger across the exterior, trailing it through a layer of white film. "You sprayed it with a dry chemical fire extinguisher?"

"There's more than one type?"

"Well, excellent work," he said, examining further. "Those things contain potassium bicarbonate. The time machine uses solid acid fuel cells, which were exposed when you crashed it through the ceiling."

"*And?*"

"Bases neutralize acids. Didn't you ever take chemistry?" Hudson tutted as he assessed the damage. "The circuitry is shot... this is going to take *months* to fix."

"*Months?* It can't take months. *Nothing* takes months."

"This will. I'll have to gather the materials, get a crew to bring this thing to my lab, recalibrate the..." He stopped himself from rambling, and eyed them with suspicion. "Why, what's the rush?"

"Our fathers are missing," Patience said.

"That's too bad," he said and—without missing a beat—added, "you ladies need a place to stay?"

Lemon looked at him with disgust. "Not even. Any more offers like that and I'm telling Twitter."

The girls were stuck.

After Hudson had left, Patience paced and fretted.

"By the time months pass, Edward and Arturo's creditors will surely have seized our home."

"Nahh," said Lemon. "I'm sure future you and future me will pop in any minute and drop off a big bag of cash." She said it into the air, like she was expecting something.

Nothing happened.

"Aww, florp."

Patience allowed her voice to hit its maximum volume— that of a normal speaking voice. "We must do something to help!"

Lemon raised her brow. "We must?"

"We're partly to blame," Patience said, vexed. "If we'd visited more than once a fortnight, we might know more information on our fathers' whereabouts. I believe this means..."

Lemon sank into her shoulders. She knew what it meant.

"We gotta get jobs."

33 / ROAD RUNNER

Brooks tossed and turned on the artistic olive-green thing, in the throes of one of his recurring dreams. This one was the *A Christmas Story* of dreams, in that it starred a selfish protagonist, replayed constantly, and had little entertainment value.

The dream began with events that happened around a year ago, back in his home universe.

Brooks had, for the first time in almost a decade, gone to Confession. It had been a Hail Mary—forgive the pun—but nothing else had eased his conscience.

He stepped into a small room that smelled like oak and Italian hoagies. It was better lit than he remembered, and a bit more welcoming. Very Biscuit Bucket.

On one side of the room were a pair of chairs and a café table, in case the faithful preferred a casual confessional. On the other side—for those seeking something more traditional—was an elaborate wooden half-wall with a padded spot in front for kneeling. Behind it, the priest remained obscured, and a grate in the enclosure ensured his voice would carry.

Brooks knelt, took a deep breath that tasted of salami, and recited from memory.

"Bless me, Father, for I have sinned. It has been, uh... more than a few years... since my last confession. I'm not sure I'm even Catholic anymore. I haven't been to Mass in forever because...y'know...the Church hates me. I guess not as much as it did before, but still..."

"Why did you come here, Arturo?" The voice belonged to Father Diego, who'd known Brooks since before his Confirmation.

"Okay. Really thought this was supposed to be anonymous." Brooks pulled himself up off the floor and took a seat at the café table.

Father Diego stepped around and took the seat across from him. He was a short, chubby man with greying hair, glasses, and a mouth that always seemed on the cusp of smiling. "If you wanted anonymity, you could have gone to any other parish."

"Good point."

"You wanted to speak with me."

Brooks sighed. "I don't know what I want."

"Forgiveness?" Father Diego suggested. "That's usually why people come here."

"Something like that."

"Last I remember, you and—"

"We're married," said Brooks, cutting him off. "Not in your eyes, of course, but... no regrets there. That's not why I'm here."

Brooks shut his eyes, breathed deep to steel himself, then reopened them. "I killed someone."

"That's very serious," said Father Diego. That was an understatement.

Brooks muddled through. "I sort of work in... law enforcement... now."

"I know what you do. I've seen the ads."

Brooks felt a little embarrassed at that. "Right, well, I... I had to do it to save lives. A lot of lives."

"In that case, it's not a sin, Arturo," Father Diego said.

"I know... but the problem is... *why* I did it. I mean, I didn't have a choice, but... I wasn't thinking about saving people."

"Then why did you do it?"

Brooks shook his head, in disappointment. "Because I was pissed off. Because I hated him. Because he hurt people I love. I'm just... so full of hate right now... and I know that doesn't lead anywhere good."

"Have you been lashing out? At others?"

"No. I just... don't feel good about myself. Who I am?

What I do...? I pray to figure it out, but I don't feel anything."

"There are a lot of people going through the same, with all of the unusual events and strange creatures that have been appearing lately..." admitted Father Diego. "It's not unheard of to have a crisis of faith in times like these."

"None of that's new for me, though," Brooks said. "It's not that. It's..." He hesitated. "I died."

Though he tried to hide it, Father Diego's eyes widened ever so slightly.

"I died, and they brought me back as a cyborg," he explained. "When I was dead, there was nothing. Nothing I remember, anyway. And I can't help but think... maybe I came back wrong. Maybe... I lost my soul?"

"Do you feel that's true?"

"Maybe. Maybe I'm just realizing that I suck... but I keep coming back to... if Jesus died for me, what did *I* die for?"

"You may not figure that out for a long time, if ever."

"Well, it's driving me nuts." There was desperation in Brooks's voice, but the priest took his time before finally responding.

"Is this something you can change?" Father Diego asked.

"No...? If it were, I wouldn't be here."

"Then you can either do good with it, or do bad with it. Unlike many of God's creatures, you have free will."

"Do I?" Brooks wasn't sure. He did—at one point—have evil Puritan programming.

"You do."

That conversation really happened.

The next part of the dream—in which the priest morphed into a slobbering manticore and tried to sting Brooks with his scorpion tail—did not.

*
**

A roaring rockslide shocked Brooks into the waking world. His eyes fluttered open and took in the sunlight—it was morning already. He yawned and rolled over, extending an arm to wrap around... no one.

"Eddie?" he wondered aloud.

No response.

Brooks sat up and looked around the empty room.

"Eddito?"

His heat vision registered no one in the house. No one alive anyway.

Before dark thoughts could consume him, he heard voices outside. He sprinted out the front door to find the other Smiths loading the station wagon's rear compartment with canned goods from the abandoned snack stand.

"There's no room for my feet," Eddito whined.

"Sure there is," Phil said, pointing. "Look at that gap."

"It's tiny."

"You're tiny."

Brooks interrupted, his voice on the verge of panic. "Have you seen Eddie?"

Phil put a hand to his chin. "He's not with you?"

"No. When I woke up, he wasn't there."

"We've been at the Visitor Café all morning. Haven't seen him. I figured you two were... doin' what you do."

Eddito dropped an enormous can of peaches on the ground and chimed in. "I think he went to the hospital."

Brooks knelt down. "What makes you say that?"

The child rifled through his jacket pockets.

"Found this stuff on the stairs," Eddito said, pulling out a used syringe and empty vial.

"Holy sh—crap!" cried Leslie as she yanked them from his hands. "*Do not* pick up stuff you find on the ground! Especially used syringes."

"Give me that."

Brooks snatched the vial from her hand.

Midazolam, 5mg/ml, and then, in tiny print: Johnstown Hospital.

Thank God for proper labeling... Brooks thought, before turning to Phil.

"Where's Johnstown?"

Phil thought on it. "Maybe an hour away..."

"We're going." When the Smiths didn't hustle, Brooks added a forceful "*Now.*"

Phil fumbled for the car keys.

Brooks plucked them from his hands and marched around to the driver's seat, as Eddito looked to his parents, confused. "Are we leaving?"

"*Get in,*" Brooks demanded.

"Yep. We're leaving." Phil slammed the hatch and he, Leslie, and Eddito filed into the second row.

They barely had enough time to strap themselves in before Brooks threw the wagon into drive.

"Tell me where to go."

34 / SOME CASUAL MURDER

No one had ever driven *to* Johnstown, Pennsylvania as fast as Brooks did. The car bobbed and weaved through the country landscape and around fallen trees until it screeched to a stop in the hospital parking lot.

"Wait here," Brooks said, leaving the car idling and the Smiths still clinging to the door handles.

The medical center was the first place Brooks had seen since the mall that showed any significant signs of life. Its parking lot—lit by street lamps—housed dozens of cars, presumably belonging to hospital staff. The windows of the three-story building were aglow, but their contents were obscured by curtains and blinds.

Brooks entered through powered sliding glass doors that let out a PSSHT sound. Six baton-wielding men, all wearing orange fluro pants, navy bomber jackets, and aviator sunglasses, immediately rushed him.

This wasn't the TSA, and Brooks had no reason—except his guilty conscience—to hold back. His conscience wasn't all that guilty at the moment. Angry and reacting only on instinct, he channeled the action hero in every one of his favorite movies, including their blatant disregard for human life.

Brooks intercepted the first baton that came close, tore it from his attacker, and plunged it straight into the man's chest, killing him in an instant. He caught the body as it fell limp and heaved it at two of the guards rushing him, knocking them back onto the floor.

Two men closed in from the left, one from the right. Brooks's cyborg reflexes reacted almost instantly. With a swift kick, he swept the lone guard's feet out from under him and dodged out of the path of two incoming batons. He grabbed the men by the shirt—one in each hand—and slammed their faces together. They crumpled to the ground groaning in agony, looking like bloody ham salad.

The guard Brooks had tripped rose to his feet and lunged at the cyborg, having learned nothing from the fate of his coworkers. Brooks put a palm to each side of his head and twisted; not an instant killer, but enough to immobilize. Maybe permanently so.

Brooks hadn't forgotten the final two, who'd been on the ground playing possum. As they moved to attack him from behind, his reflexes kicked in again and he whipped around, grabbed their batons, and slammed them down into the men's skulls in a single, violent motion.

Brooks panted, his teeth bared like a blood-soaked animal. A white-coated doctor hurried over, his hands raised to his mouth in horror.

"What are you—?"

Brooks grabbed him and pinned him against the wall behind the reception desk. "Edward Smith. Where is he?"

The doctor's eyes bulged and he began to stammer. "I... I don't know who or—"

"Ahem."

The throat-clearing sound came from the end of the hallway. Brooks dropped the doctor, turned, and spotted Smith, casually standing there in blue scrubs, shooing away a familiar face.

"Eddie? And..."—Brooks realized he'd never gotten a name for the—"trucker?"

The truck driver who'd once propositioned the men now wore a pair of scrubs like Smith's, but with the waistline jazzed up by his eagle-shaped belt buckle.

"See ya later, Toe Jam," said Smith.

The trucker glanced at the carnage, gave a sheepish wave, and hurried out the front door.

"Huh?" Brooks sputtered. "What...?"

"What's confusing you?" Smith teased, then explained. "His name's Toe Jam. He got nabbed and was already mounting an escape when I got here."

"You didn't, um...?"

"No, I'm not a *service station*."

"Are you okay?"

"Yeah. You just made getting past those guards a whole lot easier, though. Holy shit, Brooksy."

"What is this place?"

"It's some kind of breeding program to make more people. Run by Shoppli, of course."

"So... they're buying people, *and* making more people?"

"Yeah."

"They didn't, um..." Brooks tried to tiptoe around it.

"Turn me into a broodmare?" Smith wondered.

"You'd be a stallion."

"You'd know." Smith winked and used his tongue to sound a CLOP CLOP. "No... but the kinky fuckers gave me a plastic cup and tried to get me to make them a fappuccino."

Brooks made a face.

"My thoughts exactly," Smith said. "Our cross-universe adoption theory is checking out, though. Who can afford to drop $50k, in cash, on a kid?"

"White people," they answered together.

"And what do white people want?" Smith asked.

"More seasons of *Frasier*?"

"Apart from that," Smith said, then he laid it out. "White babies. All the patients here are pale as shit."*

Brooks sighed. "I was kind of hoping your Mirror Hitler theory would work out so we could, you know... get to murder Hitler."

Smith leaned to peek around his husband at the bodies littering the lobby. "Uh... I think you've done enough

---

* Pale shit can be a sign of liver disease. Informative!

murdering for one day."

"I..." Brooks flushed.

Smith placed a hand on his shoulder. "This is a lawless wasteland and they're irradiated monsters. I blew up three dudes in a trailer. Just..."—he took a second glance at the bloody mess—"keep an eye on yourself, T-1000."

Brooks shook it off. "Ready to go?"

"I was born ready," Smith lied. He was actually born naked and covered in goo, like everyone else. "Let's go fuck up Shoppli."

As they exited the building, Brooks surveyed the damage he'd done, avoiding the frightened looks of hospital staff. His mind scolded him.

Great use of free will.

35 / WIDGET'S DAY

Bark. Bark Bark. Bark. Get pets. Bark. Nap. Bark Bark. Kibble. Bark. Gotta poop. Bark. Bark. Get pets. Walk. Bark. Bark Bark. Miss dads. Nap. Bark. Nap. Kibble. Poop. Sleep.

36 / BOT BLOODED

Following their detour, the remaining drive from Johnstown to Allentown was set to take over eight hours. As the sun began to set, Phil assured the group they didn't want to be in Allentown after dark. He pulled the station wagon into the parking lot of a what seemed like a deserted dollar store. Inside, they found it well-stocked with sleeping bags, blankets, and curtains that were heavy enough to act as extra blankets.

They also found some weirdos. Four people—two women and two men—lived in the store. All were dressed in nothing but black and had powdered their faces white with whatever was around... probably corn starch. The two women wore tattered fishnet veils. In the center of the store, the group had created an elaborate exhibition from the cheaply produced goods that surrounded them.

The Goths had no interest in interacting with the visitors, other than to say:

"Don't touch the art."

Their house, their rules.

With its rear seats folded, the station wagon could comfortably sleep three. Leslie, Phil, and Eddito posted up inside, while Brooks and Smith bedded in the makeshift gallery, settling in between a display of plastic lighters melted to look like a graveyard scene and a bin of VHS tapes, stacked in the shape of a skull. All were dimly lit by black votive candles, purposely placed to highlight the 'art.'

Brooks didn't need sleep to the extent that non-cyborgs do, but going without made him anxious and irritable. He lay beneath an oversized picnic blanket, staring through a hole in the roof at an ominous sky—too polluted to reveal any stars, if this universe had them. Next to him, Smith lay half under the blanket, half dangling outside. Brooks elbowed him gently.

"...stop it..."

"Are you awake?" Brooks poked again.

"I am *now*." Smith rubbed at his eyes.

"Sorry."

Smith rolled to face him. "What's wrong?"

Brooks looked troubled. "I have a bad feeling about this," he said, reciting one of his favorite movie clichés.

"How long have you been waiting to say that?"

"Since I got here," Brooks admitted. "It's just... I'm worried about you. You just got closure with Indiana and now... here we are with Leslie and Phil... I mean..."

"You think they're hiding something."

Brooks considered his words. "Maybe..."

"Yeah, me too," Smith said, staring at the ceiling.

Brooks let out a relieved sigh. "It's nothing they said or did," he clarified, "just a feeling. Maybe I'm just worried you're going to end up hurt, so I'm..."

"Brooksy... I'm not you. For me to be let down, I'd have to have hope in the first place. My parents and I are getting along, and they seem like decent people, so... of course I assume they're gonna turn out to be shapeshifters or pedos or something."

Brooks furrowed his brow. "That's not a great way to live."

"I know, but I—"

"I swear, if you say you're self-aware—"

"I am." Smith winked, but grew serious. "But what I was gonna say is... I feel like it's worse if I'm wrong. What happens if we all go back home together and live happily ever after? What kind of relationship am I supposed to have with them? Shit, what kind of relationship am I supposed to have with Eddito? Is it a Big Brothers/Big Sisters kinda thing? Am I gonna have to tell him all about how I knew I liked boys and girls?"

Brooks chuckled. "You'll figure it out."

"Nah. They're gonna turn out to be creeps. Just wait."

"Why? Because they're nice to you?"

Smith knew how it would sound if he answered in the affirmative, but that's exactly how he felt. He gave a half nod, half shrug.

"You trust me," Brooks noted.

"You're not all that nice, babe."

For some reason, Brooks felt it necessary to defend his in-laws. "Honestly, I don't think it's all bullshit because... I don't think anyone from Indiana is that good an actor."

"Brendan Fraser's from Indiana."

"*Like I said.*"

Smith shrugged. "I guess. Hotter than hell, though..."

"In the '90s, maybe... but don't change the subject. Are you going to be okay?"

"Knowing I'll never bang peak Brendan Fraser?" Smith smiled. "I think I'll manage."

"You know what I—"

"You already asked me. I already answered. Yes, I'm *probably* gonna be fine." In his newfound self-awareness, Smith turned the tables instead of becoming annoyed. "Are you?"

Brooks shook his head. "Not even. I'm terrified. Every time there's some big thing—a time machine or a temporal rift or a genie or whatever—I end up losing you."

"Only for a little bit," said Smith.

Brooks let out a laugh against his own judgment. "It's not funny," he said, then added, "I don't have anyone else."

"That's—"

"Kinda need you to let me ramble here..."

Smith shut up and obliged.

"When my dad and Tasha died, that was it for me—that was all the family I had. My dad was an only child. I never even met my mom, so I'm not exactly close with her family. My tías in Flatbush are fine, but... I used to... I had a lot of friends. But after Willowbrook Park, I... I guess I just threw myself into the work because... how can you pretend things are normal when you're dealing with monster stuff every day? Plus, as far as I knew I was set to die anyway."

Smith was about to comment, but Brooks's raised palm told him otherwise.

"Permanently, I mean." Brooks continued. "Once everyone found out about the paranormal, I tried to reconnect with some people, but they were all just pissed that I'd kept quiet about everything."

Brooks snorted, both in amusement and exhaustion. "The closest thing I have to friends now are my therapist and your ex-girlfriend, who—*by the way*—is the one who stabbed me to death. That is *so* messed up. Now I'm thirty-five, half-robot, and I hunt monsters for a living. Where am I supposed to make friends? The local cyborg society? Ask our competitors if anyone wants to start a private dick club?"

Smith snickered, then quickly choked it back.

"I have you and the girls, but they're not exactly around much these days. I think that's why I'm so invested in the adoption thing." He frowned. "You said you don't plan on dying, and I believe you. But if something does happen to you... you saw what I did at the hospital. I don't think I can control that part of myself."

"Yes, you can."

Brooks shook his head. "You know what I did when I met Leslie and Phil?"

"What?"

"I bent his cane in half." He thought back on the outburst and hung his head. "I was pissed off and I wanted answers, and I didn't care."

"So what? He probably had it coming."

"Sometimes... I think I'm a few bad days away from becoming a murderbot."

"Nah," Smith said dismissively.

Brooks pushed up into a seated position. "*Nah?*"

Smith shrugged. "If I'm not my parents, then you're not your programming."

"When I said you weren't your parents, it was under the assumption they were abusive meth heads. Now that they're Nerd Dad and Surly Puns-a-Lot..."—he stifled a snort—"you kinda are."

"I'm gonna make you take that back when they turn out to be pedos."

"*Obviously*. But that's another thi—" Brooks stopped himself. "You know what? Nevermind."

"You wanna say something that's gonna piss me off," Smith said. "Just say it."

Brooks relented. "*Okay*. We keep running into people who care about you, like Teddy and all those jello eaters at the VFW and now your long-lost parents. I never get that. But you do, and you don't even care. It's absolutely *infuriating*."

"I'd give them to you if I could," Smith said, "but... fate's bullshit." He started counting the fingers on his right hand. "You were supposed to die. Didn't happen. I was supposed to die. Found a loophole. You don't wanna turn out to be a murderbot..."—he closed his fingers into a fist—"just don't be a murderbot."

"You don't want to be a bad father, just don't be a bad father," Brooks said, pointing out his husband's hypocrisy.

Smith raised a hushing forefinger. "I believe in you. I don't believe in me. But I'm not going anywhere. You're stuck with me. And pretty soon you're gonna be stuck with me and some kid from Des Moines."

"Yeah?"

"Yeah. Now..." Smith yawned aggressively. "We have *got* to get some sleep. Shoppli tomorrow."

"I'm not sure I can—"

Smith scooted his pile of bedding closer, and draped an arm over his husband.

Brooks was asleep in seconds.

37 / SHOPPLI: THINK BIGGEST

By morning, the Goths had vacated to find a new scene, but the Smiths and Brooks paid that no mind. They piled into the station wagon and started out for their best guess at a destination.

After several hours with Leslie behind the wheel, the roads took a steep decline. At the bottom of a winding mountain road stood the remnants of an enormous, devastated city. Allentown, Pennsylvania. Former Population: 2,103,758. Current Population: 780 mole people who only emerged from the sewers in the darkness of night.

Skyscraper ruins packed the skyline. Although they were nonexistent in the city's center, where a bomb made its direct hit, the surrounding districts were littered with the twisted, empty frames of obliterated buildings, reaching like ladders into the hazy sky. Farther out were hundreds more buildings that were still somewhat building-shaped, but windowless and in various stages of crumbling.

"You sure this is Allentown?" Smith asked.

"I ought to be," Phil chuckled. "I was born here. Well... not *here* here. You know."

"It looks as big as Chicago."

Phil leaned over the passenger seat to look at his son. "Oh, it's bigger'n that. Lehigh Valley never became a thing back home?"

Brooks and Smith stared in bewilderment.

"No...?"

"DeSales University is here," Phil said, then corrected himself. "*Was* here. Every computer and semiconductor company was here. Apple. Xerox. Shoppli. This place even had a NASA facility."

"Oh." Brooks understood. "Like Silicon Valley. Ours is in

California."

Phil was aghast. "What about the earthquakes? Seems like a silly place to put the tech center of the world."

"How is this any better?" Brooks asked.

Smith backtracked a bit. "Wait a minute. You're from Allentown?"

"Born and raised."

"Why the fuck would you ever move to Indiana?"

"Leslie's from there," Phil said, silently adding a tally to his notepad. "She and I met at university and one thing led to another... She wanted to move closer to her family."

"*Wanted* is a strong word," Leslie chimed in. "My mom got Alzheimer's."

"You ever meet your grandparents?" Phil asked.

"No," Smith said.

In the back of the wagon, Eddito perked up—almost making the connection.

"That breaks my heart. Wonder what happened to—" Phil realized he was about to give things away to Eddito, and censored himself. "What do you think ever happened to *your* parents, Les?"

"I assume mom died, what with the Alzheimer's. And dad would be in his nineties in 2018, so... he's probably dead too."

The matter-of-factness of her tone reminded Brooks of Smith's reaction to the O'Gradys passing. He let out a small laugh.

"Oh my God. It's not funny. I'm so sorry."

Shortly after the inappropriate remark, Leslie pulled the station wagon up to a group of buildings near the city's perimeter. At the center stood a concrete eyesore whose design could best be described as fuck-it architecture.

A precursor to modern tech campuses, Shoppli HQ sprawled across nearly twenty acres of Allentown. Most of it consisted of parking lots, or buildings that had been leveled to parking lots. The main building, however, still stood six stories high, looking as though someone had haphazardly stacked cement boxes of varying sizes. All of the windows had been blown out, but the holes they left behind on the building's front were shaped like the letters on children's wooden block toys. They spelled:

SHOPPLI

Below the windows was the company's slogan, in rusted wrought iron:

Think biggest.

Smith kept his eyes on the decaying building. "This place isn't working on shit."

"There could be people working in there," Brooks said. "Reticent HQ looked like a dump..."

"Yeah, but it wasn't collapsing. And it had power."

He had a point. Not one window was lit up, and the cement cubes leaned at angles they definitely weren't supposed to. Floors on one corner of the building seemed to be sinking into the floors beneath them. Still, the pair had gone far enough out of their way not to let an OSHA hazard stop them.

Brooks walked toward the entrance's bright red doors. They were covered in green, blue, and yellow dots, and all of the scratched and smudged coloring looked like a self-harming clown's attempt at clawing off his makeup.

Smith followed, and alerted his family.

"Heading into the shithole!"

"We'll stay here and keep the car running," Leslie reassured him.

"Okay..."

That single, weak word represented a lot of trust for Smith to put in his newfound parents. He hoped it wasn't misplaced as he and Brooks made their way in.

Shoppli HQ didn't look much better on the inside, at least not anymore. Across from an empty reception desk, the remains of wicker-framed hanging chairs dangled from the lobby ceiling. A grand, split staircase welcomed visitors deeper into the world of Shoppli, and signs on the wall provided directions to rooms called Rigel, Betelgeuse, and Alnitak A. They were named after stars in the constellation Orion, but the words meant nothing to the detectives.

"Ugh. I wish I had Wi-Fi," Brooks complained. "Where do we start?"

Smith shrugged. "If you were an evil company involved in human trafficking, where would you hide your dirty laundry?"

"Sub-basement," they said together.

Ignoring the grand staircase that would only lead to astronomy-themed conference rooms with broken windows, they went for the emergency stairwell around the corner. "In Case of Fire, Break Glass" said a broken glass container near the entrance.

The stairwell was pitch black. Brooks gave his Costco flashlight a shake, but it had already died. Solar-powered items didn't work great in a world with so little sun. As they crossed the threshold, Smith tripped on something in the darkness and yelped.

Brooks caught him by the belt and pulled him steady, preventing him from plummeting down the stairs.

"Stop almost dying," he chided.

"Want me to finish the job?"

Smith couldn't see the unamused look on Brooks's face.

"Just stay close behind me," Brooks said.

Slowly, deliberately, and clinging tightly to the handrail, they made their way down three flights of stairs into the building's fallout shelter of a basement. At the bottom, a metal vault door prevented them from going any further.

"Oh no, I guess we'll have to go home," Brooks said, before shattering the locking mechanism with his closed fist. The door cracked open, revealing a silver glimmer.

"We've got lighting!"

Stirred by his husband's feat of strength, Smith adjusted himself as he followed Brooks through the doorway. "And I've got a raging—"

"*Eddie*."

Four-inch square lighting, spaced every six feet or so, gave the basement hallway a dim glow, just enough to illuminate the rat droppings all over the tile floor. Reinforced metal doors dotted the entire hallway, and Brooks broke each one open on their way.

Door one: bathroom.

Door two: break room.

Door three: ping pong room.

Door four: kitchenette.

Door five: ice cream station.

Each room had sat unused for a long time, judging from the thick layer of dust that coated everything inside.

"Jesus, did these fuckers ever *work*?" Smith wondered.

The sixth door answered his question. Brooks kicked it open, revealing an open office concept. Rows of tables stretched across the building. Beige desktop computer stations were crammed in along them, each with a complete set of beige accessories. Even fresh out of the box, computers from the 1970s looked dirty. These were hardly brand new.

On the wall, a half-peeled poster bore the face of a grinning cartoon rat with the caption 'Bring your pet to work!' and in smaller text: 'Shoppli cares.'

Brooks and Smith doubted that.

This cubicle farm was still functional and, even stranger, fully staffed. Illuminated by each glowing computer monitor was a ghostly pale, emotionless face, staring at numbers on the screen in front of it. Despite the hundreds of workers, not one looked up to acknowledge the two men who'd intruded on their workspace. They cared about nothing but Shoppli.

Smith faked a cough to announce their entry.

No one answered. Their fingers just kept typing away.

"Well, I guess we're not gonna have to fight 'em—"

Brooks stepped behind an office chair and looked down at the figure seated in it. "Move."

The Shoppli employee's eyes never left his monitor. Brooks gave the man's shoulder an aggressive shove. "Move!"

The employee adjusted himself and resumed typing. Based on the screen, it appeared to be standard data entry. On the table next to the keyboard was a three-inch-thick, spiral-bound book. Every once in a while, the Shoppli employee glanced down at it before typing a series of numbers with no discernable pattern.

Brooks wrapped an arm around the man's neck.

"What the fuck," sounded Smith in alarm. "What happened to keeping an eye on yourself?"

Brooks continued applying pressure. "What? It's just a quick nap..."

Twenty seconds later, Brooks gently lowered the unconscious Shoppli employee to the floor and commandeered his seat.

He stared at the computer setup and frowned. It was a bulky beige unit, with a twelve-inch CRT monitor attached to a thick mechanical keyboard. To the side, attached by thick cables, were two floppy drives, a boxy two-button mouse, and a dot matrix printer.*

BOOP. The computer emitted a tinny alert as the entire

---

* Look it up, zoomer.

screen went blue.

**Logged out due to thirty seconds
of inactivity. Log in or
insert boot disk.**

"Ugh. Everything is so old," Brooks griped. "I'm not compatible with floppies..."

"Lemme try?" Smith suggested.

"What are *you* going to do?" Brooks asked. It came out sort of smug.

Smith ignored him. "Move?"

Brooks threw his hands into the air as he rose up out of the chair. Smith slid in to replace him and hovered his hands over the keyboard.

"What are you doing?" Brooks asked.

With horrible, one-fingered typing form, Smith keyed in a word: p-a-s-s-w-o-r-d.

"You really think they're that dumb..."

BOOP. They weren't.

"Told you."

Smith pondered, then tried again: p-a-s-s-w-o-r-d-1.

A friendly beep let him into the Shoppli system.

Brooks huffed. "Are you kidding me?"

"Sometimes you overestimate people. My password back home is just 'Passw0rd' with a big P and a zero for the O."

"Yeah. I know."

Smith stared at him and narrowed his eyes.

"*Relax*," Brooks assured. "I had to log in and close your accounts when you were dead. I didn't snoop. I don't want to know what else is on there."

"No. You don't." Smith laughed and pointed at the monitor. "Oh my god, look. Their computers are like the ones on TV with the obvious icons."

The screen was solid grey, with four pixelated, black and

white icons: Clock, Calendar, Data Entry, and Search. It was primitive and ridiculous.

"Anything about portals?"

"No..."

Smith rolled the mouse back and forth a few times before the ball inside decided to cooperate. When it did, he clicked the large icon of a magnifying glass labeled 'Search.'

It prompted fields for First Name and Last Name. Smith typed in his own.

15,670 results.

"Did I ever tell you how much I hate my fucking name?"

"You can have mine if you want."

"Oh yeah," Smith said sarcastically. "Come to the office of Brooks & Brooks & associates... Country club douchebags specializing in financial planning—" He tapped at the keyboard. "Oh, thank fuck. I can sort by middle initial."

He sorted by L, and used the arrow keys to navigate down to his name.

FILE RECORDS
Smith, Edward Lock (B) b. 4/12/1976
1. Shoppli Superior, Exp. 1/2019
2. Shopper Profile
3. Wishlist
4. Product Reviews
5. Search Data, 2004-Present
6. Contacts, Personal
7. Ad Targeting
8. Biometric Data
9. Shoppli+ Watch History
10. GoMart Rewards
11. Adopt Shop Application

The two stared at the screen, slack-jawed.

"I wasn't born in April..."

"Euro format," clarified Brooks, "but look at the files.

They have everything. They have your biometrics. They even have our adoption paperwork."

Smith rolled his eyes, less concerned with his own personal privacy and more with the spirit of adventure. "We came all this way just to find out they're using this universe as a data center?"

He typed in the number 11 and hit Enter. Their adoption forms popped up on the screen.

"It's brilliant if you think about it," Brooks said. "No internet, no security leaks." He put a hand to his chin. "But to get information in and out quickly... they'd need permanent interdimensional access."

"Portal gun?" Smith suggested.

"Wouldn't be the stupidest thing we've ever seen." That honor belonged to a werepigeon.

Smith tapped the Print key. Brooks shook his head.

"Those things never work—"

BZZT BZZT BRRRP.

The noises coming from the ancient printer disagreed. They stirred the Shoppli employee on the floor, who groaned, rolled over, and fell back asleep.

CLICK. BZZT BZZT BRRRP.

CLICK. BZZT BZZT BRRRP.

While they waited for what seemed like an eternity, Smith backed out and continued to explore his profile. Number 7.

AD TARGETING
Smith, Edward Lock (B) b. 4/12/1976
1. Drugs, Antidepressants
2. Drugs, Fat Burners
3. Music, Metal
4. Novels, Sci-Fi & Fantasy
5. Novels, Romance
6. Nudity, Female
7. Nudity, Male
8. Therapy, Online

9. Zane, Godwin

"Shoppli called me fat," Smith complained.

"That's the part you're concerned about? They know your prescriptions, who you've slept with—they've got more information on you than we have in most of our case files. They know you read... romance novels, apparently."

"That's a mistake," Smith said defensively.

"Is it though?"

Smith scoffed. "Have you even met me?"

"You once quoted Nicholas Sparks."

Smith turned the accusation around. "And how would *you* know that?"

"I'm *connected to the internet*."

"So what? You google everything I say?"

"No," said Brooks, sulking. "I have a built-in plagiarism detector."

"Fuckin' narc."

Smith tapped 5. This time, he was met with his entire online search history, in reverse chronological order.

SEARCH HISTORY
Smith, Edward Lock (B) b. 4/12/1976
1. Trout pro ammo
2. why do i hate nice people
3. Directions to kraft cemetary
4. help me fall asleep
5. order pizza online clarksville
6. biscuit bucket rewards login
7. old glory inn trip advisor
8. whats a carpetbagger
9. hobbit remake shoppli+
10. translate spanish apretadito
11. what counts as road rage
12. omega airlines bag fees
13. how many kids named khaleesi
14. Bream a Little Bream of Me cast

```
15. Dog groomers park slope
16. therapist nearby
```

The list went on.

"You didn't type any of that into Shoppli, did you?" Brooks asked.

"No, babe. I wasn't shopping for depression."

"They even have access to search histories from other websites. When did you search for Trout Pro ammo?"

"Maybe two minutes before I got sucked into the portal."

"So, it's *extremely* up-to-date."

Before Brooks could comment on the rest of the search queries, Smith backed out to the list of Smiths. The next entry looked identical: Edward Lock Smith. He clicked.

FILE RECORDS
Smith, Edward Lock (C) b. 4/12/1976
```
1. Shopper Profile
2. Ad Targeting
3. Biometric Data
4. Adopt Shop Exemption
```

Eddito's file was decidedly lighter. The detectives ignored the implications of a multidimensional conglomerate targeting ads to undeveloped minds, and focused on number 4.

"Exemption?" wondered Brooks.

Smith squinted and opened the file. Before he started reading it, he reflexively tapped Print.

"It says he's exempt from being given out for adoption because... his parents worked for Shoppli?"

"Which ones?" Brooks asked. "If his birth parents... the people who raised you—"

"—the Assholes—" Smith corrected.

"—if it's the *Assholes* who worked for Shoppli... maybe they took you on purpose. If it's the other ones—the Smiths sitting outside in a station wagon—we have a problem. It also means we should get back out there ASAP."

"Told you they're probably dicks."

"You said pedos," Brooks reminded him, "but we don't know that yet."

Smith followed that up by printing the records for Leslie and Phil—both sets—then, as an afterthought, the records for Brooks. Back on the main screen, he clicked the icon for Calendar. What appeared on the monitor didn't look much like any calendar he'd ever seen.

A	0500 Data Xfer Site 16	0500 Data Xfer Site 12	0500 Data Xfer Site 7	0500 Data Xfer Site 19	0500 Data Xfer Site 21	0500 Data Xfer Site 4
B	1900 Staff Xfer Site 1	2100 Staff Xfer Site 9	2300 Staff Xfer Site 25	0100 Staff Xfer Site 7	0300 Staff Xfer Site 9	0500 Staff Xfer Site 1
C	1750 Adopt Shop Site 6	1030 Adopt Shop Site 6	0310 Adopt Shop Site 6	1950 Adopt Shop Site 6	1230 Adopt Shop Site 6	0510 Adopt Shop Site 6
D	1100 Data Xfer Site R	1445 Data Xfer Site X	1830 Data Xfer Site P	2215 Data Xfer Site Q	0200 Data Xfer Site R	0545 Data Xfer Site N
E	0400 Staff Xfer Site 7	0200 Staff Xfer Site 8	0000 Staff Xfer Site 7	2200 Staff Xfer Site 8	2000 Staff Xfer Site 7	1800 Staff Xfer Site 8
F	2700 Data Xfer Site Σ	3000 Data Xfer Site Ω	3300 Data Xfer Site Σ	3600 Data Xfer Site β	0300 Data Xfer Site Θ	0600 Data Xfer Site Ω

Smith stared. "The fuck am I looking at?"

"A calendar," Brooks said dryly.

"No kidding. You said Clarksville was Site 1 and Akron was Site 2. But now there's a whole alphabet, and some of the sites are in Greek..." Smith tapped Print again.

Brooks stared at the F row. "I don't remember days lasting thirty-six hours..." Suddenly, a thought struck him. "Wait. Go back and click the Clock..."

"Wondering how long we've been clicking links?"

"No..."

Six digital clocks appeared on the screen.

A	B	C
11	30	8
January	May	April
2022	2018	1984
0707	2107	1957

D	E	F
7	19	7
September	Mercedonius	Μάρτιος
1997	21	3078
1307	0607	2907

"Fuck me," Smith stammered. "A multiverse?"

"Looks like it."

"—and we're from Earth... *B*?" Smith let out a disgusted sound.

"What's wrong with being from Earth B?"

Smith threw his hands down on the desk. "Have you ever watched *anything ever*?"

Brooks sighed and prepared for the incoming rant.

"—It means we're disposable. Crisis on Infinite Earths? The Tournament of Power? Rise of the Cybermen? Shrek Forever After? We exist to be erased."

Brooks raised a finger to object. "Not as long as Shoppli's

profiting from us."

"That—" Smith saw no counterargument. "—that's a good point, actually. So, we're from B and we're in... C..."

He tapped Print once again.

"You can't print a clock—"

CLICK. BZZT BZZT BRRRP.

While the dot matrix printer proved Brooks wrong, the detectives passed the time perusing the rest of the office. Each disinterested face they walked by remained focused on data entry—the clacks of their keyboards echoing in a near synchronous score.

As they moved down the rows, the detectives tried but failed to elicit any sort of reaction from the mindless workers. One by one, they'd shake a shoulder or lean in to block their view, always with the same result. Brooks pushed one worker until he was tilted nearly sixty degrees to the right, but the man's eyes remained glued to the screen, and his hands kept typing. When Brooks let him go, he sprung back into place like a weeble.

In the two hours they spent at Shoppli HQ, the most interesting thing that happened was the retrieval of the sleeping worker. About forty-five minutes after Brooks had rendered him unconscious, a self-driving forklift appeared out of nowhere, rolled down the aisles, scooped up the useless employee, and drove away.

BEEEEP. BEEEEP. BEEEEP.

The detectives followed the forklift through the dimly lit corridor to another metal door, labeled Waste Management. This one opened automatically and inside, amongst several large pieces of machinery, was an incinerator. The forklift drove up to the furnace, dumped the man's unconscious body, emitted a friendly chime, then shut itself off.

"Does that count as a murder?" Brooks asked, frowning.

"Nah. That guy's been dead inside his whole life."

An hour later, Brooks and Smith emerged from the

building, each carrying a thick stack of continuous, perforated printer paper.

The station wagon was gone.

38 / GOOGLING QUESTIONS OF EXISTENTIAL DREAD

The shadow of the Shoppli building had grown long and thin, and the already-gloomy sky was darkening. Smith used his lighter and a little effort to turn Shoppli's stylish wicker chairs into a small fire in the parking lot. He and Brooks sat cross-legged on the pavement beside it, shuffling through reams of paperwork. Every so often, cackles echoed from somewhere nearby—somewhere beneath—and the detectives knew it wouldn't be long before they weren't alone.

Brooks tried—for the umpteenth time—to broach the subject of what had happened.

"You know, it's okay if—"

"No."

"Very mature."

"Who ever said I was mature?" Smith wondered. His eyes showed he was hurting, but he wouldn't let his words do the same. "I told you they were gonna turn out to be shit. Not surprised, and I don't want to talk about it." He rifled through the paper. "I do want to talk about your search history, though..."

Brooks flushed red. It was clear, even in the firelight.

"It's... excessive."

SEARCH HISTORY
Brooks, Arturo Gene (B) b. 19/8/1982
1. Current GPS location
2. Sync current time
3. News headlines
4. Sync current time
5. Current GPS location
6. Current GPS location

```
 7. Price compare SKU 6468243
 8. Sync current time
 9. = 3.99/6
10. = 6.99/12
11. = 14.49/24
12. Price compare UPC 016000264601
13. News headlines
14. Sync current time
```

The first thirty pages of Brooks's search history went on with mechanical queries like those, until Smith finally reached something he recognized.

1731. Directions to Green River Mall

Smith handed his pile of papers over to Brooks. "How long were you in our universe after I came here?"

Brooks thought on it. "A few hours. Enough time to call the girls, go to dinner with... everyone, get a ride back to Clarksville..."

"So... in a few hours, you searched over seventeen hundred times. That's like..."

Brooks did the math. "Over five hundred and seventy-six searches an hour, or almost ten searches a minute."

"You think that's healthy?"

"Healthier than googling questions of existential dread." Brooks poked at the fire with a sprig of wicker. "If you were a cyborg, your search history would look like that too."

"I dunno. Can't really see myself checking the time and location every goddamn minute. Or the latest news. Or cost comparing prices on whatever the fuc—"

"Granola bars."

"Christ. That's basic math. Can't you do it in your head?"

"Yeah, I can. *I do. I myself* am connected to the internet, Eddie. It's not like I'm going over to Google and typing all of this in. These are my *thoughts*, okay? Shoppli knows my thoughts."

Brooks realized what he'd just said, and repeated it for emphasis.

"*Shoppli knows my thoughts.*"

"Which means...?"

Brooks rifled through pages upon pages of his search history until he found the train of thought he was looking for. "Look." He pointed at the page. "Shoppli Adopt Shop acquisition. Adopt Shop reviews. Shoppli lawsuit. Shoppli malfeasance. Shoppli records retention. Shoppli corporate login. Adopt Shop Manhattan floorplan. Adopt Shop Manhattan security. Breaking and entering laws. Whistleblower reports. 401k withdrawal process... they knew exactly when we started investigating them and why."

"And every plan we ever made," added Smith.

"They're not just generally shady," Brooks continued. "They *targeted* us. And they've got a portal schedule. They probably opened that one that brought you here in the first place..."

Smith stared down at the burning embers. "I wonder how the Smiths and Assholes fit into this..."

Brooks tilted his head to hear something in the distance. It was a station wagon.

"Let's ask them."

Smith heard the car a few moments later, but found no relief in the sound. He set his paperwork down, and rose to a standing position.

Leslie and Phil pulled the vehicle around and emerged, unprepared for the vitriol about to greet them.

Smith stomped across the parking lot, practically spitting. "*What the fuck?*"

Eddito tried to hop out of the back, but Leslie waved him back.

Smith slammed a hand on the side of the car. "Where the hell were you?"

"Refilling the tank?" Leslie squinted.

"She's a beaut," said Phil, "but she only gets about six kilometers per liter."

Smith's eye twitched.

Brooks answered the question before his husband could get it out. "Fourteen miles per gallon."

Phil appeared puzzled. "You didn't think we were gonna abandon you fellas, did you?"

"Probably would have been a smarter move," Smith said. He pointed at the decaying building. "You work for Shoppli!"

"What?" Phil objected. "We sure as heck do not."

"Files say otherwise," Brooks said, shaking the papers in his hand for emphasis. "You work for them, in exchange for the kid being exempt from cross-universe trafficking." He wasn't certain, but stating speculation as fact was a tried-and-true detective technique.

Leslie sighed. "We *did* work for Shoppli," she relented. "Back in the 70s. *Back home.* Before we moved to Indiana."

"Doing what?" Smith asked.

She hesitated before answering. "Researching wormholes."

"Miniature wormholes," Phil clarified. "You know, the sort of thing that got us here in the first dang place."

"In theory, if you could create wormholes between two points, you could get deliver goods and materials from one place to another instantaneously," Leslie said.

"Like a transporter on *Star Trek*," Phil added.

Leslie rolled her eyes. "Right. Shoppli would save a sh— crap ton on shipping costs. But it turns out the stupid things were interdimensional. They scrapped the project, or so we thought."

Smith eyed his parents with suspicion.

"Everything else we've told you is true," Phil said. "And I'm telling you now... we never signed any agreement with

Shoppli about our little Eddie."

"Then why didn't you ever mention you used to work for them?" asked Brooks, with an accusatory tone.

"We signed an NDA," Leslie said. "Those things are *seriously* binding. When people break a Shoppli NDA, bad shi— bad stuff tends to happen.

"Bad stuff... like getting tossed into another universe?" Brooks wondered, as their situation started to make a bit more sense.

Phil tilted his head. "Why? You fellas didn't break one, did you?"

The detectives exchanged a look.

"Maybe," Brooks admitted.

Smith added, "It was really long."

Phil brushed the sweat from his forehead. "Well, cat's out of the bag now. Hope you two aren't too mad."

"Mostly confused," Smith said. "You two were scientists?"

"Yeah," Leslie said derisively, as if her son were stupid for not getting it.

"And the other Smiths too?"

They nodded as Smith began to piece things together.

"Meth lab... huh," he muttered.

"Wh—"

Before Brooks could ask for an explanation, Smith gestured at Leslie and Phil and said, "If *these two* didn't get their kid—me—an exemption, that means *the Assholes* did. For Eddito—their real son."

He continued. "They weren't cooking meth. I bet they were trying to recreate their work at Shoppli outside of the lab. To get their real son back. Either they fucked it up and blew themselves to bits, or Shoppli really didn't want them breaking the agreement."

"That tracks," Leslie confirmed. "We tried running similar experiments at first, and the end result was... also an explosion."

It was obvious they were hiding something.

Brooks quizzed them. "An explosion?"

Leslie looked sheepishly at her husband and scrunched her nose. "It... *may* have given the US government the impression we'd been bombed by the Soviets, which *may* have led them to retaliate, which *may* have then led the Soviets to launch their own attack."

Smith stared at them. "You doomed an entire world trying to get me back?"

"Maybe..." said Leslie with a shrug.

Phil threw up his hands. "Didn't mean to!"

Brooks was as stunned as his husband. "That doesn't weigh heavily on you at all?"

Leslie shrugged. "Why should it? It was the government who fu—screwed it up. Not our fault they can't tell a lab accident from an exploding H-bomb."

Brooks elbowed Smith. "Too bad you didn't inherit your parents' lack of contrition."

"Har har," said Smith, rolling his eyes.

Brooks delved deeper. "When you still worked for Shoppli, where was your lab?"

"New York."

"Specifically?"

"Manhattan," said Leslie. "Um... East 33rd."

"Son of a bitch," said Smith. Another for the swear jar.

"That's where Adopt Shop HQ is," Brooks said.

Smith hurried over to his pile of papers and retrieved the calendar printout. He brought it back and showed it to his parents. "There's an Adopt Shop event every few hours at Site 6. I'm betting that's in Manhattan, and I'm betting that's when Shoppli sends over all the orphans they're cranking out in this shithole."

While Smith caught his parents up on their history with Adopt Shop, its acquisition by Shoppli, and everything they'd discovered in Shoppli HQ, Brooks got another funny feeling;

a twinge pulled at the back of his brain.

He looked past the Smiths, down an empty street full of empty buildings.

No matter what his scans said, they didn't feel empty.

39 / GROWING PAINS

Barista was a natural vocation for Lemon. It was a job, so she disliked it out of principle, but it wasn't the worst one in the world. The constant stream of foot traffic and the sound of clacking keyboards—along with a steady flow of espresso—kept her energy levels high. Sometimes, the manager even let her put Pop Tart & the Activation Energy on rotation. It didn't make her want to put the band back together, but it did make her reminisce fondly.

The job only became stressful when a customer dropped an order like the one she'd just received: one extra-large, quarter-whole milk, quarter-nonfat milk, half oat milk, extra hot no-foam butterscotch latte—add two shots of espresso (ristretto), add whip, add matcha powder—with two packets of sugar substitute and one packet of sugar, topped with cinnamon powder, nutmeg, and rainbow sprinkles.

While she reviewed the order slip to make sure she'd remembered everything, the bell above the door jingled and her sister entered the café.

"One sec!" Lemon shouted over the sound of steam.

Patience always looked a bit silly in her old-timey frocks. Wearing a knee-length khaki romper underneath a hand-sewn grey cloak, she looked extra silly. She approached the counter as Lemon handed the elaborate beverage to a businessman who eyed it with skepticism, took a sip, then walked away, satisfied.

"The usual?" asked Lemon.

Patience nodded. "Yes, please."

Lemon could pour a glass of milk with her eyes shut, but she kept them open as she stared at a collection of green and brown stains all over Patience's uniform.

"Trouble at the zoo?" Lemon asked.

Patience nodded. "I was hosing away a fallen slushie from the floor of the ape exhibit when a chimpanzee threw its feces at me. Then a child threw another slushie at me."

"That sucks," Lemon said, handing her the milk.

Patience took a deep swig, then wiped the white moustache from her upper lip. "How is your baristawork faring?"

"Awful," said Lemon. "These creepin' glorbdinks aren't tipping at all." She directed her voice toward her earlier customer, seated in a nearby booth. "*Not even when they order stupidly complicated drinks.*"

"I'd hoped for good news." Patience frowned and took another sip. "My ledger shows we've not earned even a third of what we owe the mortgagers."

"We're gonna get repo'd," said Lemon. The espresso machine made a loud spurting sound in agreement. "Where the *florp* are Turo and Eddie?"

"Ms. Burroughs hasn't heard from them either. Do you have any further knowledge as to when the time machine will be ready?"

"Last I heard, it was still weeks out, but Paysh... if it's gonna get fixed... it should've shown up by now. There's no way future me wouldn't do something to get past me out of having to have a job."

Patience frowned even harder. "Are you suggesting the machine may never be repaired?"

"Not suggesting," Lemon said, looking serious. "I'm saying it's for sure."

"Then... how are we to keep our home and locate Edward and Arturo?"

Lemon didn't respond.

Due to the prolonged silence, Patience wasn't sure whether her sister had heard the words. She also wasn't very familiar with the concept of rhetorical questions.

"Erm... Lemon? How are we to keep our home and locate Edward and Arturo?"

Lemon still didn't respond. She froze in thought. That, Patience decided, was worrying.

As she stood behind the counter in a pool of Italian blend, Lemon was locked in a convenient flashback.

A year ago—give or take—she'd begrudgingly accompanied Brooks to Shakespeare in the Park. Smith and Patience had gone to see some abysmal sci-fi movie about time travel, which Patience would absorb as a documentary. Since her fathers seemingly had no friends, Lemon got stuck with High Culture Duty.

She emerged from Central Park, carrying a Big Gulp, feeling duly cultured and a little peeved. "So, why was Shakespeare always killing characters off-stage?"

"Couldn't tell you," said Brooks. "Maybe he thought that... whatever the audience's imagination could come up would be cooler than anything he could put on stage."

"Oh, Lady Macbeth is dead," she mocked in a low-quality British accent. "You wouldn't be interested in seeing that. Oh, Macbeth got decapitated. You wouldn't wanna see that either."

"Any other critiques?" Brooks asked.

"Nah. It was fine, I guess," Lemon said, like a typical Moonlennial.

"*You guess?*" Brooks blinked in disbelief. "A play that's endured for four centuries is *fine?*" He used the opportunity to make an extremely awkward transition.

"Are you?"

Lemon was taking a big gulp of her Big Gulp. She stopped, mid-gulp. "Huh?"

"I mean, are you doing... fine?"

"Uh, yeah. I'm grape jelly," Lemon replied.

"Are you sure?" Brooks asked, pressing the issue.

Lemon sank into her shoulders and rolled her eyes. "Yes. I'm sure."

"I just... I know what it's like to lose—"

"You know what it was like *for you*," Lemon corrected.

Unspoken between the two was that Lemon's brother, Tangelo, had recently died during his conscripted service in the Lunan Army. That wasn't unexpected. Lunans were weak, malnourished hipsters, and their army had an eighty percent casualty rate. But Tangelo had been the last surviving member of Lemon's family, following her parents' deaths in the Craft Beer Wars. He'd basically raised her up to the moment she moved into the Brooks-Smith home.

"It's fine," Lemon said. "We have a time machine. I can visit him any time I want."

"But you'll never experience anything new together." Brooks didn't want her to dwell, but he did want her to be honest with herself. And with him. "You already know how everything he's ever done will play out..."

"I'm good," she said curtly. "You know what? I think I'm gonna go back to the 1600s and ask Billy Shakes what he was thinking."

"You're running..."

Lemon soured. "I'm strolling at a casual pace."

She pitched her drink into a nearby trashcan and quickened her pace. "Now I'm running." As she did, she pulled out her phone and texted Patience.

Idea. U wanna meet bill shakespeare?

Brooked started after her. "Where are you going?"
Her phone screen flashed.

I'm not familiar with a Bill Shakespeare. That is, unless you are shortening William Shakespeare's first name as though you two are acquainted. If that were the case, I believe you would have mentioned your friendship at some point in the past. For I have never known you to refrain from what Edward refers to as "humblebragging."

Lemon let out an exasperated sigh, then turned back to Brooks. "Gotta go!"

He could have caught up to her—he was a cyborg, after all—but Lemon knew her father was an anxious mess. Just the optics of him chasing down a black teenager would keep Brooks from following her. That, and the fact that when Brooks was nearby, Lemon was mortal.

Brooks slowed to a walk, and Lemon escaped without having to learn anything.

40 / THE ONLY THING BILLY JOEL EVER GOT RIGHT

Billy Joel is a liar. For starters, he was never a 'backstreet guy.' William Martin Joel grew up in Oyster Bay, Long Island, home to some of the oldest yacht clubs in the world. All of the love songs he wrote? Tainted by the fact that he's been married four times.* Only the good die young? Utter bollocks. Jeffrey Dahmer—serial killer, cannibal, and famed necrophiliac—died at thirty-four. Caligula died at just twenty-eight, after tormenting Roman citizens under his megalomaniacal rule. If that's still not young enough, take a long, dark look at any ill-fated high school shooter. The point is: Billy Joel is a liar.

However, there's one thing Billy Joel got right, and that's how much Allentown, Pennsylvania sucks. Following Leslie and Phil's advice, the Smiths and Brooks hightailed it out of the city before sunset. Somewhere in Earth A, meanwhile, the mole people fandom wept at not getting to see their preferred subterranean monsters.

After some more time on the road, sleep again became a priority. As the group reached the outskirts of Morristown, New Jersey, Phil pulled the station wagon up to a cute roadside inn. Nestled between the tech hub of Allentown and the financial center that was New York City, Morristown's people never had a chance of surviving a nuclear holocaust, but some of its buildings had. Former Population: 16,614. Current Population: 0.

The group approached the lilac-colored door on an old Victorian home. Smith read the sign aloud.

---

* Probably five by the time you're reading this.

"Come On Inn?"

He and Leslie shared a devilish smirk.

"*I don't even know Inn*," they said together.

Eddito scratched the back of his head and looked up at the sign again. "I don't get it."

"You will when you're older," Phil assured him.

The boy crossed his arms and harrumphed.

Though its décor was tacky—fleur de lis wallpaper and beadboard wainscoting as far as the eye could see—the Come On Inn had retained much of its charm. This was thanks to its solid foundations and thick, blast-resistant windows. Like many people of the era, the inn's original owners believed broken glass was a death omen.*

The building's interior didn't receive much natural light, but it also hadn't experienced the flooding and resultant mold growth that most Morristown buildings had. It still had that old musty smell that old musty places have, but it was tolerable. Plus, they had the whole house to themselves—with no skeletons for company.

When the bombs fell, the Come On Inn had been hosting a wedding. All attendees and hotel staff had been outside in the garden—now just dust and piles of bone marked where the corpses had found their final resting places.

Just behind where he assumed the ceremony took place, Smith spotted what looked like a small well house. This gave him an idea.

He enlisted Brooks to carry a cast iron, clawfoot bathtub from the second floor down to the front lawn, while he and his parents picked apart wicker bathroom baskets and a rocking chair to use as kindling. Smith's trusty lighter came in handy once more, and one-by-one, the group was able to bathe for the first time since Clarksville. It was essential, especially given what Leslie and Phil had been up to at every

---

* Fortunately, the only real death omen is life itself.

stop.

When they were all washed up and the Come On Inn's dusty lawn had become muddy and saturated with bathtub runoff, the group seated themselves on the wraparound porch.

Eddito stared at Brooks. "Where's your batteries?"

"I don't have batteries."

"But you're a robot—"

"Cyborg," Brooks corrected.

Phil chimed in. "I kinda wanna know how that works myself."

Brooks didn't find the question charming, in the least, and he didn't sugarcoat his answer. "I had every muscle in my body ripped apart and shot full of synthetic tissue. Then, my eyes were yanked out of my head and replaced with artificial ones. I had my skull torn open so they could shove a computer inside. There's wiring in my spine that leads from my brain to some input and output ports I'd rather not talk about." He took a deep breath. "Happy?"

"Do you have batteries in your butt?" Eddito asked with tactless innocence.

"No. I don't have—"

Brooks was drowned out by the resulting laughter. He turned to Smith with a look of disbelief, and his husband raised his hands in surrender.

"Sorry. You gotta admit that was funny."

Brooks sighed. "Maybe *a little* funny."

Come morning, Brooks, Smith and Eddito—once again roommates for the night—made their way toward the parking lot. They'd arranged to meet the Smiths outside.

"Shit," Smith said, patting his pockets. "Forgot my lighter." He motioned them ahead. "Go ahead. I'll be right back."

Smith headed down the hallway toward the bedroom his parents were staying in. As he passed the doorway, he overheard his mother's raised voice.

"It's one or the other."

"I know, but it's so darn... wrong," said Phil.

"This is the *perfect place* to do it."

"I know, I know..." Phil trailed off.

Smith's detective instincts—or his eye for fuckery—kicked in. He pressed his ear to the door and listened to the conversation on the other side.

"What do you want to do, Phil?" Leslie continued. "Stay in this hellhole for some guy—"

"He's our son!"

"He's a stranger."

Smith felt his stomach sink. This time, he couldn't blame Biscuit Bucket.

41 / LIES, DAMNED LIES, AND BALLISTICS

The conversation continued, and Smith continued to listen.

"Only one of them can go through—you know that," Leslie said. "You wanna stay here and help a stranger leave when you, me, and Eddie could get out? No."

"I'm with ya," Phil said, though his voice wavered. "I know what we have to do."

Smith couldn't take it any longer and banged his fist against the door.

Phil opened it and greeted him with an exaggerated smile. "Hey, son. I'm glad you're—"

"Shut the fuck up," said Smith.

Leslie seemed genuinely taken aback. "What's wrong?"

"Save it. I heard you."

"Heard what?" Phil asked.

"Only one of us can go through?"

"You must've misheard—" Phil began by playing stupid, until he saw the vicious look on his son's face. He sighed. "We... found a portal home a few years ago, but the other Smiths were still alive, and Shoppli doesn't allow duplicates back home in Earth C. Can't have two of the same person running around causing chaos and whatnot."

Leslie shot daggers at him, but Phil continued explaining. "We couldn't get back while the other Smiths were alive. Now they're dead, and that's great, but little Eddie..."

"Couldn't come through if I was there," Smith finished.

Phil nodded. "Initially, we were gonna go through, bring you back here, and swap. Then we found out time passes differently there..."

"So, you two lured me here in the first place?"

"Kinda. We scouted your universe and found out you were a detective and sent an email to your agency. Figured if you looked hard enough into Shoppli, you'd end up here one way or another since this world is where they stuff undesirables."

He and Leslie had been hopping portals for quite some time, waiting for Smith to go missing from Earth C so they could seize the opportunity to bring little Eddie home.

"It's not that we don't care about you," Leslie said. "It's just... at this point, he's our real son. Not you." She tried to take his hand and he brushed it away.

"I get that," Smith said. "Why the ruse, though? Why this whole stupid road trip? Why not grab the kid and take him back as soon as I fell into this world?"

"Because we ran into a *cyborg who can bend metal*," Leslie said. "Based on what you told us happened at the hospital, we made the right call."

"You could have fucked off at any time," Smith said.

"Yeah," Leslie said, glaring at Phil. "I've been trying to get him to let you go for *a while*."

"I just wanted to get to know my son a little before—"

"Whatever," said Smith.

Phil gestured toward the window. "We're gonna take the car and go now."

"No." Smith cracked his knuckles. "Brooksy and I are gonna take the car and you can stay here and experience the thrills of Morristown." When they didn't react, he added, "Like you said, he's a cyborg. He'll kick your ass."

Phil pulled a surprise from under his shirt: Smith's Chekhov 0.38.

"Wh—where'd you find that?" Smith asked.

"The BBAZ security bin," Phil said, casually moving the barrel toward his son. "I took it."

"You know the—"

"That the ammo's wrong? Yep. That's why we picked some up back in Allentown."

Leslie accentuated that with air quotes. "Filling the tank."

They didn't mention that they'd traded canned peaches with some mole people while Eddito took a nap, but this book would be remiss if it didn't.*

"*Shit*," said Smith.

Phil pressed the gun to Smith's back and escorted him through the doorway. "I'm really sorry about this."

As they exited the lilac door, he moved the gun to his son's temple and shouted, his voice more authoritative than ever before. "Get out of the car!"

Brooks stepped out of the vehicle.

"Um... what's going on?"

"Assholes, not pedos," Smith said, but there was little humor in his voice.

"We're gonna take the car," Phil said, approaching slowly. "Just let us take the car, please. I really don't want to have to shoot my boy."

Leslie overtook her husband and moved toward the station wagon. Smith shook his head ever so slightly, telling Brooks not to try anything and to let her pass.

She took a wide path around the wagon and seated herself behind the wheel, then glanced in the rearview mirror and spotted Eddito getting ready to hop out.

"Sit down." It was a demand, not a request.

The boy squirmed. "What's going on? Why's dad pointing a gun at Mr. Brooks?"

She waved him quiet. "Don't worry about it."

Outside the car, Smith spoke to Phil with a voice laced with venom. "You can let me go any day now. Just take the fucking car and go. Both of you."

"I'm sorry," Phil said.

"I don't give a shit."

Phil pushed his son away, and hurried around to the

---

* Please accept this breadcrumb, mole people fandom.

passenger's side of the car. As soon as his butt hit the seat, the car screeched and took off down the road with the door still open. An arm reached out and slammed it shut.

Brooks ran to Smith, and the two stared after the car as it disappeared into the smoggy horizon.

"What the hell happened in there?" he asked.

Smith summarized. "Something about Shoppli keeping doppelgangers out of Earth C. Either me or the kid can go through the portal, but not both of us. They chose him."

"Are you going to be okay?" Brooks asked.

"Huh?" Smith was already distracted, looking around the parking lot for a new plan.

"I said... *are you going to be okay?*"

"Oh, yeah," Smith answered nonchalantly. "Sure."

Brooks blinked a few times, then cried out in disbelief. "*Now!? Now* is when you finally say yes to that question?"

"Are you kidding?" Smith laughed and slapped his husband's arm. "I'm *so* much more comfortable knowing these versions of my parents are assholes too. And the peril? Peril is where I thrive."

Brooks considered this. "I wouldn't call it thriving..."

"Yeah, but it pays the bills." Smith grinned.

When good things happened, Smith dwelled on his misery, obsessing over how he should be happy. But when bad things happened, he could throw one hundred percent of his energy into trying to make the situation suck less.

It was time for action.

42 / SWEET SCHEMES (ARE MADE WITH EASE)

Smith's eyes darted around the inn's parking lot, searching rolled-over and rusted-out vehicles for his mark. He found it in a minimally beat-up 1978 Cadillac Seville. He walked over to the previous night's firepit, grabbed a charred rocking chair arm, and used it to bash out the cracked driver's side window. Then, he unlocked the door from the inside, and opened it wide.

"What are you doing?" Brooks asked.

"Hotwiring a car." Smith adjusted the handle to move the seat back and wedged himself under the dash.

"That's a thing you know how to do?" Brooks asked.

"Yeah." Smith tossed a piece of plastic to the ground. It skipped across the hotel parking lot.

"I can think of a few times that would have come in handy..."

Smith mumbled through a wire he held between his teeth. "It only works on shitboxes made in the last millennium."

"What about gas?" Brooks asked.

"Diesel model," Smith said.

"Do you need any—"

The car's engine interrupted his question with a thunderous roar. Smith dusted glass shards off the seat, and took the wheel while Brooks hurried around the car to the passenger's side. They sped down the road.

"Are you taking the highway?" Brooks asked, alarmed.

"Yeah. We don't exactly have a map—"

A second freak-out emerged from Brooks's mouth. "If we don't get there in time, we're going to be trapped here."

"No. *I'm* gonna be trapped here."

"Hi. Do you even know me?" Brooks said. "I'm not leaving you behind."

"Love the sentiment, but no." Smith shook his head. "Don't get me wrong. We're gonna beat my parents to the city and find a damn portal before they do. But on the off chance we don't, you gotta go back without me."

Brooks scoffed. "And then what? Kill little Eddito so you can grab the next portal home? I know that's not your plan."

"Wow, straight to child murder. Nice." Smith continued, more forcefully. "*No.* The plan is you go back and live in *not a hell world.*"

"No. I'll stay here with you. With the different time flow... eventually he'll die in our universe, and then we can go back."

"Eventually?" Smith did some basic math. "You're talking about spending like... a decade here, eating locust salad? And even that might not be enough. What if Zane Industries finds a cure for aging? What if the kid becomes immortal? Wouldn't be the first time. What if Maxwell Naples decides to use a different universe as Shoppli's dumpster-slash-orphan farm and all the portals close for good?"

Brooks repeated himself. "I'm not leaving without you."

Smith was about to argue, but Brooks cut him off. "What are you going to do, make me? Who has the superhuman strength here?"

"For fuck's sake," said an exasperated Smith. "I'm being practical. Patience and Lemon—"

"—have a time machine and can come find us whenever we reappear."

"Widget—"

"—is with Burroughs. I'll miss him, but he'll be fine."

"Stop," Smith said.

"Stop what? Being right?"

"You're only here because I'm an idiot who fell into a hole, okay? I wouldn't be able to live with myself if you ended up stuck in Hell World because of me."

"You think I'd be able to live with myself if I left you here? You think I wouldn't turn into that murderbot? If we're going to be miserable, we'll be miserable together. End of story."

"But—"

"But it doesn't matter, because we're getting out of here. I'm stuck with you forever." Brooks poked his shoulder. "You promised."

"Right..." Smith said, before trailing into an "oh, fuck!"

It now became apparent why Leslie and Phil always insisted on taking the back roads. Morristown to New York City was only thirty miles via highway, but that was the exact route survivors of a nuclear holocaust could be expected to take. They were easy targets.

Approaching from behind—at speed—was a roaring, open-top Jeep Gladiator, filled with *Mad Max* types like the ones who'd pursued Smith and Eddito a few days before. It looked as if the entire roof had been sawed off in haste, and the group hooted and hollered while shaking baseball bats and claw hammers.

The Jeep's bull bar had been crudely wrapped with razor wire and was primed to push the Cadillac off the road.

"We need to go faster," Brooks said, tapping the dash.

"I'm already pushing... two hundred kilometers?" Smith wasn't sure he'd read that correctly. "That sounds like a lot."

Brooks translated. "A little under one twenty-five."

"Yeah, and she's rattling, Cap'n."

Around them, the jalopy growled and grinded in protest.

"New plan." Smith nudged the car to the shoulder to avoid a pileup of abandoned cars. "Can you stop a moving vehicle?"

"Maybe?" Brooks hesitated as he eyed their pursuers. "I can't exactly google how much a 1970s Jeep weighs right now and calculate the force... with a lift kit and a handful of dudes in it..."—he sighed—"I guess I can try."

"Okay. You hop out and murder those guys, and I'll pick you back up," Smith said, as if he were making dinner plans.

"*Keep an eye on yourself,*" Brooks mocked.

"Yeah, well... Hell World," Smith replied. Without taking his eyes off the road, he grabbed Brooks's hand, pulled it close, and gave it a quick kiss. "I believe in you."

Smith punched the brakes and the car skidded and slowed to... whatever was a reasonably slow speed in kilometers per hour, allowing Brooks to hop out.

He hit the asphalt running and the car sped away, leaving him behind.

Brooks turned and stood defiant in the face of the approaching vehicle, but the Jeep showed no signs of slowing. The bull bar landed a direct hit to his abdomen, knocking him off balance and dragging him underneath the vehicle. The Jeep careened, swerving inches from a topped van, righted itself, and continued its chase.

Smith checked his rearview in horror.

Fuck! Great plan, dipshit. Don't be dead—

Brooks's cyborg strength was incredible, but he wasn't invincible. The collision hurt like hell—the tires even more so—and blood trickled from his mouth and nose as he rose to his feet. Nothing vital was broken, but his face had taken some scrapes and beneath his shirt, his chest screamed in agony.

Smith didn't see the details because that's not how human vision works, but he let out a relieved breath when he checked the rearview and saw his husband standing in the distance. Until the Jeep pulled in, obstructing his view.

BRRRRRRK.

Its bull bar pressed against the rear of the car, causing the whole thing to sway uncontrollably.

Smith tried to turn the wheel to little result. The shitbox skidded and he reached for the handle, flung the door open, and tumbled out—just as the Jeep plowed the car off the road into a ditch.

Brooks approached at speed, running with a limp and holding his side. He panted like someone who'd just finished running a half marathon with no training. "You... o... kay?"

Aside from some light grazing where the highway had torn through his suit, Smith was in surprising shape. He dusted some road filth from his pants and placed a hand on Brooks's shoulder.

"Yeah. You?"

"Few... broken ribs," said Brooks, wincing.

"Sorry." Smith's eyes shifted and he raised his brow. "You still have ribs?"

"You still haven't read my handbook."

"Wouldn't that be a violation of your privacy?"

Brooks groaned and clutched the side of his ribcage.

"You sure you're good?" asked Smith.

At the side of the road, three leather-bound marauders emerged from the Jeep.

"Give me your knife," Brooks said to Smith.

Smith pulled it from his pocket and handed it over.

The frontmost marauder had a thick scar across his right eye that looked like he'd stitched it up himself, and his face was badly burned. He thwacked a tire iron into his palm. "You're gonna come with us."

Brooks flipped Smith's knife open and threw it toward the marauder at full force. It landed right between the eyes— deep enough for an instant kill.

"I could have done that—" Smith cut himself off as he dodged an incoming baseball bat, wielded by a scraggly teenager who had an extra nose in the middle of his forehead. He lifted his foot, catching the teen between the legs. His attacker bent over in agony.

"Backpack," Brooks said.

Because he didn't love the idea of vigorous hand-to-hand combat while his body throbbed in agony, Brooks was busy backing away from the third attacker—a man whose mutated head had the shape of a mushroom—toward where his somewhat-crushed backpack had landed in the road.

Smith intercepted it and started rifling through.

"Here!" He tossed his partner a pair of scissors.

Brooks caught them and jabbed them right between the mushroom man's eyes.

Smith rejoined his partner as the greasy teenager righted himself. He grabbed his bat and snarled at them, the sound amplified by his extra nostrils.

"Is there *anything* else in there I can throw?"

Smith pawed around in the backpack. "Can you kill a man with a broken granola bar?" he asked, with genuine curiosity.

"Probably not."

Brooks braced himself. He took a few painful steps forward. With a labored kick, he swept the last marauder's legs out from under him. This time, when he man hit the pavement, Brooks dropped a leg on his chest for a retaliatory rib break. Then, the cyborg fell to his knees.

Smith hurried over and helped Brooks back to his feet. The two walked and hobbled, respectively, to the Jeep. Smith guided Brooks up into the passenger seat, then stepped around and took the wheel. In no time, they were back up to top speed, racing toward Manhattan.

"You know..." Smith scratched his head with one hand. "I always figured if we were gonna end up in a *Mad Max* situation with people chasing us, it would've been—"

"A gay thing," they said together.

Brooks stifled a cough.

"You sure you're gonna be okay?"

Brooks reclined his seat enough to make his chest hurt less, then snorted. "Gonna annoy me... with my own annoying question?"

"Well?" pressed Smith.

"I'm okay..." Brooks replied, catching sight of something

in the side-view mirror. "For now."

Smith checked the rearview mirror.

Once again, a vehicle larger than their own was approaching at speed. This time, it was an armored Humvee, and it mowed over the broken-ribbed teenager as its driver tried to catch the detectives.

"I definitely can't stop that one," Brooks said.

"We're almost there," Smith said, pressing the accelerator. "Think you can swim?"

"Absolutely not."

In this universe, Manhattan was still an island with limited points of entry.

"Well, I'm not driving us into a tunnel that's either gonna be pitch black or pitch black *and collapsed*. Think the GW's still standing?"

"Maybe...?"

The Humvee had outmatched their speed and was quickly gaining. Then, as rapidly as it had approached, it pulled back; or, more accurately, it slowed to a stop while Brooks and Smith kept going. As they sped away from the second set of pursuers, both men checked the mirrors. The Humvee's driver—clad in leather motocross gear and sporting shaggy black hair—stormed out of the vehicle holding a red metal canister and gesturing angrily at his companions.

"They ran out of fuel?" Smith laughed.

Brooks shut his eyes in relief, but they sprang right back open. He sat up and scanned for the fuel gauge.

"Please tell me you didn't just doom us to an ironic comeuppance..."

"We have a full tank," Smith assured.

"*Menos mal...*"

A few minutes later, the detectives approached the point where an iconic skyline would normally have greeted them. It didn't. Manhattan had been totally obliterated. With the exception of a few metal frames, the buildings now lay in pieces small enough to drive over.

"There's no way Adopt Shop is still standing," Brooks said.

"Doesn't have to be standing to have a portal. The Green River Mall was a big pile of nothing in our universe."

While that was true, Adopt Shop HQ *wasn't* a big pile of nothing. After navigating blocks upon blocks of debris, the detectives found one building still standing—or, more accurately, rebuilt. With no surroundings, the building's eight brand-new stories looked enormous.

Brooks reached over and put his hand over Smith's. "You know a movie thing I've always wanted to do?"

"Thelma and Louise?"

"What? *No.* I want to drive through a window."

Smith smiled, and accelerated. "What the gentleman wants, the gentleman gets."

43 / ANY PORTAL IN A STORM

Glass shards sprayed everywhere as the Jeep skidded to a standstill in Adopt Shop's abandoned lobby. Smith hopped out and helped Brooks do the same. They looked around for signs of anything or anyone. Nothing—no people, nor people-adjacent monsters.

Brooks groaned as he eyed the powerless elevators, then a floor chart on the wall. "Please... tell me I don't have to... take the stairs..."

"Well, you could wait here, but you know what happens when I wander off..."

That was not an option. Smith hurried toward the stairs, stopping every few steps to let Brooks catch up.

On the second floor, they found people. Dead ones. It was their former travel companions, executed in the style of William Shakespeare.

Leslie and Phil lay sprawled out on the floor, each with a fresh bullet hole in the side of their head and an expanding crimson puddle beneath.

Smith looked down at his parents' bodies, dismayed.

"Serves them right," Brooks said.

"Not really..." Smith knelt down and retrieved his Chekhov from Phil's clenched fist. "They were assholes, but... I get it. It's not like Patience and Lemon are blood relations, but I'd save them over these two any day. Same for them. Some old bastard they just met, or the little goober they've been raising for as long as he remembers?"

"Hmm." Brooks pointed at a sheet of paper sticking out of Phil's shirt pocket—placed like it was meant to be found.

Smith squatted to pick it up. "It's an old-ass NDA. It says they'll be... *terminated* if they discuss the terms of their contract with anyone..." He handed it over to Brooks. "Shoppli really doesn't fuck around."

Brooks scanned the sheet. "It's got... a no-movement clause for Eddito... but they did break their NDA, so maybe that doesn't apply anymore... maybe you can both..." Brooks's voice rasped.

Smith lowered his head, on the cusp of a realization—

A scream from the floor above interrupted him. Not Eddito, judging from the supersonic pitch, but agonizing nonetheless.

Smith sprinted—while Brooks followed as quickly as he could without passing out—up the stairs and into a huge conference room. At its center, a Shoppli portal hovered above the ground, swirling and glowing angry red. Two Shoppli guards in their fluro pants and aviator sunglasses stood watch over the gateway, while a third shoved a terrified orphan girl toward it. She was no older than three, and had no idea what was happening—thus, the screams.

THWWUP.

Her waiting cut to silence as the wormhole sucked her in. To Brooks and Smith's surprise, it stayed open. This was the scheduled portal.

"You were right... looks like this one doesn't close ASAP," Brooks said.

"Thank Sagan," Smith said. "Let's grab mini me and get the fuck out of here."

A dozen blond, blue-eyed orphans stood in a line, awaiting their turn to be pushed through for inter-universal adoption. At the end of the line was the newest draftee: Eddito.

Ignoring the guards, the detectives approached him.

Smith spun the newly orphaned child around, inspecting him for injuries.

"Have you seen my mom and dad?" Eddito asked.

"N—" Brooks began, but Smith's alternative account quickly cut him off.

"Yeah, they already went through. Told us to follow them

and meet up on the other side."

The two portal guards had noticed the men, and approached the back of the line. Before they could utter a word, Brooks looked them in the eyes.

"Listen... I've murdered like... twenty people in the last two days. This isn't who I want to be, so—"

Shoppli's finest wouldn't be talked out of a fight. The larger of the two slowly swung a meaty fist, leaving Brooks plenty of time to roll his eyes, grab the man from behind, and snap his neck. He dropped to the floor and clutched his side.

"I keep *trying* not to choose violence," he complained.

"Yeah... uh..." Smith—unable to reach his Chekhov in a struggle—was attempting to fight off the other guard with his bare hands. It wasn't going great, and he took a fist to the jaw and spat. "Principles are great and all, but..."

"You're practical..." Brooks said, rising to his feet. He grabbed the guard by his hair, balled his fist, and drove it straight through the man's diaphragm, in a visceral display that would traumatize three of the orphans for life. The rest of them were used to this sort of thing.

Brooks turned to the last Shoppli employee in the room.

"I'm just an escort," the man said, peeing himself a little. "I don't fight."

"Then *escort* the rest of these kids through."

The man nodded and began shoveling kids into the portal as quickly as possible.

Once all of the orphans and their escort had passed over to Earth B, it was Brooks, Smith, and Eddito's turn. They joined hands and stepped toward the portal together.

In what shouldn't have been a surprise, they were immediately bounced away.

44 / SHOCK AND AWW

Brooks, Smith, and Eddito stood facing a glowing red portal, with no idea how long it might remain open.

"*Shit*," said Smith. "Leslie and Phil weren't lying..."

Brooks finished that thought, softly. "Only one of you can go through..."

Eddito looked up at his duplicate. "One of who?"

"You'll find out when you're older," Smith said.

"Stop saying that!" Eddito griped.

Smith looked down at the younger version of himself—little arms crossed in consternation—and he smiled. Then he looked over to his husband. His smile faded.

"I'm staying," he declared.

Brooks's eyes widened. "What?"

"You take Eddito. I'll stay here."

"You're kidding."

Smith wasn't. "I think... I finally get the sea bream thing."

Brooks put a palm to his forehead. "*No.*"

"Try as I might, I can't find it in myself to be the guy who leaves the kid alone in a hellscape..."

Brooks shook his head. He had a better plan. "We can all stay here."

"One: You're hurt," Smith said, counting fingers. "Two: We might need people on both sides to solve this, and... Three: The kid's got potential, which is... a lot more than I can say for me. He's not gonna get to live up to it here."

"You're the one who gets sucked into portals and kidnapped when you're alone. You'll end up dead, or..."

Smith scoffed. "You know I don't die easy."

"This isn't funny," Brooks said.

"I know," said Smith. "But if I can't take care of myself, who can I take care of?"

"*Me?*" blurted Brooks. It wasn't much of an argument, and he wasn't going to win it. All he could do was let his tears flow like LaGuardia ceiling water.

Smith put a hand on his shoulder. "Brooksy. I'm not saying leave me here forever. Just go home. Get yourself patched up, take care of the kid and Widget and the girls, and when you figure out the workaround—"

"*If*," Brooks corrected.

"*When* you figure out the workaround... because you're brilliant... I'll be at the Green River Mall waiting for you to pop through that portal and pick me up. Hell, if you figure out the rest of the schedule you can pop in for kicks, or... licks. Just go to Tape World and check the S section."

Brooks's already ragged breathing grew shorter. He pulled the backpack off his shoulders and handed it to Smith. "I don't know if the flashlight will do you any good, but there's still a first aid kit and a few granola bars left..."

"And I've got the Chekhov." Smith smiled through tears.

"Eddie, don't make me do this."

"If I could *make* you do anything, we'd have a much bigger bed and a messier living room."

"I don't want to go."

"I know you don't, but I'll be okay."

Smith planted a kiss on Brooks's lips. Eddito groaned in response.

"Raise me right," Smith said, with a nod to the boy. He took Brooks's hand, guided it toward Eddito's, and shoved the two of them toward the dimensional gateway.

45 / END OF THE ROAD

Brooks automatically reconnected to Wi-Fi as soon as he arrived home on Earth B. Internet access didn't make him feel nearly as good as he thought it would. An overwhelming sense of loss struck him, even as the heads-up display in his mind beamed the current time, date, and temperature in orange Helvetica.

10:31 AM. November 20, 2018. 71°F.

Shit. It's been even longer than I thought...

The portal had closed up behind him, and Brooks found himself in a small, sterile room with one other person. The blue-haired zoomer who'd evaluated his and Smith's fitness to adopt stood before him—once again holding a clipboard.

"W—where's the kid?" Brooks asked.

"He's being taken care of," said the zoomer. "Mr. Naples would like to see you."

Brooks didn't give a damn about Shoppli CEO Maxwell Naples, or what he would like—even if he was now the richest man in the world.

"Being taken care of how?" he asked.

"He's a few floors down. He's fine." The zoomer stepped toward the exit. "He's eating animal crackers. Come on."

In silence, they rode a tiny elevator to Adopt Shop's highest floor. The building was only eight stories, just as it was on Earth C, so it wasn't a long ride. A far cry from the expansive campus at Shoppli HQ. After thirty seconds or so, the doors opened, and Brooks's blue-haired guide directed him to a simple conference room. It seemed unremarkable from the outside, but the blinds were pulled tight.

"Mr. Naples will see you now," the zoomer said.

Brooks peered at the door and windows with suspicion. His scanners picked up nothing.

"There's no one in that room," he said.

"He'll see you now."

The zoomer held the door open, and Brooks proceeded with apprehension into the threshold.

He surveyed the room. It contained a boat-shaped conference table that could seat eight. At the head of that table—behind a large stack of paper meant to lend him an air of importance—sat Maxwell Naples, in a blue suit with no tie.

Brooks took a step forward.

"Why couldn't I detect you?" he asked.

The man didn't answer. He didn't stand either, as this would have revealed his diminutive stature; he was five-foot-four, on a good day. His eyes remained fixed on the paperwork, which he rustled for effect. All Brooks could see of the man was the top of his bald head and a tuft of eyebrow.

"Shut the door behind you," he said finally.

Brooks obliged, and took a seat diagonally across from the CEO.

"Call me Max," he said without looking up.

"I didn't call you anything," Brooks pointed out.

Max finally looked up. "I know that," he said. Thick, angry eyebrows rested above his beady grey eyes. The left one blinked constantly, against his will, and the inspiration for Shoppli's winking logo became clear. An aquiline nose made a path to thin, smirking lips and a weak chin. In short, he looked like a cross between a freshwater turtle and a Wal-Mart greeter, and nothing like a Fortune 500 CEO should. That didn't stop his voice from dripping with condescension. "I was clarifying before you make a mistake."

"Where's the kid?" Brooks asked.

"Downstairs. Fine. Animal crackers. It's not important." The man was clearly used to getting his way, and he leaned back in his chair. "I don't want to discuss that. I want to discuss you."

"Why?"

"First, I owe you a debt of gratitude. Thanks to your actions, Shoppli and its subsidiaries now have better cybersecurity than any company on the planet. Interdimensional paper records are the way of the future. Totally off grid. Totally off world."

"Thanks to—"

"You. As I said."

"*How?*" Brooks was totally lost.

Max gave him the side-eye. "You remember hacking into our systems? It was for a refund on a... ceramic gravy boat, if I'm not mistaken."

"Wait, so... you keep paper records *in another dimension* because I took fifteen dollars from you for a refund?" Brooks blinked a few times. "That's moronic."

"Your action was repeatable, by any number of malicious agents. That's no longer the case. Additionally, access to your mind has given us invaluable insight into how to cloak our personnel from your... kind."

"There *were* people following us..."

"So," Max ignored the comment and gave a begrudging, "thank you."

"Uh huh. Sure. You're welcome. Now bring my husband back," said Brooks.

"No..." Max shook his head. "One can be simultaneously grateful and vindictive."

"Vindictive? Over a *gravy boat?*"

"A gravy boat, a cyberattack, numerous dead employees, pressuring others to break their NDAs, trespassing, unauthorized access to company records, thousands of dollars in property damage to Adopt Shop headquarters... You're a dangerous man, Mr. Brooks."

"You're right. I am." Brooks stared into his twitching eyes, a bit too eager to prove it. He stood from his seat and tightened his knuckles.

Max stroked his chin and his lips parted into a wide smirk. "With the right leverage, even a dangerous man can be brought to heel."

Brooks loosened his grip, not liking what was coming.

"This is what's going to happen," Max continued. "You're going to leave. You will never investigate Shoppli or any of its subsidiaries again, and you will not trespass any of our facilities or dimensional gateways. You will, however, be forthcoming with any of our requests for assistance in securing our assets against cybernetic organisms—"

"*Assistance*?"

"Studying your mind and its processes, extrapolating data," Max clarified. "If Shoppli is satisfied with your performance, I'll authorize an exception on our duplicate policy and allow Mr. Smith to pass back into this reality."

"All this over a gravy boat..." Brooks trailed off. It wasn't even a nice gravy boat. "How long until you're *satisfied*?"

"As long as it takes," replied Max. "You should be happy. Our original intent was to leave you both on Earth C."

"And now—"

"Now only one of you is stuck there, to both your and Shoppli's benefit."

Brooks hung his head. "Say I do... ignore the human trafficking and help you out—"

Max anticipated his question. "I guarantee he'll be unharmed."

Max anticipated wrong.

"—why wouldn't I just kill you once we're back home?"

The CEO smiled and laughed lightly. "Think *biggest*, Arturo." He leaned forward and—between involuntary blinks—looked Brooks square in the eyes. "You need to understand... Shoppli is everywhere. You cannot win."

That sounded like a challenge. But one for another day.*

With no alternatives, Brooks lowered his head, and half-heartedly agreed. "Fine, but one thing—"

"You're not really in a position to negotiate, but go on."

"I leave here with the kid," Brooks said.

"A reminder of your missing husband hanging around your home, Mr. Brooks?" said Max. "Are you sure that's what you want?"

"Yes."

Max thought on it. "I am grateful, as I said... I suppose we can swap him out with the child from Des Moines... Yes. Agreed." He smirked biggest. "You will, of course, still be paying the fifty thousand in cash..."

The cyborg gave a dejected nod.

Some of the paperwork on the table was legitimate, and Brooks spent a long time signing it. It would have been exhausting under normal circumstances, and it was only more so for a man with broken ribs who was accustomed to digitally signing documents with his thoughts.

When it was done, the zoomer escorted Brooks back into the elevator and down to the lobby, where Eddito stood, nibbling on animal crackers, as promised.

"Mr. Brooks..." the child started, looking eager but also hesitant to ask.

"What is it?" Brooks wondered.

"Are... the other Mr. Brooks and me the... same person?"

"Um..." Brooks fumbled. "Sort of... I'll exp—"

"—explain when I'm older?" Eddito sighed.

Brooks avoided the topic as long as he could, but during the long, awkward cab ride home, he found himself unable to keep the truth from the child any longer. He explained the situation as best as he could while keeping quiet about Leslie and Phil's deaths. Now wasn't the time.

---

* And for another book.

When they arrived at 55 Decatur Street, the house had too many front doors. It hadn't taken any time at all for some property management company to scoop up the brownstone and subdivide it into three separate units. A large, grey sign in one of the top floor windows—Patience's former bed-room—supported 'Zane for President 2020.'

Brooks's HUD flickered on and off a few times as his in-sides swarmed with panic. He had no husband, no home, and no idea what kind of fuckery was going on in the world. But he composed himself, so as not to alarm the young boy.

"Well, this is embarrassing," he said to the driver. "Looks like I gave you the wrong address..."

"You forgot where your house is?"

Brooks shrugged. "Looks like."

Eddito didn't seem convinced, but he didn't seem to care much either. "I'm *tired.*"

Not as tired as this cab, thought Brooks.

A lame pun. He sniffed a little, wishing Smith were there to say it. In his mind, he composed a short email to Bur-roughs asking whether she still lived at the same apartment in Queens. She sent a very long, very angry reply confirming that she did.

Brooks checked the scraps of cash in his wallet, and hoped his credit cards hadn't been cancelled. He spoke loudly, to the driver. "Can you make it 75 Penelope, in Queens?"

Widget ran out the door of Burroughs's apartment, barking the loudest series of barks he could muster. He leapt at Brooks, who caught the dog and lifted him up to face level.

"Hey, Widge," said Brooks, taking licks to the face. "Who's my good little scrapper?"

"Where the *hell* have you been?" asked Burroughs, as she leaned to the side to get a look around him. "Who's the kid?

Where's Eddie? Please tell me Eddie's not the kid."

"Well..."

Burroughs motioned at them. "Come in."

Once in the living room, Brooks gestured toward the child. "This is Eddito. Eddito, this is Erin Burroughs."

"It's Eddie," said Eddito. He shook her hand. "Nice to meet you, ma'am."

"He's our Eddie from another universe," Brooks explained.

"Okay," said Burroughs, familiar with these sorts of situations. "Where's *our* Eddie?"

Brooks motioned towards the kid with his head and raised his eyebrows.

Burroughs caught his drift. "Hey, Eddito—Eddie—would you like to watch something on TV?"

Burroughs flipped it on and quickly changed channels from *Gangbang Island*—her favorite reality TV guilty pleasure. She stopped at the first piece of kiddie media she found and directed Eddito to an armchair. "Hang out here for a second."

"Okay." Eddito, already transfixed by the colors and noises, climbed up into the chair. Parenting was going to be a cinch with this one.

The adults made their way into the kitchen, out of earshot. Widget followed.

"Are you sure he's an Eddie?" Burroughs asked. "He seems... agreeable."

Though Brooks had insisted he'd been mentally preparing for Smithlessness, in reality, he didn't know what to do. All of his stone-faced stares had been for nothing. He burst into tears.

Burroughs grimaced. "Oh no. Is he dead again?"

"No..." Brooks explained, wiping his eye. "He's trapped in another universe, where everything got nuked and it's the eighties and people eat rats and Shoppli wants to use his sperm to make orphans..."

"That's a lot to process—"

"And his parents were kind of okay, but they're dead, and now he's probably dead... and if he's not dead he's probably wishing he were dead... and now I'm caught up in a multidimensional human trafficking ring that I can't do anything about or I'll *definitely* be dead..."

That was enough 'dead's to set off an alert, but Burroughs and Brooks didn't notice the green glow outside the window until Lemon stormed into the room. Patience traipsed in after her.

"*Someone* better be dead this time," Lemon warned. "We *just* got the time machine back! X and I were about to—" Lemon cut herself off when she spotted her sobbing father leaned over a kitchen island. "You're... back."

"What am I going to do?" Brooks buried his head in his hands.

Lemon looked around for an explanation. "Um... kinda missed what happened, but... can we help maybe?"

"No. You're not safe with me around," Brooks said. "Nobody is."

Lemon rolled her eyes. "Please. You're not safe *without* us around."

Patience nodded in agreement. "We're quite sorry for not returning home as oft as we should have. We vow to do better henceforth."

"What she said," Lemon said. "We're gonna be around so much you're gonna be sick of us."

"Around *where*?" Brooks asked, in desperation. "We don't have a house!"

"Maybe not..." Lemon stepped out the door for a moment, then returned from the time machine dragging a heavy burlap sack with both hands. "But we can buy a new one!"

She pulled the bag to a stop and let it fall over. Thousands of gold coins clinked and clanked and bounced across the floor.

"What the *hell*—"

Lemon shrugged, then gave a wink. "Martian royalty. Deeeeep pockets. Not very bright."

Patience stepped toward the pile with a disparaging look and added a single gold coin from a pocket she'd sewn onto her dress. "I must add that I did not have illicit relations with an alien monarch. I found this in the coin return slot of a vending machine."

Lemon slapped her father across the shoulders. "Point is. We've got your back."

Brooks smiled and wiped his eyes. There was still plenty of uncertainty in the air, but one thing was clear:

Becoming a murderbot was no longer on the table.

EPILOGUE

The bunker beneath the Green River Mall was mind-numbingly dull. Donning his favorite emo wig, Smith seated himself outside, on the hood of a dead man's Pontiac, kicked up his legs, and flipped through a 1970s nudie magazine he'd stolen from Waldenbooks. In the last few months, he'd seen more bushes than the halls of Yale University.

How many months had passed, he wasn't sure. Maybe it was a year. At some point, he stopped marking passing days on the walls. It was too depressing. Living in the moment, grabbing the big rat by the horns—that's what it was all about.

He'd made several parking lot visits after Brooks and Eddito disappeared, and each one had ended with him packing up his pornos and heading back into the space between the S tapes, alone.

This time was different. Smith didn't have time to register any sights or sounds, just the feeling of a familiar—and extremely heavy—body crashing into his, knocking him back onto the windshield and sending his wig to the pavement.

"Broo—" There was no time for words either, what with a tongue jammed down his throat. It was full sensory overload for Smith as Brooks committed oral assault on his husband's face and neck. Smith didn't mind, of course, but he had questions. He gasped out words between kisses.

"What... are you... sure... time for..."

Brooks pulled back for a brief moment.

"Don't talk to me about time," he warned.

He grabbed Smith by the arm and tugged him off the hood. He ripped a back door off the Pontiac in one swift move, and tossed his husband onto the backseat. Then, they went to town.

Sometime later, as they were lying naked in a pile of their own clothing, Smith pulled out a pack of Pall Malls that bore no health warnings.

"Can I get one of those?" Brooks asked.

"You don't smoke."

Brooks stared at him with a tired face. He didn't say a word. Smith lit two, and handed one over.

"So, what was the solution?" Smith asked. "Please tell me this isn't just a conjugal visit."

Brooks drew deep, coughed, and puffed smoke through his nostrils.

"Shoppli controls all the portals, so now... I work for Shoppli..."

"Shoppli," said Smith. The cigarette drooped from his lip. "You work for *Shoppli*? For how long?"

"Five years..."

"Five years!" Smith inhaled and blew the smoke. "*Doing what?*"

"I don't want to talk about it," Brooks said.

A little smirk appeared on Smith's face, and Brooks narrowed his eyes.

"*What?*"

Smith took another puff. "Five years, huh? That would make you—" He drew the final word out, waiting for his husband to finish.

Brooks didn't. "*Okay.* First of all, it's not fair to count the birthday I missed when I was stuck here in this universe. Also, I'm a cyborg, so I don't age as quickly as you do..."

"Right, but all things considered... that would make you...?"

Brooks rubbed his cigarette into the footwell to extinguish it, then crossed his arms. "You know... *technically* you lived a few decades as an immortal so you're like a hundred..."

"Right. Sure. But what you're saying is that you're...?"

"I'm forty-one," Brooks snapped.

Smith emitted a solid cackle.

"It's not funny," said Brooks. "When I got back there, our house was gone and I had to purchase Eddito from Shoppli and I owed Waco Car Rental like sixty thousand dollars, and then there was a plague, and I had to raise a child without you, and..."

"And there's gonna be so much time for me to unpack all that trauma with you. But right now... just to be clear... I'm forty-two, and you're forty-one."

Brooks glowered. "Forty-one. Yes."

"Okay." Smith smirked. "Just one more question..."

"*What?*"

"How many is that in horse years?"

Brooks stared, Smith stared back, and the stare-off continued until they both broke into laughter.

"You ready to go home?" Brooks asked.

"I dunno, the cicada salads around here are *fire*..." Smith put out his own cigarette. "Yeah. I'm ready."

They exited the car, hand in hand, ready to return to Earth B. Home wasn't perfect, not by a long shot. But it's like a book once said—better the dystopia you know than the dystopia you don't.

APPENDIX I: MAPS

Earth B

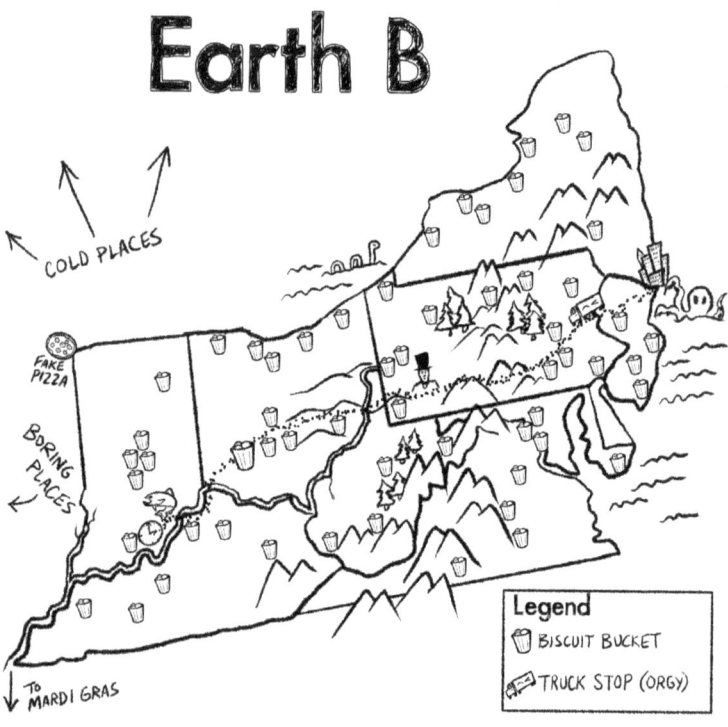

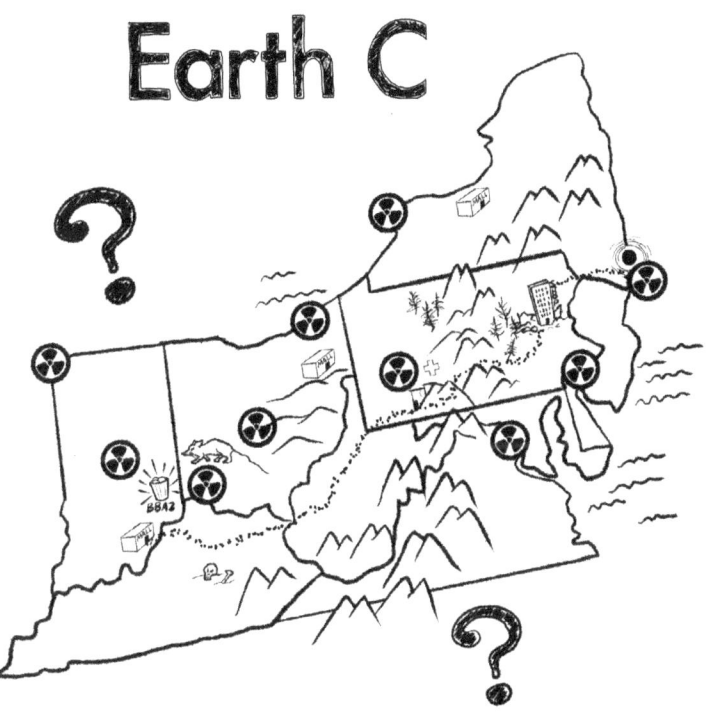

APPENDIX II: 1980s TECH PRIMER

Are you a zoomer? If so, here's a dictionary of terms that may have caused you some confusion over the course of this book. There are no secret messages in here.

Cab – A taxicab. It's a car you can hire to take you places. Think a more expensive rideshare, but slightly less exploitative. If you desire, you can probably still find these relics in major metropolitan areas.

Floppy – A piece of long-forgotten physical media. Like a Blu-ray disc, only for computer data. Their storage capacity was almost nothing. A video game could, for instance, be spread across a dozen floppy disks, and you'd have to routinely swap them out to continue gameplay.

Home – Something neither of us will ever own.

Landline – Long ago, people didn't have cell phones. Phones were connected to a little port in their home's wall. If you're unlucky, you've used it for a DSL connection.

ACKNOWLEDGEMENTS

I'd like to thank 2020 for being a nightmare and trapping me inside my house with nothing to do but plan my next few books. I'd like to thank all of my beta readers and ARC readers, especially the one who abandoned ship because of the Reagan joke on the first page. You showed me I was alienating the right people. Extra special thanks to Tom, who stepped in to edit Book 4 of a series while my usual editor was out of commission. Most editing assignments don't require three books' worth of homework, but you took the job and made the final product much, much better. Then there's Ben. I found my biggest supporter just in time for a global pandemic, and I couldn't be more grateful.

Finally, I'd like to thank everyone who has ever left a positive review for one of these books. You know what that means? It means if you go leave a review on Amazon or Goodreads, you're included in these acknowledgements. Wouldn't that make you feel special?

Brooks and Smith will return in:
Oops! All Zombies (Book 5)

For announcements about this and other projects,
sign up for the mailing list at martina-fetzer.com, or
scan this little QR code...